Praise f

The Violinist o

"This panoramic novel of composer Antonio Vivaldi's life sweeps readers into a world of beautiful melodies and forbidden passion. Palombo allows music, more than the characters, to be the key to her sumptuous novel. One can almost hear the sweet notes while reading of the passionate and tragic star-crossed lovers. Those who adore the music and history will find what they desire in these pages."

—*RT Book Reviews*

"Mesmerizing . . . So gorgeous are the relationships and music reflected here that the reader will want to spend hours listening to truly beautiful music created by both Antonio Vivaldi and Adriana d'Amato. Stunning, lovely historical fiction that is a must-read!"

—*Historical Novel Society*

"Alyssa Palombo's training as a classical musician is evident in her first novel, *The Violinist of Venice,* a historical romance set in the eighteenth century. . . . Palombo skillfully blends historical facts with innovative and colorful fiction, creating a delightful, fast-paced romance that is sure to please music lovers and romance readers alike."

—*Shelf Awareness*

"A lovely book, engrossing and realistic. In simple, spare prose, Palombo gives life to an improbable romance between Vivaldi, the 'Red Priest,' and Adriana d'Amato, the lovely daughter of a wealthy merchant. Music is Adriana's downfall—she falls deeply and passionately in love with the composer—and ultimately her salvation.

The most compelling aspect of the novel is Adriana's love of music and the author's virtuoso descriptions of Vivaldi's compositions. The passages are so evocative one can almost hear the ebb and flow of the music. We are in the hands of not only a master storyteller but also a dedicated music lover."

—Roberta Rich, international bestselling
author of *The Midwife of Venice*

"Utterly captivating! Palombo brings the world of Vivaldi to life in a sweeping tale of love in all its many forms. Beautiful, poignant, and at times heart-wrenching, this should be at the top of everyone's list to read."

—Jessica Leake, author of *Arcana* and
The Order of the Eternal Sun

"*The Violinist of Venice* by Alyssa Palombo is a warm and compelling story of the secret love affair in the life of the famous Baroque composer Antonio Vivaldi. Vivid and alive and thrumming with the exquisite strains of violin music, the novel explores the impossible choices between love and duty and the demands of art in the decadent world of early-eighteenth-century Venice."

—Kate Forsyth, international bestselling
author of *Bitter Greens*

"A passionate, heartbreaking love story between a brilliant young violinist whose father forbids her to make music and the gentle, gifted composer who restores it to her. I was utterly swept away by their impossible love and the rich worlds which grew from it in this moving novel set among the aristocrats and musicians of eighteenth-century Venice."

—Stephanie Cowell, author of *Marrying Mozart*
and *Claude & Camille: A Novel of Monet*

"Vivid, emotional, and profoundly satisfying. This marvelous debut is a sumptuous tale of a passionate affair between Vivaldi and a promising student set to a masterful musical score. Palombo has created a fascinating portrait of both the beauty and limitations of life in aristocratic Venice."

—Jennifer Laam, author of *The Secret Daughter of the Tsar*

"Debut author and musician Palombo creates a lovely fictional account of a great love affair. . . . A nicely crafted first effort that reimagines Vivaldi's life in a bittersweet narrative."

—*Kirkus Reviews*

ALSO BY ALYSSA PALOMBO

The Violinist of Venice: A Story of Vivaldi

The MOST BEAUTIFUL WOMAN *in* FLORENCE

A STORY OF BOTTICELLI

ALYSSA PALOMBO

St. Martin's Griffin New York

This is a work of fiction. All of the characters, organizations, and events portrayed in this novel are either products of the author's imagination or are used fictitiously.

 Printed in the United States of America. For information, address St. Martin's Press, 175 Fifth Avenue, New York, N.Y. 10010.

www.stmartins.com

The Library of Congress Cataloging-in-Publication Data is available upon request.

ISBN 978-1-250-07150-7 (trade paperback)
ISBN 978-1-4668-8264-5 (e-book)

First Edition: April 2017

10 9 8 7 6 5 4 3 2 1

For my dad, Tony Palombo, for traipsing through the palazzi and museums of Florence with me while I researched this book; for giving me my love of history; for loving Italy as much as I do; for spicy pizza, and gelato, and French fries at Beer and Vinyl

The MOST BEAUTIFUL WOMAN *in* FLORENCE

PROLOGUE

Florence, 1484

It was a large canvas, big enough that it had taken two men to carry it into Il Magnifico's chambers. The artist himself had supervised, concern etched across his face while he watched, as though they carried the sum of all his life's work in their hands—and perhaps they did.

The men set it down carefully, leaning it against the wall in its rough-hewn, linen-draped frame. The artist waved them away impatiently and they took their leave, shutting the door behind them.

"So this is it, is it?" Lorenzo de' Medici asked the artist. His eyes were alight with curiosity.

"It is, Magnifico," he replied reverently.

Lorenzo chuckled. "Enough with the flattery, Sandro, I pray you. You already know I will help you in whatever ways lie within my power, no matter what."

"Why, then I might ask of you anything on God's earth, I think," the artist said. This time his words were teasing, those of an old companion to his friend who has risen high, but the artist's face remained somber. For him, this was the most serious of occasions.

Lorenzo felt his face tighten into a similarly somber expression. He had an inkling—more than an inkling, truth be told—as to what was on the canvas. "Do not keep me in suspense, *amico*." He motioned imperiously at the canvas—a man not used to being kept waiting, even by a friend. "Let me see."

The artist closed his eyes, resting his forehead against the frame in a brief moment of silence before he pulled back and finally nodded. Slowly, he slipped the cloth from the face of the painting. In that instant, Lorenzo de' Medici was struck speechless—a sight no man could claim having witnessed before.

There were the colors; pale blues and greens and pinks and yellows, subtle yet somehow vibrant. And the extraordinary way the maestro had somehow managed to capture *motion*, of all things, on a canvas: the flowers tumbling to the ground, the wind lifting and tangling locks of hair, the folds of a skirt, the cloth of a robe.

But it was the center figure, the focus of the painting, which struck him most. She stood in a seashell upon the waves: with unblemished, alabaster nude flesh; soft, rounded, inviting curves; clothed only in what seemed to be miles of reddish golden hair.

And her face. It was a face Lorenzo knew well: the tilt of her chin when she laughed; the crease in her brow when she was thinking; her smile. Yet he was not, he had long suspected, as familiar with her as the artist.

Lorenzo knew, without a doubt, that what he was looking at was the artist's finest work thus far, an outstanding piece in a distinguished career that had seen commissions from the wealthy, the noble, and even from the Holy Father himself.

But he also knew that he must—for the foreseeable future, at least—remain one of the only ones to see it. He understood, now, what the artist had come here to ask of him. Yet still, he let his old friend speak first.

"It has been years in the making," the artist said at last.

Lorenzo turned to face him. "Yes," he said. "At least eight years in the making, I think." He focused again on the painting, on the woman in the center, a woman he had seen at his dinner table and in his garden and in his library. He smiled. Yes, she could usually be found in his library. "It is her," he said. "I almost expect her to step from the canvas. You have captured her, Sandro, as no one else living could have."

"It was never my intention to capture her," the artist said, his voice rough. Lorenzo was surprised to see tears in his friend's eyes as he studied the woman he had rendered in paint. "But rather, to set her free. To let her live again."

"And so you have," Lorenzo said, his voice catching. *Damn it, but Sandro will have me weeping in a moment as well.* He sighed. "I would ask why you have brought it—her—here, but I believe I already know."

"Yes." The artist's eyes were earnest as he faced Lorenzo. "I cannot keep it. Even if I could bear it, the Church . . ."

"Indeed," Lorenzo said. "Holy Mother Church would find much here to censure you for, even if you did just paint His Holiness's little chapel."

"Yes," the artist said. "But you can keep her safe. I could not bear to have this work confiscated, or . . ."

Lorenzo put a hand on his shoulder. "Worry not, old friend. I shall put it in one of the country houses, out of the way, where no one goes except by invitation. And if people talk, well . . ." He shrugged. "I have been accused of keeping far more scandalous secrets."

The artist embraced him. "Thank you, Magnifico."

"As I said, none of that," Lorenzo said, returning the embrace. Both men stepped back to contemplate the painting again. After a moment, Lorenzo added, "After all, by now I can tell when you are trying to get into my good graces. You are wanting me to pay for a better frame for your masterpiece, are you not?"

The artist smiled. "You know me too well. But look at her!" He gestured. "Does not Venus deserve the most splendid frame Medici money can buy?"

Lorenzo smiled. "That she does. Well, I shall choose such a frame for Venus, then. For Venus and for Simonetta."

PART I

LA BELLA SIMONETTA

Genoa and Florence, April–December 1469

1

Genoa, 1469

"Simonetta!"

I heard my mother's voice drift down the hall as she drew nearer. Not too loud—a lady never shouted, after all—but the urgency in her tone was more than enough to convey the importance of this day, this moment.

I met the gaze of my maid, Chiara, in the Venetian glass mirror. She smiled encouragingly from where she stood behind me, sliding the final pins into my hair. "Nearly finished, Madonna Simonetta," she said. "And if he wants you that badly, he will wait."

I smiled back, but my own smile was less sure.

My mother, however, had a different idea. "Make haste," she said as she appeared in the room. "Chiara, we want to show off that magnificent hair, not pin it up as though she is some common matron."

"*Si,* Donna Cattaneo," Chiara responded. Dutifully, she stepped back from the dressing table and my mother motioned for me to rise from my seat.

"*Che bella, figlia mia!*" my mother exclaimed as she took me in, dressed in my finest: a brand-new gown of cream silk, trimmed in fine Burano lace, with roses embroidered along the collar and hem. A strand of pearls encircled my neck, and the top strands of my gold hair were artfully pinned back, allowing the majority of it to spill down my back to my waist. "As always," she said.

I smiled the same uncertain smile I had given Chiara, but my mother did not notice. "He is already quite taken with you, and when he sees you tonight, he shall be positively smitten."

I had only met Signor Marco Vespucci once, and at Mass, no less. He was a Florentine, sent to study in Genoa by his father. He was known to my father, somehow, and approached us in the church of San Torpete that day with, it seemed, the intention of being introduced to me. He had bowed and kissed my hand and paid the same extravagant and foolish compliments to my beauty that all men did, so I had scarcely paid him any mind. He was handsome enough, but then many men were handsome.

Apparently, though, he had not forgotten our encounter as easily as I had. He had written to my father shortly thereafter, asking if he might pay court to me.

"But, Mother," I began, thinking that this might be my only opportunity to air the doubts that had been fogging my head, but uncertain how to do so.

"But nothing, *mia dolce,*" my mother said. "Your father and I have discussed it, and Signor Vespucci is a wonderful match for you—why, he is an intimate of the Medici, in Florence! Do you not wish to help *la famiglia nostra* as best you can?"

"Of course," I said. What else could I say?

"Of course," she echoed. "Then let us go downstairs and meet your suitor. There is no need to fear; you need not say anything at all, if you do not wish to. Your beauty is enough and more."

It was all I could do not to roll my eyes—another thing ladies did not do. As if I would not speak to the man who wished to marry me. And what a foolish notion, that he did not need to hear me speak—did men wish for wives who were mutes, then?

Possibly, I thought, a wry smile touching my lips as I contemplated all the times my mother would chatter on and on, not noticing the somewhat pained expression on my father's face.

Well, if he married me, Signor Vespucci would not be getting a mute for a wife, that was certain, and I would make sure he knew that right off.

I followed my mother down the stairs, Chiara trailing discreetly behind in case I should need anything. Our *palazzo* was of a decent size, though perhaps not as large as some of the *palazzi* owned by other members of the Genoese nobility. It was situated far enough inland that one could not quite see the sea from the upper balconies, but I could always smell it: the scent of the sea pervaded the air, the breeze, the very stones, all throughout Genoa. It was the smell of home.

Once on the ground floor, we went out into the open-air courtyard; it was a lovely and mild late April evening, and so my father had seen fit to greet our guest out of doors.

"Ah, here she is," I heard my father say as my mother and I appeared. "Simonetta, *figlia*, surely you remember Signor Vespucci?"

"Of course," I said, offering my hand. "How do you do, Signor Vespucci?"

"Abundantly well, *donna*, now that I am in your presence once more," he said, bowing low over my hand as he kissed it. He straightened up, a small, nervous smile playing about his thin lips. I cast my eyes quickly over his person again. Yes, he was handsome, and young; perhaps nineteen or twenty to my sixteen years. His dark hair and pointed beard were neatly trimmed, his eyes were large and kind, and his nose proportionate to the rest of his features. His clothes were sober grays and browns, but made of the finest stuff.

"Do come inside, Signor Vespucci," my father said, "and take a glass of wine with us."

"I would be honored, Don Cattaneo," he said.

We adjourned into the receiving room, and my mother sent a

servant for a bottle of our finest *vino rosso*. I sat on one of the carved wooden chairs, careful not to wrinkle my skirts.

I could feel Signor Vespucci's eyes on me, but directed my gaze modestly to the floor, pretending not to notice. *Are you going to speak to me, signore, or merely gaze at me all evening as though I were a painting?* I wondered crossly.

"You are a vision, truly, Madonna Simonetta," Signor Vespucci said at last. "I wonder that the sun dares shine and the flowers dare bloom in your presence."

I bit forcefully on the inside of my cheek to stop myself from laughing. All men, it seemed, fancied themselves poets, but few were worthy of the name. Signor Vespucci was no exception.

"I thank you, signore," I said after a moment, once I had mastered myself. "Your words are too kind."

"And quite lovely," my mother interjected, from a seat at an angle to my own. "Ah, you young men and your poetry!"

I bit down on my cheek again and was glad to return my gaze to the floor.

"All men—young and otherwise—can only dream of such a muse to inspire them," he said, still looking at me. Despite decorum, I lifted my eyes and met his straight on, trying to read his sincerity. He surprised me by holding my gaze for a moment, as though he were appraising something other than my beauty, if only briefly. Yet then I saw his cheeks flush, and he looked away.

"So tell us how your studies go, Signor Vespucci," my father said, once the wine had been poured.

My suitor took up this topic eagerly, telling us in great detail everything he was learning about the art of banking, and how he hoped his new skills would serve him well when he returned to Florence, the city of those famous master bankers themselves, the Medici.

I could not bring myself to be interested in his talk—numbers and ledgers and accounts were hardly my forte. Yet what intrigued me was the light in his eyes as he spoke, the life in his voice and his enthusiastic hand gestures. He sat on the edge of his seat as he went on, leaning forward toward my father, as though his excitement was such that it was all he could do to keep to his chair.

I softened a bit toward him then. Maybe he found in his numbers and ledgers the same thing I found in poetry: a love of something outside oneself that nevertheless felt like it was a part of one's very being. And at that moment, that spark of recognition, as though I could see his soul, was far more attractive to me than his handsome face.

As the hour grew later and the conversation dwindled—perhaps through my parents' design, I had not, in fact, had much chance to say anything—Signor Vespucci noticed the book left on the varnished wood table nearest him. "Ah, of course," he said, noting the title. "*La Divina Commedia*. And who is reading Dante?" He glanced up at my father, assuming he already knew the answer to his question.

"I am," I said.

Signor Vespucci looked startled as he turned to me. "You, Madonna Simonetta?"

I had received only a rudimentary education: reading and writing, and simple figures. Yet I had often persuaded my tutor—an old and kindly priest—to let me read the histories of such figures as Julius Caesar and Alexander the Great. And from there we went, naturally, to poetry.

Yet when I'd reached the age of thirteen, my parents had sent Padre Valerio away, saying it was an unnecessary expense to continue to pay him. I had already learned as much and more as was needed to be a lady and a wife. "No man wants a wife as well learned as he is," my father had said, with my mother nodding emphatically beside him. "And a girl as beautiful as you has no need of books."

They would not let me continue my lessons, no matter how I begged. So I began to read on my own, my father's volumes and those I asked him to purchase for me. The copy of Dante that had caught

Signor Vespucci's attention, however, had been a gift to me from Padre Valerio—one of several such gifts, bless him.

"Indeed. I wonder at your surprise, signore. Because so many noblewomen are uneducated, did you assume that I was among their number?"

My father frowned at me in warning, but I paid no heed.

"Why, no," Signor Vespucci said, recovering. "It is just that it is quite the tome, and one does not always expect a young lady—"

Narrowing my eyes at him, I quoted, "'Good Leader, I but keep concealed/From thee my heart, that I may speak the less/Nor only now has thou thereto disposed me.'"

My mother laughed nervously. "Simonetta . . ."

Yet Signor Vespucci ignored her, and again met my eyes. "'So I beheld more than a thousand splendors/Drawing towards us, and in each was heard: "Lo, this is she who shall increase our love."'"

Neither of us looked away for a long moment, longer than was appropriate. I felt a strange skip in my heart. It was nothing like the tormented passion Dante described, and yet still I felt my skin flush and my breath quicken.

This time it was I who looked away first.

"You would be in high favor among the Medici circle, Madonna Simonetta," Signor Vespucci said after a moment of heavy silence, a faint huskiness in his tone. "You have in abundance the two things most prized there: beauty and poetry."

"Indeed?" I asked, struggling to compose myself.

"*Si*. Lorenzo de' Medici is following in the tradition of his grandfather, the great Cosimo, and is gathering about him the brightest and most gifted minds he can find: poets, scholars, artists. Nowhere in Italy—in the world, no doubt—are the arts held in such high esteem."

I allowed myself to imagine it. Brilliant men, artists, all in attendance on the Medici, discussing their ideas and their art. Would they welcome a woman in their midst? Perhaps, for even here in

Genoa we had heard of the formidable Lucrezia dei Tornabuoni, mother to the Medici brothers Lorenzo and Giuliano, an intelligent and well-read woman in her own right.

"I should like to see it," I said, smiling at my suitor.

I did not realize it then, but in the weeks that followed I would look back on that moment as the one in which I had made my decision.

2

Of course, it was not as simple as that. Signor Vespucci dined with us again after that, at which time—once my mother and I had retired for the evening—he made his intentions known to my father. Before he could make a formal offer, however, he had to return to Florence—he was almost finished with his studies, in any case—and receive the permission of his family. Apparently he foresaw no difficulty, once he told them of my virtue, my goodness, and my beauty. Especially my beauty.

And so I waited, as was, I supposed, the lot of women.

In those first days after Signor Vespucci's departure from Genoa, I found myself missing him. Our discussion of Dante had left me with a fondness toward him, and I appreciated that my cleverness in such things was not off-putting to my suitor—quite the reverse, in fact.

And so I missed him and perhaps, more so, I missed the conversations we had not yet had. I knew that we would have nothing but time for such things once we were married, but even so.

And yet, as the days wore on, and we did not hear back from him, that very idea of marriage began to grow ever fainter and more alien to me, like the page of a book one has pored over so often that the ink begins to fade. Perhaps it would be for the best if I heard no more from him, for what did I know of marriage, or of men? Or, more specifically, of this particular man? Knowledge of poetry, a fine mind, and a handsome person did not a good marriage make. Or did it? What more was there, really? I knew I was lucky to have such a young and handsome suitor. Most girls my age were married to men much older than they.

And every so often I would remember what he had said about Florence, about the society there, and about what I could expect to find. I did want that: to meet those wise and learned men that Signor Vespucci had spoken of. I did not want to remain in Genoa with my parents all my life, seeing and learning nothing more of the world than my own town.

Yet who knew if Signor Vespucci had spoken in earnest about taking me to Florence, and presenting me to the Medici's circle? Why should men like Lorenzo de' Medici care about a simple nobleman's daughter from Genoa? Signor Vespucci had spoken no more than a few words on the subject, and I was ready to tumble right into the marriage bed. As far as wooing went, he had not needed to try very hard. And perhaps that's all his words had been—weightless words meant to woo a naïve maid.

Just over a week after Signor Vespucci's departure, my friend Elisabetta came to visit me. Quite the gossip, she was a year older than me and still unmarried, which perhaps accounted for our friendship more than anything else: we were the only noble girls of age who had yet to be married or confined to a cloister. Elisabetta was nice enough to talk to, and to visit the merchants with, but often I could only spend so much time in her company before the spite that worked its way into her gossip began to wear on me.

We sat outside in the courtyard, wearing wide-brimmed hats to shield our faces from the sun, yet with the crowns cut out so that our hair could be pulled through and left to fall down our backs, that it might lighten to a dazzling shade of gold. That was what the Venetian ladies did, anyway, and it was said Venetian women were the most beautiful in the world.

"Any word from your handsome suitor?" she inquired as soon as we were seated.

"No," I answered. "And what of you? Does your father still have his heart set on Count Ricci?"

Elisabetta made a face, and I saw that my words had stung her in a manner I had not intended. The latest gossip about town (for I had Chiara to keep me informed when too much time had passed since Elisabetta's last visit) was that Elisabetta's father, after failing to broker her a marriage between any of the younger scions of the local families, had offered her to Count Ricci, a childless widower nearing fifty. I had not thought there was any truth to the tale, but the look on Elisabetta's face told me otherwise.

"God forgive me, but I should rather be a nun," she said, primly crossing herself.

I laughed off my discomfort. "Let us hope it does not come to that. Do not worry yourself, *amica*. Surely your father will look elsewhere for a match for you—Pisa, perhaps, or Florence."

Elisabetta waved my words aside. "Bah. Pisa is full of nothing but scholars and priests. Florence, though—Florence, it seems, is the place from which husbands hail." She very nearly leered at me. "As you would know, my dear Simonetta."

"I have no husband as yet, from Florence or elsewhere," I said.

"You will soon enough, or so I hear."

I shrugged in a rather unladylike way. My mother would be appalled. "Perhaps."

I could feel her eyeing me from beneath the brim of her hat. "Was he not pleasing to you?" she asked.

"Pleasing enough," I said, remembering that strange moment of kinship. "It is just . . . I do not know that I want any husband yet."

Elisabetta laughed. "What else could you do but get a husband?"

"What else indeed," I murmured, but I knew the answer as well as she did: nothing. The most I had ever dared hope for was that I might find a husband tolerant enough to permit my continued study and reading of poetry, and wealthy enough to keep me supplied with books. Signor Vespucci was just such a one.

"You could never be a nun," she continued. "You are far too pretty." When she said it, it sounded as though she were accusing me of being a witch.

"A convent might not be so terrible," I said, leaning my head against the wall behind us and closing my eyes. I knew even as I spoke that my parents would never allow me to take holy vows. As the only child of the family, I was expected to make an advantageous marriage—and with my beauty, so I had been told many times, I would no doubt be able to make the most fortuitous of matches. Yet the nuns were allowed to read, and the most skilled of them even copied manuscripts.

Elisabetta was still watching me. "I heard he has a mistress," she said suddenly.

I opened my eyes. "Who? Count Ricci?"

"No," she said, her gaze still fixed on me. "Your Signor Vespucci."

I felt as though the pleasant feeling Signor Vespucci had planted in my stomach suddenly went sour. "What of it?" I asked, belying my discomfort—or so I hoped. "Most men do."

"She is a courtesan in town," Elisabetta went on, as though I had not spoken. "Her name is Violetta. Apparently she is very beautiful, and much sought after for her particular . . . gifts."

I could not believe Elisabetta was insinuating such things—it was as near to vulgar as I had ever heard her. "And so?" I asked, my voice a bit sharp. "What am I to do about it? Not marry him because he once bedded a courtesan? If such were grounds for refusing a husband, every woman in the world would remain a spinster."

Elisabetta turned her head away slightly. "I just thought you should know."

I narrowed my eyes. I knew jealousy plain enough when I saw it. Yet Elisabetta seemed to credit me with having more control of my own fate than I did. I may have fancied that I had made a decision in regard to Signor Vespucci, but so long as my father saw an advantage to the match, betrothed I would be. Really, the only thing for me to decide was how much resistance I would offer up.

I closed my eyes again, face tilted up to the sun, the creaminess of my skin be damned. Neither of us spoke again for a long while, and when I finally broke the silence it was only to ask Elisabetta if she might like some wine.

Three days later, a letter arrived from Florence. Signor Vespucci had spoken to his parents and was returning to Genoa, so the missive went, where he hoped he might have the privilege of coming to call upon my parents and me at once.

I scarcely heard my mother exclaiming in happiness, nor my father proudly booming about what an excellent match it was, an excellent match indeed. No, instead I felt that same warmth sprawl through my lower abdomen, accompanied by something else, something that—I thought—might be joy. And if it wasn't, perhaps it would be, one day.

3

Signor Vespucci arrived one fine spring morning, and immediately sought a private audience with my father. I was awake, dressed, and groomed as perfectly as a queen—my mother had seen to that—for we had known that Signor Vespucci would come this day. My mother paced my bedchamber restlessly while we waited to be summoned downstairs to my father's office.

"What can be taking so long?" she burst out, after half an hour had passed. "Surely they cannot be haggling over the dowry already?"

I said nothing, having no answer and knowing my mother did not expect one from me. What if he had come to tell us he had changed his mind? It was the question I dared ask only of myself. Or to tell us his parents had not given their consent? What then?

Well, at least Count Ricci is still available, as he remains unmarried to Elisabetta or anyone else. Yet at this, my heart only began to beat harder. Surely Signor Vespucci brought good news. Why else would he have been so eager to return?

I fought the urge to get up and pace with my mother.

Fifteen minutes later, my father's manservant came up to fetch us. "Madonna Cattaneo, Madonna Simonetta," he said, bowing, "Don Cattaneo requests your presence in his study with his guest."

My mother could not quite stifle her unladylike cry of glee, but managed to compose herself. "*Grazie*, Giorgio. We will be along directly."

He bowed again and left the room.

My mother came to me and clutched my hand in hers, pulling me from my chair. "This is it, *mia bella* Simonetta," she said. "Are you ready?"

She did not wait for an answer, but chattered on. "You are about to become betrothed! Your life is beginning!"

I smiled. "Perhaps we should go downstairs now, Mama. It would not do to keep my . . . suitor waiting."

She waved a hand dismissively. "It does not do to appear too eager. We shall go, then, but slowly. A lady never runs."

I followed my mother, my hand still in hers. We descended the stairs to the first floor, where my father's study was. My mother paused outside the door—squeezing my hand for just a moment—before pushing it open and stepping inside.

My father and Signor Vespucci both looked up as we entered, nearly identical expressions of delight on their faces. They had a decanter of wine between them on the desk, with just a splash left in each of their glasses. "Ah, there they are!" my father said. "Ladies, do come in, so we might share the good news."

Signor Vespucci drew up chairs for us, sweeping a bow as he returned to his own chair. Once we were both seated, my father spoke again. "Simonetta, Signor Vespucci has, having received the blessing of his parents, just now made me an offer for your hand, and I have accepted." He seemed not to notice my mother's sigh of happiness, and continued on. "The formal betrothal shall take place posthaste, and you shall be married before the end of the year. What say you, my dear?"

"I am quite pleased, Papa," I said, my eyes modestly on the floor. Yet for just an instant, because I could bear it no longer, I glanced up at Signor Vespucci, allowing him to see my eyes, my smile, so that he might know I spoke truly.

His face was positively rosy; his joy a visible, living thing. I looked back down, almost afraid to look upon his happiness, and afraid of my own response. Was this what Dante had written of, then? He had, after all, only ever loved his Beatrice from afar. Was it this feeling that had inspired him to write, this sensation as though I had stepped off of a high cliff and was falling, tumbling, yet with the sure knowledge that when the moment came, I would be able to spread wings and fly, like a bird soaring over sparkling blue waves?

My father was speaking again, and I had to struggle to pull my mind from my delicious descent. "We thought we should pour ourselves some wine and toast the happy occasion," he was saying. "We've glasses for you two as well; go on, then, signore, pour for your future bride, won't you?"

Signor Vespucci obliged, filling my glass, then his own. He lifted it to me, and tapped it against my own. "To your health, Madonna," he said. "And to our future happiness."

"Indeed," I murmured, holding his eyes as we both drank. Then I looked away, flustered. What could I be thinking, making cow's eyes at a man in the presence of my parents?

Oh, for heaven's sake, we were to be husband and wife. What did it matter anymore?

"Marco," my father said, familiarly addressing his future son-in-law, "tell my wife and your intended about the offer you and your family have so graciously extended to us."

"Of course," Signor Vespucci said. He shifted in his chair to more completely face my mother and me. "Once they had given their blessing to my marriage, my parents asked that I invite the three of you to Florence. That way the details of the betrothal contract can be worked out in person, and Madonna Simonetta can begin to become accustomed to her new home. We have already found a house at which to lodge you."

"Why, we should be delighted!" my mother exclaimed. "We will be able to make the journey, will we not, my dear?" She directed her question to my father.

"I am certain Genoa can spare me for a few months," he said. "I told Marco we are honored to accept."

Signor Vespucci's eyes sought mine again. "I shall be able to introduce you to my circle in Florence, Madonna Simonetta," he said. "And, of course, I shall present you to the Medici brothers, as well as their esteemed parents."

I felt my wings begin to stretch, to flex, ever so slightly. "I should like nothing better, Signor Vespucci."

He took my hand and kissed it. "Please," he said, "just Marco."

I knew that, very soon, I would be flying.

4

The household was, naturally, thrown into complete upheaval following Signor Vespucci's—Marco's—momentous visit. There was much to do in preparation for our departure for Florence, and my parents were determined to go sooner rather than later. "My family and I will be ready and delighted to welcome you at any time," Marco had said.

Yet we could not go too soon—not only because of all there was to be done, but also because my mother and I must receive calls from the rest of the ladies in Genoa, who sought to congratulate us and give me their best wishes (and, of course, marriage advice).

Each of these visits was much the same: glasses of watered wine with a matron whom I scarcely knew, and who was usually a great deal older than me. They advised me in everything from running a kitchen to choosing the best kinds of cloth to choosing a wet nurse for my children. Almost without variation, they exclaimed over how beautiful I was, and how I was certain to make Signor Vespucci the happiest of men, their tones and expressions hinting at something dangerous, scandalous, something of which we were not to speak.

Of course, Elisabetta and her mother came to visit as well. Once the usual congratulations had been made, our mothers drew their chairs up next to each other and began to chat away happily, paying us no mind.

Elisabetta smiled thinly at me. "So it is as I said. You have got your Florentine husband."

I smiled, in the open, honest way I had not allowed myself to when speaking to all the noblewomen of the city. "Yes," I said. "Or will have, at least. The betrothal is not yet signed, of course, so it is not official, but . . ."

She waved away my words. "Oh, come, Simonetta, do not be so coy. It is official, for all intents and purposes. You have won."

"Won?" I laughed. "What contest was I entered in without my knowledge?"

"The contest of being a woman, of course," she said, and I was surprised to see a hint of a sneer around her lips. "It has ever been a competition between us women, from the moment that Lilith was cast out of paradise in favor of Eve. You have your beauty, of which no one ever ceases to speak, and now your fine Florentine husband with his Medici friends. You, Simonetta, have won it all."

I was taken aback. "But I do not—"

"No need to know you are in a contest if you are always winning, is there? It is of no consequence. But mark my words, Simonetta Cattaneo—the Florentine women never forget what game it is they are playing, and they know the rules as well as they know their catechism. So beware."

Anger flared in me. "And what do you know of Florentine women and their rules, Elisabetta Abruzzi? You have never left Genoa any more than I have. What is this nonsense you speak, of contests and competitions and winning? If there is any victory here, it is not of my doing."

I paused, seeing Elisabetta's face flush red. I bit my lip in consternation. "I am sorry," I said. "I do not mean to speak harshly to you, my friend."

"Nor I to you," she said, the color still heightened in her cheeks. "It is just that . . . I will miss you. I am sad you are going. Truly."

I reached out and took one of her hands, where it lay in her lap. "Come to my wedding," I said. "I shall send you an invitation. You must come to Florence. It will be wonderful."

She remained still for a moment, then withdrew her hand. "I will see if my parents agree," she said softly.

I knew, right then, that it would be the last time I saw her.

Marco only remained in Genoa for two short weeks following his offer of marriage. Amidst all the congratulatory calls and visits, he came to take his leave of me one quiet afternoon. Now that we were betrothed, my parents left us alone in the receiving room with only Chiara for a chaperone.

"I am back to Florence at first light, to make everything ready for you," he said, once we were both seated. "I am afraid we have spent more time apart than we have together in our acquaintance, and it grieves me, but soon we will have our whole lifetimes to be together."

"Indeed," I said, before adding boldly, "And even so I shall miss you." The excitement of my parents, my neighbors, and everyone outside of this room meant little to me, I had found; what I wanted most was Marco's company. If only, I sometimes felt late at night, to reassure myself that I was not making a mistake.

No, I thought as I smiled at him. *This is no mistake.*

"I shall miss you, Madonna, more than words can express—even Dante himself could not find the words!"

I laughed. "Now you go too far, signore. There were no words so far to seek that they could not fly to Dante's pen."

"Then I must apologize to Signor Alighieri, and hope that his spirit does not take offense," he said. "Though as he was never in the same room with you, we will never truly know the extent to which he was able to capture beauty in his verse."

"More blasphemy! You would have me more beautiful than the divine Beatrice, then?" I asked, enjoying—and flattered by—our lively conversation.

"I would, and to the spirit of Beatrice I will offer no apology."

"Let us hope that she does not come to haunt us in our new Florentine home, then."

"No," he said. "I shall not allow it. Only happiness shall we have there. I promise you."

I smiled at him again as our eyes met. "I look forward to the fulfillment of your promise, signore."

"Ah," he said. "As I said, you must call me Marco."

I hesitated for a moment. I had not yet spoken his given name aloud before him, and it felt almost too intimate. "Marco," I said softly.

He rose from his chair and came to kneel beside mine. He was tall enough that, with him kneeling and me seated, our eyes were level. "Yes," he said. "I am yours to command, Simonetta." He took my hand and kissed it, his eyes never leaving mine.

What I did not realize right away amidst all the preparations was that I would not be returning to Genoa before my wedding, and thus perhaps not ever. It did not occur to me until I came into my chambers one afternoon to find my mother consulting with Chiara about the packing.

"Not the bed, nor the coverlets, of course—we shall buy her all new linens in Florence for her trousseau, and they shall have a bigger bed—they will need one." She giggled. "But, yes, we must have the dressing table sent, and the wardrobe . . ."

"Why?" I asked, stepping into the room behind them.

My mother turned, starting slightly. "Goodness, Simonetta, what are you doing, lurking at doors like that? A lady never eavesdrops like a common servant."

"I have only just now come in," I pointed out, a slight peevishness in my tone that I could not always master when speaking to my mother. "Why shall we need to take all my furniture to Florence with me?"

"For your new home, of course," my mother said. "What else? Not that Signor Vespucci will not provide you with some marvelous new things, naturally, but no daughter of the Cattaneo name shall come into her marriage looking like a pauper, I promise you!"

"But . . ." my confusion must have shown on my face, for my mother sighed as if in distress.

"Oh, Simonetta, surely you knew you would not be coming back here?"

"I thought . . ."

"Oh, my dearest, no. There would be no reason. We shall go to Florence, draw up the betrothal, then set ourselves to planning the wedding. Then you will be married, and move to your new home with your husband. There is no need for you to come back here."

"I see." I sat on the dressing table stool, picking up a ribbon that had been left to lay there and twining it idly through my fingers.

My mother came up behind me and placed her hands on my shoulders. "It will be better this way," she said. "Indeed, once you are in Florence, you will no doubt never wish to come back."

That night I prayed, as I had not all throughout the last weeks, that Florence would be everything I dreamed, that it would be the paradise of poets and painters that Marco had told me it was. Please, Lord, let me love it there, I thought, feeling too uncertain and childish to even speak the words aloud. Let me love it there at least a little.

And, I reminded myself as I climbed into bed, dragging my cloak of hair behind me and arranging it upon my pillow, Marco would be there. That much I could rely upon.

5

The city of Florence lay sprawled out below us, a mass of both brownstone and red-tiled roofs nestled among the brilliant, vibrantly green, rolling Tuscan hills. Above it all rose the massive dome of Santa Maria del Fiore, Brunelleschi's wonder, famous the world over. The cathedral rose above the city like a great sleeping dragon, watching over its domain even in its slumber.

We had heard of this modern wonder in Genoa, of course, but seeing it in person was an entirely different matter. The dome was egg-shaped, and had been finished with reddish tiles beneath the great white ribs of its supports. A cross sat at the very top, blessing those who beheld it from below as well as pointing upward into the heavens. As I gazed upon it, I marveled that so great a structure could stay upright without collapsing in on itself. It seemed a frightening thing, that lowly mankind had dared to build something that ascended so close to God.

My father came up beside me. "Beautiful, is it not?" he asked. "It is a lovely city. And every time I see *il Duomo,* I am struck anew by the majesty of it. Who knew that human hands could build such a thing?"

"God makes all things possible," I said, "especially such a great work, in His name. The city of Florence must be especially blessed."

My father was silent for a moment. "One might think so," he said at last. "And yet there are startling stories coming from the city of late, as well." He turned a stern face to me. "You must be careful, daughter. A part of me thought it was perhaps not wise for you to marry into this city, and yet we could not refuse such an offer."

"What do you mean?" I asked, perplexed. "What manner of stories do you speak of?"

He waved a hand dismissively. "It does not do to trouble women with such things. I should not have spoken of it." He walked away from me and returned to his horse. "Back into the carriage, ladies," he called to my mother and me. "We shall want to reach our lodgings before nightfall." Behind him were the two wagons carrying the luggage and our servants—save for Chiara and my mother's maid, who rode in the carriage with us—and at his words they began to slowly roll forward once again.

I did as I was told, still unsettled by my father's words. Surely my parents would not send me anywhere dangerous, regardless of how good the match was? Something in his tone, however, had suggested that these "startling stories" were of a danger other than the physical.

I would not think of it now, I decided, pushing such thoughts firmly aside as the carriage began to move down the hill toward the city. I was ready to embrace my new life in this place, and while I was sure it would not be without its difficulties, I would deal with them as they came.

We were a greater distance away from the city than it had appeared from our perch atop the hill, and it took us the rest of the afternoon to reach our rented house, which was near to Marco's family home in the Ognissanti district of Florence, on the banks of the river Arno. Once we entered the city proper, I craned my neck out the window to see the narrow cobblestoned streets, the tall buildings of terra-cotta and stone and wood, the laborers whom we passed and who had to jump out of the way to avoid our carriage. I was thwarted in my desire to see all of the city that I could, though, by my mother admonishing me to bring my head back inside the window. A lady never gawps, after all.

The sun was beginning its descent by the time we reached our rented lodgings. It was not a large house, with its tall and skinny façade squeezed in between the two larger neighboring buildings.

"This is it?" my mother asked dubiously, poking her head out of the carriage window. I had to bite my lip to keep from telling her not to *gawp*.

"It is just for a few months," I reminded her. "Did you expect us to take up residence in a *palazzo* the size of the Medicis'?" Of course, I had never seen the Medici *palazzo*, but based on what I knew of them I assumed it was large.

"Of course not," she huffed. "Do not take everything I say so literally, Simonetta."

Then why do you say such things? I wanted to ask.

We went inside, while my father remained in the street, supervising the unloading of our luggage. We explored the house with its small rooms, which did not take long, then ascended to the top floor to select our bedchambers. "Baths, I think, to wash away the dust of the road," my mother said to Chiara, following me into one of the smaller rooms that I had deemed as good as any other. "For myself and Simonetta. You shall need to wash Simonetta's hair, as well." She turned to me, grinning widely. "We want you looking perfectly fresh tomorrow, when we go to meet Signor Vespucci's family."

I had nearly forgotten that the next day we would go to call on my future in-laws. I shook my head slightly. I was far too tired from travel to think about it now. Instead, I napped on my borrowed bed while waiting for Chiara to locate a washing tub, find a source of clean water, and fill it so that she might bathe me. As soon as the ordeal was over I fell back into bed, not caring that sleeping on my wet hair would make for at least another hour of work on it in the morning.

The next day, Marco came to call for us in a carriage and took us to his large family home, the same home where he and I would also be residing after our wedding, for the customary dinner with our two families. It was during this time that I would be presented with my betrothal ring. His parents were very kind to us, and made much of my beauty and of me. His mother was rather quiet, and spoke only when she was spoken to—a womanly art that my own mother had never mastered, nor had I. His father seemed the sort to be a stern taskmaster, who had no doubt raised his son to know exactly what was expected of him. His parents had clearly spared no expense on the meal, and we dined well on sliced melon, a rich vegetable stew, fresh trout, and veal. They introduced us to a curious, pronged implement that was all the rage among Florence's well-to-do set: called a fork, it allowed one to spear and pick up bits of food without dirtying the fingers. It was rather odd to eat with, but I did appreciate the cleanliness it afforded—as well as what I guessed would be additional decorum, once I'd grown more comfortable with it and did not drop morsels back onto my plate quite so often.

The conversation consisted mostly of my father and Signor Vespucci speaking of business and politics, those of both Florence and Genoa. Every now and then Marco would catch my eye across the table and smile at me, and I would try to smile back as much as I dared without seeming immodest. Something about his smile made me wish that the two of us were quite alone, with no parents or chaperones near. Soon enough, I told myself, dropping my eyes from his. The first time we would be alone together, I knew, would be our wedding night, when whatever mysterious thing it was that took place between a married couple would happen between us. Well-read for a woman though I was, I had not come across the details of the marriage act committed to paper, though I was inclined to believe that that was more a result of the literature I had been exposed to rather than any delicacy on the part of writers at large. I was curious, intensely so, yet knew that I would need to wait for my mother to impart this forbidden knowledge to me, like a reluctant serpent whispering in the ear of an all-too-eager Eve.

After the meal, I was given my ring—a modest diamond set in a gold band—and our fathers adjourned to Signor Vespucci's study for more wine and to begin to discuss the terms of the betrothal. I did not know how long such things took, but I knew the wedding plans would not be delayed in any case—our mothers had already made passing mention of what cloth should be ordered for my trousseau and who should make my new gown for the occasion.

Marco's mother led us into the receiving room: a rather bare stone room, as any tapestries and wall hangings had no doubt been put away in the heat of summer. Even so, the simple wooden furniture that was there—chairs with embroidered cushions and a few small side tables—was of the finest craftsmanship. Once we were all seated, Signora Vespucci engaged my mother in conversation—something that entailed my mother doing most of the talking, while Signora Vespucci nodded and murmured politely in response—so as to allow Marco and myself to speak to one another without interruption. He drew his chair nearer to mine and leaned toward me.

"I have wonderful news for you, Simonetta," he said. "I wanted to tell you myself, before anyone else knows. I think you will be honored and excited, as I am. But you must not speak of this to your parents, mind, until we have received the official invitation."

"Dear Marco," I said, smiling, "whatever it is, have mercy and do not leave me in suspense!"

His eyes took on a merry glint. "Anything you wish, dearest lady. Upon my return I was invited to the home of the Medici family to dine. They were all so captivated by my accounts of your beauty—understated, as they shall see—that Lorenzo has invited you to dine as well. As soon as our betrothal is made official, I am to present you to him and the rest of his family."

Why I should be so excited for the esteem and notice of a man I had never met, I could not say—I only knew that my heart began to pound with excitement and nervousness in equal measure. "Truly, Marco?"

"Indeed." He lowered his voice a bit further. "Lorenzo's father, Piero, is quite ill—an invalid, for all intents and purposes. Gout—it runs in their family, sadly. As such, Lorenzo has largely taken over as head of the family." He reached out and squeezed my hand lightly. "You will make a wonderful impression on such an important man."

I was hardly listening, though I knew his words were important. "Whatever shall I wear? I do not know if I have a gown fine enough. . . ."

Marco laughed. "You could dress in a nun's habit and still be the most beautiful woman the world has ever seen. Do not fret, Simonetta. And remember, Florence is a republic. The Medici are not royalty."

I heard his words, but could scarcely bring myself to pay them any mind. This promised evening—whenever it took place—would be important, I knew it. I was no longer the little Cattaneo girl, the only daughter of a minor noble family. This was my chance to be seen. To be a woman of note and learning, to speak and perhaps be heard in this enlightened city. To be somebody, if only I had the courage.

6

After that first evening with Marco's parents, the betrothal negotiations continued on unimpeded, as far as I knew, for I was not privy to any of the particulars. All I knew was that before long the agreement was signed and sealed, and Marco sent me a bracelet of small pearls with a gold clasp to commemorate the event.

We settled into our life in Florence—a temporary diversion for my parents, but a true transition for me. Our first Sunday in the city, we went to Mass at Santa Maria del Fiore. The massive dome seemed even more extraordinary when beheld from the ground beneath it; I had heard that though it had stood for years now, many Florentines were still waiting for it to collapse at any moment. I could see why.

The entire structure was enormous, not just the great dome. Up close I was able to admire the intricate marble detailing on the outside, completed in not only white stone but also in stripes and blocks of green and pink. Tall, narrow windows were set into the sides, framed with elaborately carved stonework. Beside the cathedral stood its *campanile,* nearly as tall as the dome, built in the same multicolored stone as the cathedral itself. The bells rang an urgent yet melodious toll, calling worshippers to Mass.

It was a bit intimidating to step into such a large, grand structure—it made me feel quite small but reverent—and perhaps that was the point: one should always feel unworthy of stepping into God's house, yet this structure, with its somewhat plain yet mammoth interior, heightened that feeling. Light spilled into the sanctuary from the windows in the walls and set high up near the ceiling, and this, along with the simple, if massive, columns and arches, created a vast, airy space in which to hear the Word of God. Yet, for all the space and light, there was something a bit oppressive about the cathedral as well—perhaps due to the sprawling, elaborate fresco that graced the inside of Brunelleschi's dome. It depicted the last judgment and, in addition to the Lord welcoming the righteous into the glory of heaven, there was also, as might be expected, depictions of hell and the torments that await the damned. Sinners tumbled naked into hell, where demons tortured them and Satan stuffed them into his mouth, devouring them with his gnashing teeth.

The beauty and horror of the fresco captivated me, and I confess I spent much of that first Mass craning my neck to look upward, unable to tear my gaze away, trying to take in every detail of the beautiful and hideous artwork. I could not even begin to count the numerous figures in the fresco, from saints and angels and kings sitting in attendance on the Lord Jesus to the human souls being judged and the demons of hell; it was a riot of color and activity. Several times my mother pinched my arm, a not-so-gentle reminder that my mind should be firmly on the service. Yet for what other purpose was the fresco there, I reasoned, than to fascinate and terrify the faithful? To both inspire and instill fear? It was, I thought, much more effective than any sermon.

A few days after my betrothal gift arrived came a note. *We are invited to dine at the Medici* palazzo *a week from tonight*, so it went.

I shall come to escort you, with your maid for chaperone, if that is pleasing to your parents.

At the bottom of the parchment he had written, *Do not worry. No matter what you say or do, you shall enchant them. There is no woman, on earth or in Heaven, more charming than you.*

My mother, when I showed her the note, was quite beside herself. "In the name of all the saints, whatever shall you wear?" she exclaimed. "Nothing too elaborate, no; they have such pesky sumptuary laws in Florence. The cloth must be of the best quality, though; yes, these Florentines are cloth merchants all, they will know inferior quality from a yard off when they see it. We've no time to have anything made, have we? What have you brought with you? Quickly, let us see—Chiara! Come, child, we shall need your help. Simonetta, you must try a few things, and we shall see what flatters you best."

I had, of course, brought all my clothes with me from Genoa, save those that were too worn or no longer fit. As such there were several possibilities from which to choose, and my mother had Chiara lace me into all of them so that we might best decide.

In the end we chose one of pale pink silk, of the finest cloth but simple design. The bodice and long, wide sleeves were embroidered with small sprigs of flowers, and a cream band ran beneath my breasts, with the same floral embroidery. It was determined that this gown flattered my creamy skin and golden hair better than any of the others, as well.

When the appointed day arrived, I rose early, so that Chiara might bathe me and wash my hair. I then sat in the sun on the roof of our house, my trusty hat in place, so that the sun might dry my hair. Once it was dry—hours later—Chiara sat me in front of the dressing table and artfully twisted up and bound certain strands, pinning them about the crown of my head, while leaving the rest to flow freely down my back, as was appropriate for an unmarried woman. The final result took much more time than one would guess from looking at it, which was perhaps the point. She then dressed me in a clean shift, petticoat, and, finally, the gown. My neck was left bare, but I donned a pair of pearl earrings of my mother's, and finally clasped Marco's bracelet about my wrist.

The entire process took most of the day, and the afternoon sun was slanting its light down the streets and alleys of Florence by the time we were finished. I was exhausted, despite not having done much of anything at all. Yet I had to keep my wits about me for the upcoming gathering.

Marco came for me right on time, and Chiara and I were waiting in the receiving room for him with my mother. He came in and swept us a bow as we rose to our feet. "Simonetta, *mio cuore,*" he said. "You are a vision. I did not believe you could possibly look more beautiful, but today you have managed it."

I smiled. "I shall have to try something quite new for our wedding day, then."

"It does not matter, for I will be just as in love with you no matter what," he vowed. He offered me his arm. "Shall we, then?"

My mother trailed out behind us, offering me last-minute advice on etiquette and posture and "Do not blather on about your poetry in such company, Simonetta." Again, it was all I could do not to roll my eyes. I had not come to Florence to *not* talk about poetry. "*Si, Madre,*" I called over my shoulder as Marco handed me into the carriage, with Chiara following behind me. And then we were off.

7

The Medici *palazzo* was situated in the Via Larga, a stone's throw from the great cathedral, baptistery, and *campanile* in the Piazza del Duomo. The *palazzo* had been constructed, so Marco told me en route, by the great Cosimo de' Medici, father of Piero and grandfather of Lorenzo and Giuliano. "One of the greatest men this city has ever known," he told me, his eyes shining with pride in his homeland. "It is quite the building, as you will see. Many have tried to emulate and even surpass it, though none, in my opinion, have succeeded."

I only smiled encouragingly as he went on. Marco did not seem to notice that I was too nervous to reply.

I longed to turn my head to peer out of the carriage windows at the houses, shops, churches, and streets as we passed. I was so curious about this city of which I had heard so much, and taking in my new surroundings would have been a good way to keep my mind off of the importance of the evening ahead. But it would have been rude to so blatantly ignore Marco, even though he was doing nothing to put me at ease with his accounting of the accomplishments of Cosimo de' Medici, and even those of Lorenzo himself, just back from a very successful diplomatic visit to Milan, where he had apparently been very well received by Duke Galeazzo Maria Sforza himself.

And now, home in Florence, this supposedly great Lorenzo shall receive a simple noble girl from Genoa, I thought, my heart doubling its pace.

Thankfully, before too long, the carriage rolled to a stop, and Marco hopped out in order to help me down. "Here we are," he said cheerfully.

The building I beheld upon stepping out of the carriage was more like a fortress than anything else. Taking up the entire block on which it sat, it was a massive rectangular configuration of sandy-colored stone, allowing it to fit in nicely with the brown and yellow buildings and reddish-tiled roofs that covered Florence. Two neat rows of arched windows marched in orderly fashion across the top half of the façade, marking the second and third floors. At ground level were two massive doorways cut into the stone.

All in all, the exterior was intimidating, exuding force and power without being particularly beautiful or elegant. Perhaps these Medici—whom I had been told are not royalty, even though Marco spoke of them with all the awe and honor that I imagined one would accord to royalty—must be careful not to appear too ostentatious, as though they are setting themselves up too grandly. Perhaps it was fine for others to speak of them as royalty in this republican Florence, so long as they did not seem to see themselves that way.

As we approached the center door, Chiara following behind us, it swung open to reveal a servant standing behind it. "Welcome, signore, signorina," the man said, stepping aside to allow us in. "It is Signor Vespucci, is it not?"

"*Si*," Marco replied, "and my betrothed, Simonetta Cattaneo."

The servant nodded, though I noticed him sneaking another glance at me. "Very good. The party is just through the courtyard in the gardens, signore."

"*Grazie,*" Marco said, taking my hand and placing it on his arm. "I know the way."

The servant bowed, withdrawing and gesturing for Chiara to follow him, no doubt to the kitchens.

We stepped into a small but elegant courtyard, ringed with arches supported by simple, smooth columns topped with elaborately carved capitals. Above us, windows of the interior rooms of the *palazzo* looked down upon the courtyard. Directly across from the entrance, above the center arch, was a large stone carving of what I had learned to recognize as the Medici crest: a coat of arms with six balls arranged upon it.

In the very center of the courtyard, upon a pedestal, stood a magnificent statue in bronze of David. He wore a wide-brimmed shepherd's hat but was otherwise naked, and carried a great sword in his right hand, with his left hand resting confidently on his hip. As well it should: at the shepherd boy's sandaled feet rested the head of Goliath.

I drew away from Marco and stepped closer to the statue, intent on examining it further. Unfamiliar though I was with the male nude—real or rendered in art—I could still appreciate the detail, the lifelike quality of each line and curve of muscle and flesh. So lifelike was this David that I half expected him to step down from the pedestal and begin to converse with us.

Marco came to stand next to me. "Magnificent, isn't it?" he said softly.

"I have never seen anything like it before," I breathed.

"Nor will you, I shouldn't think," Marco said. "It was sculpted by the great Donatello." He turned to look at me significantly. "David is one of the symbols of Florence, of course."

"Is he?" I asked. "Well, this is a most worthy representation—more than worthy."

Marco smiled at my appreciation. "Come," he said, taking my hand again. "Let me introduce you to the family. Then you shall be able to discuss art to your heart's content."

We moved past the statue of David and stepped through an archway at the opposite end of the courtyard, emerging into a lovely garden ringed by the stone walls of the *palazzo*. Straight stone paths cut through the carefully tended grass, with small trees and flowers planted along the walkways, and more statues interspersed among the plant life. At either end of the garden was a fountain, sending streams of water bubbling peacefully into the basin below. On the grass in the center of the garden a long table draped in a gauzy tablecloth had been placed, with perhaps twenty chairs arranged around it. Some of those chairs were occupied, while other guests wandered about the garden.

So captivated was I by my surroundings that I did not immediately notice that the attention of every individual in the garden was fixed on me. Once I did, I began to blush. So much for appearing the consummate sophisticate.

"Marco, you scamp!" a voice rang out. An exceedingly handsome dark-haired young man—of about my age, I thought—came toward us. "This cannot be your betrothed!"

Marco laughed. "Indeed she is," he said. He brought me forward slightly. "May I present my affianced bride, Simonetta Cattaneo of Genoa. Simonetta, meet Giuliano de' Medici."

So this was the younger Medici brother. "An honor, signore," I said.

He took my hand and kissed it, bowing low over it. "The honor and pleasure are all mine, signorina," he said. His eyes roved appreciatively up my person, settling on my face, as though he was transfixed. "You have no idea."

A laugh sounded behind him. "Trust Giuliano to monopolize the most beautiful woman in any company," another man said, coming forward. "Signorina Cattaneo, I must apologize for my younger brother, and assure you that not all Florentines have such appalling manners." He, too, took my hand and kissed it. "Lorenzo de' Medici, at your service."

When he straightened up again, I got my first good look at this Lorenzo, the bright light of Florence. It was apparent that his brother had gotten all the good looks in the family, for Lorenzo himself could certainly not be described as handsome—indeed, one would not, perhaps, be wrong to describe him as ugly. His features, surrounded by almost black hair that came nearly to his shoulders, were too strong, too forceful: his chin jutted forward sharply, and his nose was large and almost somewhat flattened, as though it had been broken in a fight. His eyes were dark and deep, set beneath thick black brows. Yet even so, he radiated warmth and charm, and his eyes sparkled with intelligence and conviviality. For all Giuliano's almost godlike handsomeness, I knew that Lorenzo was the brother whom I would rather think well of me.

"I am honored to make your acquaintance," I said, favoring him with a smile.

For a moment his face, too, took on the same transfixed look as his brother's had. Then he chuckled and shook his head. "I do not even want to know what black arts you practiced in order to get such a beauty as your bride, Marco," Lorenzo said, turning to my betrothed and greeting him with a friendly embrace. "But, mind you, run straight to your confessor."

At first I was shocked to hear such a joke, but when all those around me laughed, Marco included, I pushed my discomfort aside. This Florence was a new world; if I wanted to belong here, I would have to listen and observe and acclimate. I must embrace it.

"Come, Signorina Simonetta," Lorenzo said, offering me his arm. "Allow me to introduce you to the rest of the party."

He led me the rest of the way into the garden. Behind us, Marco had been drawn into easy, jovial conversation by Giuliano, and for a moment I felt adrift without him, alone among strangers. Yet this, too, I cast aside. If I was to make my home here, then I must make friends of my own. I stood a bit straighter, head back, as Lorenzo began to make introductions.

"My new bride," he said, gesturing forward a petite, pale woman with fawn-colored hair and wide eyes. "Clarice Orsini de' Medici."

The name *Orsini* seemed familiar. If I recalled my lessons with Padre Valerio correctly, the Orsini were one of the leading noble families of Rome. The Medici had brokered an advantageous match for their heir, indeed. "Signora," I said graciously. "It is a pleasure. And I must thank you for your kind invitation."

"Of course," she said in a soft voice. "I shall be glad to meet more women amongst my husband's circle."

"And my esteemed mother," Lorenzo continued, walking me around the table. "Lucrezia Tornabuoni de' Medici."

Lucrezia, the formidable Medici matriarch, surprised me somewhat. She was quite tall, with her brown hair—a few shades darker than Clarice's—pinned up modestly. Her face however, was serene and inviting, much like paintings of the Madonna I had seen. Yet I knew that she was as able a politician and businesswoman as her husband—perhaps more so, some said. I also remembered a remark made in passing by Marco's father that the Medici matriarch was an accomplished poet, and had penned many lovely devotional verses. "It is my honor, signora," I said. "I have heard many wonderful things about you."

She laughed, and the sound was bold, somewhat belying her gentle appearance. "I thank you for saying so," she said. "My, but what a beauty you are! I have scarce seen your like all over Italy. Though I expect that I am not the first to tell you so. Signor Vespucci is a lucky man indeed."

My jaw felt a bit tight from smiling so much, from appreciating the same compliment over and over again, no matter how sincerely it was meant. "I thank you for saying so, signora," I said. "You are very kind."

The introductions continued, a few scholars and writers as well as other friends of Lorenzo's and Giuliano's. I knew that I would never remember so many names, nor which names went with which faces. But perhaps that is one of the advantages of beauty, I realized, my lips curving into what no doubt seemed to be a mysterious smile. A new sense of boldness flooded through me. These men would be falling all over themselves to remind me of their names, and with pleasure, so long as I engaged in conversation with them for a brief moment. I had been told all my life—subtly and not so subtly—that beauty was a weapon, a tool, a source of power—sometimes the only one available to a woman. Yet it was not until that first evening among the Medici that I began to consider—rather innocently—how I might use it as such.

At some point, Marco had reclaimed his place at my side. "Signorina Cattaneo was very taken with the statue of David in the courtyard," he told Lorenzo. "She is a lover of art as well."

"Ah!" Lorenzo said, turning to regard me with renewed interest. "And do you prefer sculpture or paintings, signorina?"

I flushed slightly at having his undivided attention. "In truth, signore, I favor poetry," I confessed. "But I have never seen such artwork as here in Florence—the fresco in the great *Duomo,* and now your statue."

"Then it is my fondest hope that Florence shall continue to oblige in your desire to see, and to learn," Lorenzo said. "Indeed, I shall contribute to your education further right now, if I may."

"Please," I said eagerly.

He motioned for me to take his arm again and led me to a statue in the center of the garden. "Yet another by the great Donatello," he said as we stopped before it. "Commissioned, as was the sculpture of David, by my grandfather Cosimo." He fell silent, presumably giving me time to study the work, for which I was grateful.

This statue, too, was in bronze, though it seemed to me that it must have been gilded with gold, so brightly did it gleam in the light of the setting sun. It depicted the biblical heroine Judith, her sword raised high above her head as she pulled back the head of the drunken Holofernes with her other hand, baring his throat for her to strike.

A look of grim determination was carved onto her face, and it was as if one could see in her eyes both her distaste for the bloody task ahead of her and her resolve to see it through anyway, to save her people no matter the cost.

"It . . . She is glorious," I said finally, knowing that Lorenzo was waiting to hear my thoughts. "She is . . . so brave, and yet so sad at the same time."

Lorenzo cocked his head, studying the statue again. "I confess I have never thought of it quite that way before, although now I do think I see what you mean," he said. "Perhaps it takes a woman to notice it. You see her cares and worries and struggles as a man may not."

"Perhaps," I said. "Is it not amazing how two people can stand side by side and look at the same work and see two different things?"

Lorenzo smiled. "You have just articulated my very favorite thing about art, signorina—be it statuary, painting, or poetry."

He fell silent again, giving me another moment in which to study the statue. This time, I noticed two small panels propped up at the base of the statue. Each was a small painting depicting the story of Judith. In the first, she was walking through a landscape that looked very like the Tuscan countryside, a curved sword in her hand. She glanced back over her shoulder, as though about to speak to her maid, who carried the head of Holofernes. Judith's dress looked much like one my mother owned, and her long blond hair was artfully styled and pinned about her head, just like a sophisticated Florentine lady. I felt myself smiling as I beheld her: her expression was troubled, upset by the assassination she had carried out; yet, unlike in Donatello's statue, there was relief there, too, and hope. Hope that the future would bring better things, hope that the bloody deed she had committed would not be in vain.

The second panel was much more gruesome. It depicted Holofernes' generals and guards finding his beheaded corpse within his tent. The viewer's eye was immediately drawn to the lifeless body in the bottom center of the small panel and, more specifically, to the blood that oozed from his neck, now relieved of its head. The body was contorted in such a painful way that one could feel the agony of his last moments. No doubt the reactions of most viewers would mimic the shock and horror on the painted faces of those discovering the body.

"Ah," Lorenzo said, noting where my attention had landed. "I am glad you noticed the panels. They are a recent commission by my father, as a gift for my mother. They have only just been completed, and so she and I thought to show them off beside their companion statue, if you will."

"Who is the artist?" I asked, my eyes slipping back to Judith's face.

"His name is Sandro Botticelli," Lorenzo said. "A recent discovery; in fact, it was one of your betrothed's Vespucci cousins who recommended him to me. A very promising young artist, as no doubt you can see." He chuckled. "Though I doubt he will thank me for placing his work next to that of a master like Donatello."

"His work can stand the comparison, though, I think," I said.

Lorenzo turned to look at me, quite seriously. "Do you think so, signorina?"

Inwardly, I cursed myself for feeling the need to voice my ignorant, uneducated opinion. "I am only a novice in appreciating such things, as I said," I excused myself.

"No, no," Lorenzo said. "Please, signorina. I welcome your thoughts most gladly."

I hesitated for a moment before speaking again. There is nothing for it now, I told myself. I may as well be bold, and hope that Lorenzo is as fond of opinionated women as he seems to be. "Donatello's statue draws the eye first, of course," I began. "It shines so in the light; how can it not? And I can certainly see why Donatello was a master, for this work is surely a masterpiece. And yet, even so . . ." I allowed my eyes to drift back to the painter Botticelli's panels. "Donatello's Judith is fearsome, distant, even though one can see the emotion in her eyes. She is magnificent and glorious, but intimidating for all that." I pointed to Botticelli's Judith. "Here, she is . . . different. More lifelike. I feel as though I could know her, as though I might pass her in the street. As though she could be me. Signor Botticelli has managed to capture such detail and feeling in only a small space. It is wonderful." I smiled, a bit sheepishly. "As I say, I know not much of art. I only know what it makes me feel."

"That is all one needs to know, Signorina Simonetta, truly," Lorenzo said, his voice soft. "Thank you for sharing your thoughts with me. They were most illuminating. You have given me much to consider."

I felt a flush of pride at his words, at his sincere tone. What a strange, wonderful place this Florence was.

"You must give your compliments to the artist himself, as well," Lorenzo added. "I know he will be pleased to hear your reaction."

I felt myself flush again as I peered around the garden. "Is he here?"

"Not yet," Lorenzo said, "though I expect him at any time. He has been a guest of ours often, of late."

I cast a glance at the entryway to the garden, as though willing this Signor Botticelli to appear. Having seen his work, having been so captivated by it, I found myself both eager and nervous to meet the man himself. An unexpected warmth found its way into my heart as my gaze made its way back to his paintings once more. Who was this man, able to bring such life to his art?

"But how rude of me," Lorenzo said. "Here I have pressed you for your opinion, and sought to impress you with my family's treasures, and I have not even offered you a refreshment." He glanced over his shoulder and, summoned by this merest of glances, a servant appeared. "Signore?" the man said, bowing.

"A glass of wine for Signorina Simonetta, if you would," Lorenzo said. "If that is agreeable, signorina?"

"Very much so," I said, smiling up at him.

His eyes widened slightly as they took in my face, then he chuckled and shook his head. "The men of Florence had best guard themselves now that you are here," he said. "That smile of yours is quite the weapon."

I preened slightly under Lorenzo's attentions, even though a part of me preferred it when he was praising my artistic insights. That praise, at least, I felt I had earned.

The servant returned almost immediately, bearing a crystal goblet of the dry red wine that was the pride of Tuscany. I took a sip, unsurprised at finding it to be of very high quality. "*Grazie,*" I said to Lorenzo.

"My pleasure," he said. "I should return you to your betrothed, I think. No doubt he does not relish being parted from you for any length of time, and who could blame him?"

He led me back to the rest of the party, who was gathered near the table. I took my place at Marco's side, causing him to turn and smile at me. "I see you are making friends," he murmured in my ear. "I knew you would be quite popular."

"Lorenzo is wonderful," I said, keeping my voice low. "Just as you said."

He squeezed my hand. "I could not lie to you, my Simonetta," he said. "You see, it is all just as I have said. The Florence I have brought you to is in good hands."

"Indeed," I said. "And I think Lorenzo de' Medici shall leave Florence a great deal more beautiful than he found it."

Marco and I sipped our wine, which was continually refilled by the Medici servants, and mingled happily with the other guests. Giuliano regaled me with tales of Marco as a boy, including a time that Giuliano had written a love note for a girl and asked Marco to give it to her after Mass—which my affianced husband did, only to pretend that it was from himself. "He has ever been a rascal, this man of yours," Giuliano teased. "Of course, it worked out perfectly for me in the end, as within the hearing of everyone the lady declared that swine could write finer verse!"

I laughed aloud along with Marco. "Ah, well, such were my just rewards for so dishonorable a trick," Marco said, wiping away tears of mirth.

"Indeed," Giuliano said. "Tell me, Signorina Simonetta, did he need to turn to tricks to win you?"

"He did not," I said, looking fondly up at Marco. "He was just his most charming self."

"I can be charming as well, my lady," Giuliano said, dramatically dropping to one knee before me. "And my skill at poetry has greatly improved, I swear to you!"

As we all laughed together, Lorenzo appeared at my elbow again. "Pardon my intrusion," he said, "but, Signorina Simonetta, there is one more person whom I should like you to meet, if you are willing."

"Of course," I said. "Do excuse me, Marco, Signor Giuliano."

I stepped away from the mirthful pair to where someone else—a striking blond man—waited. "Signorina Simonetta, let me present you to Sandro Botticelli," Lorenzo said. "Sandro, this is Simonetta Cattaneo, the betrothed of our dear friend Marco Vespucci."

So this, then, was the artist whose work I had been admiring. He bowed over my hand briefly, then straightened and allowed his light eyes to flick back to my face. "You are very beautiful, Madonna Simonetta," he said. Yet the words were not delivered in the honeyed tones of compliments to which I had become accustomed in my brief sixteen years; rather, this artist Botticelli spoke as one simply stating a fact, as though he must acknowledge what so many others had already acknowledged.

My answering smile was uncertain. "So I have been told, signore," I said. I found myself studying him—his face, his eyes, his hands, as though by doing so I could discover how he managed to create such marvelous works. "It is a true pleasure to make your acquaintance. Signor Lorenzo was kind enough to share with me your two panels of the story of Judith. I was quite taken with them."

"Were you?" he said, sounding surprised. "I must thank you for saying so. Judith is a most worthy heroine, and so I could only hope I might do her justice."

"You did that and more," I said. "You show her not only as a heroine, but as a real woman, too. I felt that I might step into the panel and begin to converse with her."

"Then I have achieved my aim." He paused as he continued to contemplate my face, yet not with the avaricious desire with which men usually studied it; nor with the envious, calculating gaze of most women. Rather, he considered my face as though he would unlock its secrets; as though he would solve the puzzle of *how* I was so beautiful. "I should like to paint you," he said finally.

My face grew warm. I felt all of the courtly worldliness I had worked so hard at cultivating since entering this *palazzo* beginning to dissolve, when faced with this strange, handsome man and the odd, forward things he was saying. Outrageous flattery I was quite used to; this bluntness, this plain acknowledgment of my beauty and, furthermore, what purpose it may serve was very new, and very much beyond me. I struggled to find words with which to respond.

Thankfully, Lorenzo came to my aid. "Why, Sandro," he said, laughing, "the lady has only recently arrived in Florence, and only just arrived amongst this company. Let us not overwhelm her entirely just yet." He lifted my hand, which had been resting on his arm, and kissed it, his eyes meeting mine. "Though I must agree that you would make a most exceptional subject for a portrait, Madonna."

I glanced quickly toward where Clarice Orsini de' Medici stood, to see if she had noticed her husband's impromptu kiss and, more importantly, the look in his eyes as he turned to me. But she was deep in conversation with her mother-in-law—or, rather, it looked as though Lucrezia was in conversation with *her*, and it was all Clarice could do to follow along with the rapid stream of words.

I exhaled slightly, relieved. It would not do to make an enemy of a woman whom I hoped might become a friend and confidant. Back in Genoa, I often did not see my friends again once they married, especially once they saw how their husbands looked at me. But perhaps here in cosmopolitan Florence—where I would soon have a husband of my own—things might be different.

"I thank you, Signor Lorenzo," I said. "You are most kind." Without thinking, I turned my body slightly to bestow a smile on the artist, who was still watching us closely. "And you have taken a most worthy painter under your patronage, I think. He is always looking for a chance to create art."

"Indeed," Sandro Botticelli said, before his patron could answer. "For what else gives meaning to life but art?"

"What, indeed?" I responded. "And do you include the works of the great poets in your definition of art, signore?"

"Signorina Simonetta is much enamored with poetry," Lorenzo interjected.

"I should be a fool not to," he replied. "What words are more beautiful than those of Dante? I can only wish to communicate so much through my brush as he does in a single stanza."

"I believe the priests would have something to say about this discussion," Lorenzo said, interest sparking in his eyes. "They would no doubt say that the Lord God gives all meaning to life, and the life best lived is the one which dedicates itself to worshipping and glorifying Him."

"And does not art, in its many forms, do just that?" I asked.

"Indeed it does," Lorenzo replied. "Yet Sandro, here, would speak of art as the highest aim in and of itself, without the glorification of God."

"That all artists glorify God in their work need not be said," Botticelli replied. "For it is from Him that all our talent comes. Yet do you not find art for its own sake to be worthy as well, Lorenzo?"

Botticelli's casual use of his patron's Christian name surprised me; the two men were obviously much closer than I had first realized. Yet they were, after all, of an age, and perhaps had more in common than their stations would suggest. "You know I agree with you, and then some," Lorenzo said, smiling.

I felt myself relaxing more than I had since arriving—since coming to Florence, in truth. Relaxed enough, in fact, that my tongue felt much looser than usual—perhaps I had the wine to thank for that as well. "I notice, Signor Botticelli," I said, looking at him, "that you are not surprised that I should have a knowledge of poetical writings, as so many men are when I speak of such things."

His blue gaze held mine, firm and unyielding. Here, I realized, was a man who had no doubt of his abilities nor of his place in the world. "It follows that where God has created so beautiful a face and form, He would have created an equally beautiful mind," Botticelli said.

I blushed. With this sort of compliment I had no experience and therefore no response.

"Well said, Sandro," Lorenzo said. "We shall make a courtier of you yet."

At that moment, Giuliano de' Medici appeared at his brother's elbow. "Now I find *you* are monopolizing the most beautiful woman present, brother," he said, grinning impishly. "Beware of making your new bride jealous!"

I blushed again, yet all three men laughed, so I did my best to join in. "Lay the blame for stealing away Signorina Simonetta at the feet of Sandro," Lorenzo said. "I believe he is already mapping out a canvas for her in his mind even now."

The two brothers laughed, but this time Botticelli did not join in. Rather, his eyes held mine again for a moment longer, and then he nodded briefly, so small a movement that I was almost not certain as to whether I had actually seen it.

But I had. And though I knew not then what secret accord I was entering into with the painter, I nodded ever so slightly in response.

Dinner was served shortly thereafter at the table in the garden. As his father was indisposed, Lorenzo sat at the head of the table, with his mother, as the lady of the house, opposite him. Clarice sat at her husband's right hand, and I was shown to the seat immediately to his left, with Marco right beside me.

"Do sit by me, Signorina Simonetta," he said. "You and Marco are our guests of honor, after all."

I gave what I hoped was a gracious smile at the honor and took the chair he indicated. Giuliano sat across from Marco, and with us thus placed the rest of the company found their seats.

As the pasta was served, Lorenzo engaged Marco in a lively discussion of Florentine politics, and soon the majority of those at the table had joined in, especially Lucrezia dei Tornabuoni. As I knew not of the issues of which they spoke, nor had I met any of the dignitaries to whom they referred, I kept silent and listened, hoping to learn as much as I could of my new home so that one day I might join in such discussions. Lucrezia, I noticed with surprise and admiration, more than held her own, and was listened to attentively by the men present, especially her eldest son. The mothers, daughters, and wives of Genoese noblemen were expected to stay silent when political matters were discussed, and they always did, at least in my experience. Yet I smiled as I listened to the discourse and to Lucrezia in particular. She certainly lived up to her reputation, as did this Florence of which I had heard so much.

One other guest, I noticed, who did not contribute much to the discussion was Sandro Botticelli. He was seated closer to Lucrezia's end of the table, and on the opposite side from myself. He spoke rarely, and several times I noticed him watching me. His gaze held the same intensity I had noticed earlier: as though I were a mystery for him to solve, as though he sought to see past my face and my skin and my hair to what lay underneath. As though he sought to see my mind, my soul.

Once I caught him studying me, and held his gaze in a challenge. Yet rather than look away, as would have been polite and seemly, he boldly met my eyes, as if he had been waiting for this moment all along. After several heartbeats, it was I who blushed and looked away.

My other admirer—though he at times took his attention from me long enough to join in the conversation—was Giuliano de' Medici. Out of the corner of my eye I would catch him stealing appreciative glances at me, though never was he so bold as Signor Botticelli—indeed, no one else at the table but I likely noticed.

I was used to such attention, but tonight, in this new and unfamiliar place and among new and unfamiliar people, it set me on edge more than usual. I sought Marco's hand beneath the table and took it in mine for a moment, and he squeezed my fingers, smiling his handsome smile at me. Instantly I felt better, more sure of myself.

The main course was wild boar—abundant in the Tuscan hills, so Marco informed me—seasoned with spices from the Indies, imported via Venice. On my first bite, I had to stifle a most uncouth exclamation of delight. My family had always dined well in Genoa, of course, but I had never tasted anything quite like this before—rich and flavorful and spicy. I forced myself to take small, ladylike bites, even as I became aware of just how hungry I was—I had not eaten since breaking my fast that morning, and staying poised as I met so many new and important people had left me quite famished. *A lady never shovels food in her mouth like a peasant,* my mother's voice admonished me in my head.

As the dessert was being served—a flaky, cream-filled pastry, along with a much sweeter white wine—Lorenzo sat back in his chair and beamed at Marco and me. "I am so glad you are able to be our guests tonight," he said. "I hope that as you settle into married life, we may see much more of you."

"We would be honored, as we are by your invitation here tonight," Marco said.

"Tell me," Lorenzo said, leaning forward in his chair again, gently spinning the stem of his delicate crystal wineglass between his thumb and forefinger, "have the arrangements been made for your wedding yet?"

"Not as yet," Marco said. "Our parents are in the process of doing so."

"Why, then," Lorenzo said, "we must host your wedding. Do you not agree, Mother?" he asked Lucrezia.

"A lovely idea," she agreed.

"Yes," Lorenzo said, becoming more excited the more he thought about it. "Yes, you can be married here at the chapel in the *palazzo,* and then perhaps a country reception at Villa Careggi? If that is agreeable to you both, of course, as well as your families."

I could scarcely believe my ears. "Truly, signore?" I asked.

He smiled at me. "Please, do call me Lorenzo."

"You do us too much honor," Marco said, taking my hand. "We would be delighted, and I am sure our parents will be equally so."

"It is settled, then!" Lorenzo said. "Consult with your parents, and then you shall name the date." He lifted his wineglass. "To the bride-and-groom-to-be, Marco Vespucci and Simonetta Cattaneo!"

The rest of the party lifted their glasses to toast as well. "To Marco and Simonetta!" they cried as one, and drank.

Clarice Orsini de' Medici had a somewhat pinched, sour look on her face as she drank the toast. I thought how her husband had, before all those present, consulted his mother about his plan, but not his wife. I felt a stab of pity for her. It could not be easy to be married to such a man as Lorenzo de' Medici, nor to be under the thumb of such a mother-in-law as Lucrezia dei Tornabuoni. For all the prestige that Clarice's own name garnered, she did not rule in Florence and never would.

Yet I was too happy, in that moment, to pay her much mind. I smiled at Marco as he squeezed my hand, his cheeks flushed with wine and excitement. Our lives in Florence were off to a much grander start than I could ever have anticipated.

As the dishes were cleared away and we rose from the dining table, Lorenzo again turned to Marco and me. "Perhaps you would like to see the chapel where you are to be married?" he asked. "I hope it will meet with your approval and that you do not change your minds upon seeing it."

I laughed. "I think that nothing could dissuade us from accepting your kind and generous offer, but I would very much like to see it."

"Indeed," Marco said.

Lorenzo led us out of the garden, back through the courtyard and past the statue of David, and up a staircase located to the right of the main entrance. We climbed two flights and then followed him down a short corridor, at the end of which was a door on the left-hand side.

"Here we are," Lorenzo said, opening the door and motioning for the two of us to precede him inside. I could not help but gasp as we entered.

It was a very small room, but such was the artwork that adorned its walls that it seemed quite grand indeed. Covering three of the walls was a series of paintings depicting the procession of the Magi, in glorious, vivid colors.

Lorenzo smiled at my reaction. "Beautiful, no?" he gestured to the frescoes. "My great-grandfather, Piero, commissioned the frescoes from Benozzo Gozzoli."

"They are incredible," I said, moving toward the wall across from me to more closely inspect the work. The detail was astonishing; each face with its own individual expression, each color gleaming brightly down at the viewer. And such a large work: there were scores of people, of animals, all processing through the familiar Tuscan countryside toward the Christ child.

"It never ceases to astound me what man is capable of," I murmured, walking along the wall, following the steps of the Wise Men. "To conceive of such beauty, let alone to capture it for eternity . . ."

I trailed off, and paused to look back at the two men, still standing near the door. Both of them were staring at me with an expression of naked adoration. I turned my gaze back to the frescoes, uncomfortable.

"Your intended is a most intelligent and perceptive woman," Lorenzo said to Marco, though I could feel that his eyes were still on me. "She is a true child of this *renascimento*."

"Indeed," Marco murmured. "This is a beautiful place for a marriage ceremony. I can think of none better. I shall never be able to thank you enough, Lorenzo."

Lorenzo waved his words aside. "It is quite enough for me to be able to make you and your bride happy."

I paused before the altar and genuflected. Then I took a step closer, that I might better see the painting that hung over it. It depicted the Virgin, blond and delicately featured in her robe of blue, kneeling beside the Christ Child. The Holy Child lay on a lush green forest floor, with a copse of trees surrounding them, and angels watched over the Virgin's worship.

"Ah," Lorenzo said, moving toward me. "The altarpiece is entitled *Adoration in the Forest*, by Fra Filippo Lippi. It was commissioned by my esteemed late grandfather, Cosimo." He chuckled. "Grandfather had quite the job in getting the work he paid for out of the monk, of course."

"Why is that?" I asked, turning back to Lorenzo.

"Surely you've heard the stories of Fra Lippi."

I shook my head.

He smiled. "It is perhaps not suitable conversation for a chapel. But Fra Lippi was a monk who absconded with his favorite model, a young nun named Lucrezia Buti. She quite distracted him from his labors, not to mention his vows."

I gaped at him, shocked at such a tale, and shocked that Lorenzo would speak of it so casually.

He seemed not to notice my reaction, but instead stepped closer to the altar. "She later bore him a child," he said. He pointed to the figure of the Blessed Mother in the painting. "And she can be seen there. He has immortalized her in many other paintings besides this one, so I am told."

I quickly forced myself to recover. That monks with their nun mistresses should be so openly spoken of—that a monk should use his mistress as a model for the Virgin, no less—was something else I must accustom myself to about this Florence, it seemed. Was this what my father sought to warn me of, when we arrived in the city? I wondered. Yet since Lorenzo clearly thought nothing of the tale, nor did Marco seem at all scandalized, I knew I must master myself. I stepped closer to the portrait. "She is quite beautiful," I said softly, studying the figure that Lorenzo had identified as Lucrezia Buti.

"Indeed," Lorenzo said. "It is easy to see how she may have tempted Fra Lippi from his vows, no? Ah, but," he said, taking notice of the deep blush that still clung to my cheeks, "I have offended you, Signorina Simonetta."

"No, no," I assured him. "I have just . . . never heard such a tale before, that is all."

"Indeed," Lorenzo said. "Sadly, Holy Mother Church is beset by such tales often enough. Celibacy is a difficult thing to ask of a man." He turned to face Marco, who had come up behind us. "You shall have yourself a wife who is a pillar of virtue, *amico mio*," he said jovially.

"Indeed," Marco said, his eyes seeking mine. "She is beautiful in her soul as well."

"That she is," Lorenzo said. "Come. Let us rejoin the others."

I followed the two men to the door of the chapel, but before I left I felt my eyes drawn back to the altarpiece again, and to the face of a woman so beautiful she had made a man forswear his vow to God. Was such beauty a gift or a curse?

And would the punishment from God that surely awaited this woman be worth what she had gained in return: being immortalized in such a work of art?

Still, I thought, in spite of myself, in a place I did not think I could ever share with anyone, it is a terribly romantic tale.

8

"There is one more thing I would show you, Signorina Simonetta," Lorenzo said as we left the chapel. "If you would allow me."

"Of course," I said, curious.

He led us back up the hallway down which we had come, up another staircase, and down another corridor before stopping in front of a set of double doors. "You mentioned your love of the written word, signorina, so I thought you might particularly appreciate our library." He flung open the doors in a wide, showy gesture, and I breathed a happy sigh at what was beyond.

Rows and rows of shelves stretched back into the narrow room, stacked one atop the other, higher than a man's head. Scarcely was there any empty space; books and manuscripts and papers were crammed—neatly so—into the confines of each shelf. I had never seen so many books in one place in all my life. It seemed to me that all the knowledge in the world must be in that room, waiting for those who would seek it out.

I felt my pride in my own small book collection wither and die. What must it be like to have so many books in your own home, for your own learning and pleasure, at your fingertips whenever you may choose to peruse them?

Openmouthed with wonder, I turned back to Lorenzo. "Have you read all these?" I asked, astonished.

He laughed. "I am afraid I have never had the time nor the leisure to read them all, much as I may wish to. I have read a good number of them, though; either in the course of my lessons as a boy or for my own edification. I have begun to add to the library myself, and plan to do so as much as I can."

I began to wander along the shelf-lined wall to the left of us. I resisted the urge to let my finger trail down the spines, and instead merely peered at each volume, imagining all the things that they might contain. Some were bound in worn, faded cloth; others in rich cloth of the brightest, most vibrant colors; others were bound in brown or black leather; still others were just bundles of papers held together with string.

"I do not know that any of my friends, learned as they are, appreciate this library quite as much as you, Signorina Simonetta," Lorenzo said. He clapped Marco on the back. "Beautiful and pious and learned, eh? Truly you are the luckiest of men, *amico*."

Marco nodded. "Simonetta and I share a love of Dante," he said. "It was one of the many, many things that made me fall in love with her."

I turned from the shelf and caught his smile with my own. I felt my heart flutter in that strange way I had begun to get accustomed to.

"Indeed," Lorenzo said. "No doubt Florence's greatest son. And tell me, Signorina Simonetta, have you also read the works of Francesco Petracco?"

"I have not heard this name," I confessed. "My formal education ceased a few years ago, and so I have had to make do with such books as I can find in Genoa."

"I have heard the name, but cannot recall any of his works at present," Marco said.

"Well, now you are here in Florence, signorina, the center of poetry and art and philosophy in all the world," Lorenzo said, as though Marco had not spoken. "We shall remedy this immediately." He began to move across the room toward one of the shelves.

I smiled as I watched him. "You speak of Florence as if it is like to Athens," I said.

He retrieved a book from the shelf and came back toward me with it in hand, grinning. "Precisely, signorina. You have divined my dearest wish perfectly—to make of this city of Florence a new Athens, where learning and beauty are prized above all. And you, who have both, may well be the jewel in Florence's crown before long." He bowed and presented me with the book. "A gift, signorina. For you and your betrothed. A book of Petracco's poetry."

"Oh, but I could not accept—not from your own library!" I protested, even as Marco stepped forward and took the book on our behalf.

"You need think nothing of it, signorina. I have several copies of these particular poems, and so do not deprive myself or my household the pleasure of reading them by making you such a gift," Lorenzo said. "And I wish to extend to you—to the both of you—an invitation. I pray you to make full use of my library whenever you like."

I was quite overwhelmed by Lorenzo's generous offer—and to a woman he had met just a few hours ago.

"That is most kind and generous of you, Lorenzo," Marco said, finding words when I was not able to. "I thank you, on behalf of us both."

Lorenzo nodded, but he was looking at me. "You are most welcome. I am happy to share these treasures my family has acquired, and to make such friends happy." He began to lead us back to the doors. "Now we must return to the party, before I am accused of being derelict in my duties as a host!"

"You are anything but, my friend," Marco said, falling into step beside him, and I followed the two men out. I placed a hand on Marco's shoulder and gestured to the book, which he handed to me wordlessly, even as he engaged Lorenzo in a new topic of conversation.

Walking behind them, I took a moment just to enjoy the feel of the book in my hands. It was bound in coarse leather, and the paper was thin; it was not as fine as some of the volumes I had glimpsed on the shelves. Yet it mattered not at all. To hold a book, any book, in one's hands, to smell the leather and the paper and feel the smooth pages beneath one's fingers, to anticipate the pleasures contained within, was a gift and a blessing. I could not resist the temptation of opening it and reading a few lines of the first poem. Yet before I could get any further, we had returned to the courtyard where the evening had begun, and I could read no more. In spite of such illustrious company, however, I could not help but wish that I might take myself off to a chair in a corner and devour the entire volume in one sitting, so entranced had I been by just the few lines I had read. From the smile that Lorenzo gave me when he saw me clutching the book tightly, protectively, lovingly, I knew that he, at least, understood.

We took our leave not long after that, and Marco called for our carriage to be brought around. Lorenzo bid us an effusive farewell, and I received smiles from Lucrezia and Clarice, who both said that it had been a pleasure to meet me, and that they would come to call on me soon. We passed the painter Botticelli again, and he bowed deeply and kissed my hand without a word.

Giuliano de' Medici saw us out. "I shall look forward to your wedding, though the occasion shall break my heart," he said. He clapped Marco on the back, then turned to me. "Signorina Simonetta." He clasped both hands over his heart. "The mere sight of you has ruined me for all other women, for all time."

I laughed; Giuliano, it seemed, managed to put everyone at their ease. "Away with you, signore," I said. "Would you so cavalierly break the hearts of all the women of Florence?"

"Ah, that you should speak of heartbreak, when I must watch you marry my friend!" he exclaimed. "If only I had found you first!"

I glanced at Marco, to see what his reaction to this was, but he only laughed, prompting me to do the same. "Such a devoted chevalier!" I said, warming to this game of courtly love. "I shall remember your broken heart in my prayers, signore."

He took my hand and kissed it, his lips lingering longer than was proper. I felt myself flush; and who could blame me, when Giuliano was so very handsome? "May the Lord take pity on me," he murmured, low enough that only I could hear, and there was something very different about his tone this time.

Fortunately, though, our carriage came around, and Giuliano released me. Marco helped me in before climbing in beside me, followed by Chiara, who had been summoned from the kitchens. Then, with a flick of the reins, we were away, and the grand Medici *palazzo* faded into the night behind us.

"How did I do?" I asked Marco, a bit breathlessly, as the carriage bore us home.

He smiled broadly. "You were marvelous, *amore mio*. Better than even I had imagined. They were all enchanted with you, and rightfully so." He shook his head. "That Lorenzo de' Medici and Lucrezia dei Tornabuoni should offer to host our wedding . . . I had never dreamed of such an honor."

"Nor I," I said. "Are they always so generous, these Medici?"

"With those they consider their friends, yes," Marco answered. "And we are blessed that they should consider us so." He smiled at me again, pride in every curve of his lips, his eyes. "You were wonderful, Simonetta," he said again. "Truly." Yet, as he sat back against the cushioned seat of the carriage, a subtle frown creased his forehead.

I thought to ignore it, but when his expression had not changed after a moment, I spoke. "What is it, Marco?" I asked softly. "You look as if something is amiss."

He glanced up at me, and his expression cleared like clouds fleeing before the sun. "It is nothing," he said. "Only . . ."

"Yes?" I prompted eagerly. If we were to be husband and wife, then we must learn to confide in each other. I hoped that soon Marco would do so without hesitation. Suddenly dread slid down the walls of my stomach; perhaps something about my conduct gave him pause? Perhaps I did something foolish, or inappropriate, and have embarrassed him. Perhaps he was even then trying to find the words to reprimand me, as he had every right to do as my future husband.

But when Marco spoke, his words were not what I had expected. "Lorenzo introduced you to that painter, I believe, *sì*? What was his name? The blond one?"

"Sandro Botticelli," I supplied.

"Yes," he said, and that troubled look returned. "Perhaps I should not speak of it, but . . ." he glanced up at me. "I do not suppose that you noticed, but I should say that I did. He was staring at you for much of the meal, quite blatantly so. It was inappropriate and rude. I should have thought that anyone enjoying the patronage of the Medici family would know to behave better."

"I am used to such attention from men," I said, uncomfortable, as though I myself had done something wrong. I curled my fingers tightly around the book that sat in my lap, picking at the leather binding. "It may trouble you, and rightfully so, but I fear it will not cease." I smiled. "Not until I am old and wrinkled and all my hair is gray, in any case."

Marco smiled at this, and leaned over and kissed my cheek. "Even in your old age, you will still be the most beautiful of women," he said. "But . . . no. This attention was something quite different, I think—quite different from even the attention paid you by Lorenzo and Giuliano."

I wondered, fleetingly, if he had noticed the obvious appreciation with which both Medici brothers had regarded me, and how it made him feel. Perhaps he felt that, as his social betters, they had the right to look on his future wife in any way they chose, and there was nothing he could say to censure them.

The painter Botticelli was not Marco's social superior—quite the reverse. Yet I knew precisely what he meant when he spoke of the painter's gaze upon me, for I had felt the same way myself, upon noticing him observing me. His was a different sort of regard altogether; yet I could not confess to Marco that I had noticed. Nor could I confess that I had been deeply flattered, having fancied myself his next Judith in one of his paintings, perhaps. "Lorenzo had shown me some of his work, and so introduced me to the painter when he arrived," I said. "He—Signor Botticelli, that is—said he wishes to paint me. Perhaps that was why he studied me so closely."

"Oh, he does, does he?"

"Yes, I believe so," I said.

"Hmph." Marco sat back again and crossed his arms over his chest, like a petulant boy. "Even worse. That he should speak to you of such a thing before getting permission from me, your future husband."

"I did not agree, nor make any promises as to my cooperation," I hurriedly assured him. "Though I was indeed flattered by his suggestion that I am fit to sit for him."

"Hmph," Marco huffed again. "He will never have had such a subject as you, I should think." But he had begun to smile a bit. "If you wish to have your portrait painted, you need only ask. Florence is full of artists who will be falling all over themselves to paint you."

I did not agree, nor make any promises as to my cooperation, I had said to Marco. But, later that night, I remembered that strange intimate look that had passed between the painter and myself, that odd and unbidden moment of accord, and knew that my words had not been quite true.

9

The next afternoon—after I had already described every detail of the previous evening to my mother over breakfast—one of the servants came into the sitting room with a message. "A caller here for you, Madonna," he said.

"Indeed?" my mother said. "Who could it be? I have yet to make any acquaintances in Florence—other than dear Marco's parents, of course—"

"Not for you, Madonna Cattaneo," the man said. He turned to me and inclined his head. "For Madonna Simonetta."

"For me?" I asked, surprised.

"Yes. Clarice Orsini de' Medici."

"My word!" my mother tittered. "Such an illustrious guest! And you only made her acquaintance last night!"

"Indeed," I said. "She did express her desire to call on me, though I had no idea it would be so soon." I summoned my dignified, sophisticated persona again, and wrapped it about me like a heavy, fur-lined mantle. "Do show her in without delay."

The man bowed his head again. "Very good, Madonna Simonetta."

He disappeared, and reappeared again a few moments later, bowing as the slight figure of Clarice entered the room.

I rose from my chair, and my mother did the same. "Signora Medici," I said, coming to meet her. "You honor me with your visit."

"The honor is all mine," she said, removing her cloak and handing it to the servant. "I hope I am not intruding, to arrive unannounced like this."

"Not at all." I turned to my mother. "May I present my mother, Cattocchia Cattaneo. Mother, this is Clarice Orsini de' Medici, wife of Lorenzo de' Medici."

"A pleasure to meet you, Donna Cattaneo," Clarice said.

"A pleasure and an honor to meet you as well," my mother responded. "And welcome to our house, temporary though it is."

"It is a lovely house," Clarice said. "I hope you all are comfortable, and are enjoying your stay in Florence?"

"Oh, very much," my mother said. "Simonetta has told us of your husband's very generous offer to host her wedding to Marco—to Signor Vespucci, that is. So very kind. We are honored beyond words."

"It is our pleasure, that we might bring joy to our friends," Clarice said softly, and I remembered, with some discomfort, her look of pique the night before when Lorenzo, together with his mother, had spontaneously offered to host the wedding.

"In any case," my mother said as, much to my surprise, she began to move toward the door, "I shall leave you young women to your talk. So very lovely to meet you, Donna Medici."

"Likewise," Clarice murmured, and my mother left the sitting room.

I had thought for certain that my mother would wish to stay, to listen in on our gossip, and to cultivate a connection of her own to the Medici family. Yet perhaps she wished for me to become accustomed to receiving and entertaining my own callers, as I would soon need to do as Marco's wife.

"Please, sit," I murmured, and Clarice took the seat my mother had just vacated. "I shall send for some wine."

"That would be lovely," Clarice said.

I quickly stepped outside the room and sent one of the maidservants to the kitchen with instructions. Then I returned to the sitting room and took up my chair again.

"I thank you for your hospitality," Clarice said in her soft voice.

"Not at all," I said. "I must thank you again for yours last night. It was so wonderful to meet some of my future husband's friends."

"Indeed," Clarice said. "And no doubt you shall be seeing much more of them from now on. Lorenzo likes to keep his friends close."

"I gathered as much. I was also introduced to a few writers, I believe, as well as a painter, Sandro Botticelli."

"Yes," Clarice said. "Signor Botticelli is a new find of my husband's. Lorenzo has yet to favor the man with a commission himself, but he has been about a good deal of late. I believe he is establishing his own studio in Florence."

"How lovely," I said, not sure how else to respond, nor how to inquire about him further without seeming improper.

"Indeed," Clarice said, as though she did not care one way or the other about Signor Botticelli and his work. "And you no doubt met Marsilio Ficino as well, the scholar."

"I believe so," I said. "In truth, Madonna Clarice, I was introduced to so many new people last night that I do not know if I could identify the face which belongs to each name."

She smiled. "I am not surprised," she said. "Signor Ficino was a great friend of my husband's grandfather, and was one of Lorenzo's own teachers. He keeps him and many other scholars and artists always about." She sighed. "I have found it somewhat wearisome, being always in the company of men."

I found it telling that she did not mention Lucrezia dei Tornabuoni, but I kept my silence.

"This is why I was so happy to make your acquaintance, Madonna

Simonetta," she said, her expression brightening. "It will be so nice to have another woman to converse with."

I smiled. "And I was equally delighted to make your acquaintance," I said. "What friends I had I left behind in Genoa."

"Of course," she said. "And I cannot imagine—" she broke off. "Forgive me. I do not mean to be so forward."

"No, please," I said. "If we are to be friends, you must speak freely, Madonna Clarice."

"If we are to be friends, you must call me Clarice."

"Only if you will call me Simonetta," I said, smiling. "But I pray you, Clarice—you may say whatever you wish."

"Indeed," she said. "This may be quite inappropriate of me, but I—well, I shall be frank, as you wish. Upon seeing how beautiful you are, I thought that I should hate you. But that would be quite wrong of me, because you—why, you are lovely, both within and without." She blushed. "I am sorry. I should not have—"

"No, no," I said. "I confess that I have never been able to count many female friends—I suppose for jealousy. Though God in His wisdom has given me a face and form that many consider beautiful, there have been times when I wished that He bestowed His blessing—if indeed it is—on someone else."

Clarice laughed. "And so the beauties of the world pray to be plain, and the plain girls pray for beauty."

I laughed as well. "Perhaps it speaks more to the contrary nature of women than anything. Though I would venture that men are contrary enough, in their own way."

"I can promise you they are."

"As I will learn, soon enough," I said. "I do not know much of men nor their ways at present."

"As a wife, you shall learn all too quickly," Clarice said.

Here our conversation paused, and we both smiled at each other good-naturedly. Here was a woman—a friend—who would understand my concerns, my troubles, perhaps even my sorrows, and could teach me to fit in within Florentine society in a way that Marco never could, recent arrival though she was herself.

Just then, the maidservant came in with the carafe of wine and two glasses, and she served my guest first, then me. She curtsied and withdrew, and Clarice and I each took a sip, letting the silence continue.

"You must tell me of Rome," I prompted after a moment, remembering that she had come from one of the great noble families of the Eternal City.

Clarice smiled, pleased to be reminded of her home. "To be frank, I had thought that when I left Rome, I would not miss it in the least." She wrinkled her nose slightly. "It is not half so beautiful as Florence. There are beautiful churches, of course, and the *palazzi* of the great nobles—my family included—are sights to behold. Many of the cardinals live in splendor as well, though no *palazzo* is so grand as that of the Holy Father, as is only right."

"And have you visited the *palazzo* of the Holy Father?" I asked, diverted. "Have you had audience with him?"

"Oh, of course," Clarice said, "with more than one pope. My family—the Orsini—are second only to His Holiness in Rome." She wrinkled her nose. "No matter what any of the Colonna might tell you."

I hid a smile. In his history lessons, Padre Valerio had made many mentions of the Orsini and Colonna families of Rome, and their fight for dominance over the Eternal City and even over the pope himself.

"No, but . . ." Clarice trailed off, as though beginning to lose herself in the past. "Despite its occasional splendor, Rome is quite different from what you must be imagining, Simonetta. It is dirty and violent and dangerous. The Tiber floods and kills people every year, and when it does not flood it is a cesspool of waste and garbage and things a good woman should never think of. The popes and their court were in Avignon for far too long, and when they returned, the city was nearly past saving, it seems. One pope after another has striven to set the city to rights, but it will take much more time than I am likely to be granted in this lifetime. It will be many years before Rome is worthy of the title Holy City again."

I remained silent, disappointment washing over me. I had always been taught that one must strive to see Rome in one's lifetime; to go and pray before the site of St. Peter's burial; to seek an audience with the Holy Father and ask for his blessing. The picture Clarice painted was not at all what I had expected.

"And so, as I said, I did not expect to miss it," she went on. "Especially not once I saw how beautiful Florence is, and how clean in comparison. And when I saw the state of my husband's family, well—I thought I should be quite happy here." She cast a sad smile at me. "But perhaps this is yet another example of those contrary ways of women you spoke of. I miss my home, even if it is not what it ought to be. Even if there is nothing here but reasons for me to be happy."

"Surely no one can fault you for missing your home," I said. I noticed she had spoken of all the reasons she had to be happy in Florence, but had neglected to mention whether or not she was truly happy.

"Perhaps not, but a woman must do her duty no matter what she feels inside," Clarice said. "It may be that I am as yet not completely used to Florence. I do not know. The society here is so different. The things my husband and his friends speak of sometimes, why . . . no one speaks so in Rome. No one could. It is heresy, the things they say."

I was unsure how to respond. I was fairly certain that I had engaged in just such a conversation last night, with Lorenzo and Signor Botticelli. I could hardly admit that to Clarice, nor could I confess that I hoped to engage in such talk often enough in the future, for it thrilled me to the core, even as it made me nervous.

"But that is enough of my melancholy," she said, reaching for her wine again. "You must tell me of Genoa."

I warmed to the new topic instantly, describing for my new friend the bustling, busy port; the way the sun sparkled and shimmered on the sea; the way the sun set into the sea each night, bathing the water and the buildings in a brilliantly colored glow.

"It sounds beautiful," she said when I had finished. "Far more so than Rome. I should like to visit sometime, with you as my guide." She smiled. "If our husbands can spare us, of course."

"We shall implore them to do so," I said, "for I should very much like to show you my city, and my parents would be honored to have you as a guest."

Our talk then turned to other things, of what foods Clarice recommended I try, and what seamstress she recommended for my wedding gown. We laughed and sipped our wine, and the maidservant, unbidden, brought us a plate of olives and cheeses as well. Soon, half the afternoon had passed without us so much as noticing.

"Goodness," Clarice said, taking note of the slant of light through the windows, "I suppose I must take my leave and not impose upon your hospitality any further. I am to dine with my husband and his mother and brother soon, in any case."

"And Lorenzo's father?" I inquired. "I have heard that he is not well."

"He is not," Clarice said bluntly. "I fear that he will not last the year, though—" she broke off, as though she had been about to say something she should not. "It would be a great sadness for Lorenzo and Giuliano and their mother, and for me as well," she said instead. "Piero has been nothing but kind to me since my arrival in Florence."

"How sad, that he should be so ill," I said. "You and your family have my sympathies."

"I thank you," she said, rising to take her leave. "It has been difficult."

I rose to see her out. "Do give my regards to your husband, as well as to Giuliano and their mother."

"I shall," she said. "And I shall see to it that you are invited to dine with us again soon."

"I will look forward to it," I said, as we moved to the front entryway. "Your husband probably told you, but he also extended use of his library to Marco and myself. I do not wish to trespass on his generosity, but I hope very much to take him up on his offer."

Clarice went still, for just a moment. "He did not mention it," she said lightly, "but it does not surprise me. Lorenzo is very generous to his friends. And I do hope you will make use of the library. It shall give us another excuse to spend time in each other's company."

"Then I should like nothing better," I said. "Books and companionship are two of life's greatest pleasures, I find."

Clarice laughed. "What an interesting creature you are, Simonetta. I have never been one for books myself, and I cannot see that you, beauty as you are, have much need of them."

I smiled. "So I have always been told, but I cannot seem to help myself."

She laughed again. "When next we meet we shall drink a toast to books and companionship, then." She stepped out into the street and clasped my hands in hers. "I thank you again for hosting me, and I hope to see you again very soon."

"I hope for the same," I said, squeezing her hands. "And it was my pleasure."

Clarice climbed into her carriage and waved one hand out of the window, then was gone.

I turned and went back into the house, unable to stop a smile from spreading across my face. A friend—and a female friend, at that. Hopefully she would prove to be a true friend.

Elisabetta's words before I left Genoa returned to me, unbidden: *Mark my words, Simonetta Cattaneo—the Florentine women never forget what game it is they are playing, and they know the rules as well as they know their catechism. So beware.*

Clarice Orsini de' Medici certainly did not seem to fall into the mold of Florentine women of which Elisabetta had spoken. Of course, I thought, as I had asked Elisabetta at the time, what would she know of fashionable Florentine women? She knew no more and less than I, as Clarice had just proven.

10

With a chapel for our marriage ceremony and a villa for the reception, the wedding plans began to move forward at a much more rapid pace, and I, for one, was glad. I had come to Florence to make a marriage, and I was eager for it to take place so I could step into the new life I was building for myself.

I had virtually nothing to do with the arrangements. My father selected the fabric from which my gown would be made—something rich and fine enough to show off our family's status, but nothing too outrageously expensive. I met with the dressmaker for my fittings, and took her recommendation as to the cut and style, so that the gown would be as fashionable as possible while also setting off my beauty to its greatest advantage.

My father and Marco's also met to devise a guest list. I did not see it myself, but no doubt it was full of mostly Florentine dignitaries, from government officials to important and wealthy businessmen. Invitations were likely also sent back to our friends and acquaintances in Genoa, though how many of them would make the journey for the wedding remained to be seen.

Marco also sent me a trunk full of carefully selected fabrics, some sumptuous for formal occasions, and some plainer for everyday wear. *My wife must be well outfitted as befits our station, in the finest cloth that Florence has to offer,* his accompanying note said. *Have these fashioned in whatever styles you please—no doubt Clarice Orsini de' Medici can advise you. These fabrics shall be as the petals on a flower, and only serve to make you even more beautiful than you already are.* He signed it *Yours, Marco.*

I took his advice and, in the days leading up to the wedding (set for the beginning of August), I sent Clarice a note begging her to call on me, that she might help me make some fashion decisions.

"My goodness," she said, as I opened the trunk containing the fabrics, which had been carried up to my dressing room. "Dear Marco certainly thinks much of you." She raised an eyebrow. "Perhaps he fears that if he does not lavish you with gifts, you will cast him aside for some wealthier, more attentive suitor."

I straightened up and turned to face her, offended—did I seem like the sort of woman who would go back on my word, on my honor? Who cared for nothing more than money and gifts? But I saw from the sparkle in her eye that she was simply jesting with me. "I do not know that I could find a more attentive suitor than Marco," I said, relaxing. "And, indeed, I find my heart is quite set on him."

Clarice studied me carefully as I spoke. "You do love him," she said. "I can see it."

"All that I know of love is what I have read in poetry and stories," I confessed. "But I find that I can no longer imagine my life without Marco, nor do I wish to."

She smiled. "That rings of love enough to my ears. But, as to a more attentive suitor," she said, "I think you do not give my brother-in-law enough credit."

"Giuliano?" I said, surprised and diverted from the riches in the trunk. "Whatever do you mean?"

She drew a folded piece of parchment out of her sleeve and handed it to me, her eyes bright with mischief. "When he learned that I was coming to visit you, he bade me give you this. He has not ceased speaking of you since you dined with us."

"Indeed?" I said. I unfolded the paper and read through it. It was an elegantly penned love poem, though Giuliano was certainly no Dante. "Flattering, to be sure," I murmured. "But what am I to make of this?" I brandished the paper at Clarice, and she took it and read it as well.

"Why, nothing," she said. "It is courtly love, nothing more. It is all the rage amongst my husband and his set. They write words of love and worship to the most beautiful women they can find. It is chaste enough—" She paused, then took a deep breath. "Usually, that is."

"And so what is my role in all this?" I asked her, feeling like a gauche, unsophisticated child. "Am I to write back, to respond? Should I tell Marco?"

Clarice laughed. "Dear Simonetta, your role—as near as I have been able to tell in observing such games—is to simply be adored, and to enjoy yourself. Revel in it!" She grinned. "Indeed, you had best ready yourself to be so adored by every man in Florence."

"Away with you," I said lightly to Clarice, casting Giuliano's poem to my dressing table, ready to forget it. "Now, back to these fabrics. I quite like the cut of the gown you are wearing. Would you permit me to have a copy made?"

"Indeed I shall," she said, "though low necklines are coming back into fashion, so keep that in mind. It is a style that shall flatter you particularly well, I think."

And so we spent a happy afternoon sorting through Marco's gift to me. Clarice accepted my invitation to stay for dinner, and she was her perfectly charming and gracious self toward my parents, making for a merry evening for all.

In those days preceding my wedding, it also fell to my mother to explain what would occur on the wedding night, and what would be expected of me in the marriage bed. I could not conceal my shock and horror when she first outlined the details of the marriage act.

"But that is disgusting," I said. "How can I—"

"Simonetta," my mother interrupted, covering my hands with her own. "I can see how it might seem so, but it is your duty. It is your duty as a wife to bear children, and to give your husband pleasure so that he need not seek it elsewhere and fall into sin."

I was silent. For a young woman with such a thirst for love poetry, I could not believe that the knowledge of such things had completely eluded me for so long.

"In time," my mother said, hesitantly, "you may come to enjoy it. Some women do."

I blushed at the thought.

"But your pleasure is of no consequence," my mother said quickly. "Your only objective must be to please your husband. And so, on your wedding night, when he comes to your bed, you will still be dressed in your shift, and you will simply lie back and let him complete the act."

I mulled this over, trying to picture myself and Marco engaging in such an animalistic act, yet unable to do so. My breath hitched.

My mother patted my hand, noticing my distress. "You shall get used to it in time," she said. "And you have a few days yet to prepare yourself, and to get accustomed to the idea. It is necessary, I am afraid. God in His wisdom has decreed that this is how children must be brought into the world, and so we women must endure."

With that, my mother left me alone in my bedchamber, to contemplate this new and heretofore forbidden knowledge I now possessed.

Once again, the picture unfolded in my mind, of Marco and me alone together. And yet . . . as moments passed and my imaginings continued, the thought of him touching me, of his hands on my body, of him kissing me freely with no one to censure us, caused heat to rise in that very spot between my legs.

Quickly I crossed myself and knelt to pray, realizing that this must be the sin of lust. I must now list this sin among the rest when next I went to confession. Yet, before the words of prayer could come to my lips, I paused. Surely it could not be a sin to feel desire for one's own husband, could it? Even if he was not yet my husband, he would be, and for us to engage in this act would be holy and blessed; commanded by God himself, just as my mother said.

A slight smile curved my lips as I rose from my knees. I would not speak of this to my confessor.

11

The day of the wedding, I rose with the sun, as did Chiara. I bathed, then put on a soft dressing gown and sat before my mirror for Chiara to put up my long hair. For my wedding day, the longer-than-waist-length tresses must be styled much more elaborately than for any simple dinner party, even one with the Medici family. Today all the eyes of Florence—all the eyes that mattered, anyway, or so I'd been told—would be on me, and I must look a goddess. Nothing less would do.

It took Chiara a few hours to braid dozens of strands of my wavy hair, and to pin each one perfectly into place about my head, like a crown. Woven through these braids were fine strands of pearls, each one carefully nestled amongst my tresses so as to shimmer and catch the light no matter which way I might turn. Between the pearls and the natural gold of my hair, I would have a halo of light around my head in the candlelight.

Once my hair was complete, Chiara helped me dress in my new silk shift—purchased especially for my wedding, and for my wedding night—and then in my gown, of pale yellow satin with elaborate cream silk brocade: embroidered flowers and vines wove their way all over the fabric, finely worked so as to draw the eye and enhance the cut of the gown, but not to distract from my face, my form. The seamstress had assured me so when she had delivered the stunning final product.

My mother was in the room as Chiara laced me into the gown, and her eyes, when they met mine in the mirror, were rimmed with red. "You have never looked more beautiful, Simonetta," she said, voice wavering, once Chiara had finished and stepped back. She came to stand beside me, brushing two fingers against my cheek, as though to reassure herself that I was still her daughter, even in my new finery befitting a goddess. "You are a woman now. You will make your father and me very proud today."

"I hope so," I said. I knelt for her blessing, which she gave.

She smiled through her tears as I rose. "Now let us go downstairs to present you to your father. Then it will be time for us to go to the chapel." She placed her hands on my shoulders. "You are ready, *si?*"

At her question, doubt stabbed through my breast, just for an instant. I was but sixteen; what did I know of love or marriage? But my parents had wanted this match, had arranged it; and I had to trust that they knew what was best for me, even if I did not know myself. Besides, it would be Marco waiting for me in that chapel—my dear Marco, and he would not change into some different, hostile man to fear simply upon becoming my husband. Quite the reverse, surely.

But since confessing my doubt would change nothing in this moment—perhaps only cause my mother grief—I only smiled and said, "*Si,* Mama. I am ready."

The close confines of the chapel only permitted a few witnesses to the ceremony itself—my parents, Marco's parents, and Lorenzo, Clarice, Giuliano, and Lucrezia. They all rose from their seats as I entered, and I seemed to hear a collective gasp at the sight of me. Standing by the small altar with the priest, Marco took me in as I moved toward him, his eyes as round as coins.

He was dressed as richly as I was, in a silk doublet of vibrant red trimmed with pale yellow to match my gown. He looked awestruck as he beheld me, fear and desire and pride and disbelief all mingling on his face. As I approached him, he reached out to take my hand gingerly, carefully, as though he was afraid that in touching me he would find me not real after all, only some vision. I smiled reassuringly at him as he began to lead me the final few steps to the altar, wondering if he could hear my heart pounding beneath all the fine fabric I was wearing.

We knelt before the priest, and the nuptial Mass began. The Latin words blurred together as I tried to steady my breathing and slow my heart. Before I knew it, we were standing again, and I was facing Marco and promising to love and honor and obey him, and he was promising to love and honor me, and then there was a ring on my finger and Marco was kissing me and the witnesses were applauding.

And we were married. We were husband and wife, before both God and man.

And my future was set.

We traveled to the Medici villa at Careggi in a litter with Lorenzo and Clarice. From the way that Marco kept my fingers twined with his and cast me longing glances, I was sure that he wished we had a litter to ourselves, but I was glad of our friends' company. Lorenzo paid extravagant compliments to my beauty, and soon he and Marco were talking of business, leaving Clarice and myself free to chatter on as we would.

"It was a most touching ceremony, truly," she told me, "and I am sure you do not need me to tell you that you look a vision. You look as though you are not quite real."

I smiled. "I am all too real, I'm afraid. And I must confess, I do not remember much of the ceremony. This day has already been . . . a bit overwhelming."

"I know what you mean. My wedding day was much the same. Still, try to enjoy it. Do not let yourself become too preoccupied with . . ." She cast a glance at the men to make sure that they were safely absorbed in their own conversation and lowered her voice. "With what comes later. Tonight, that is."

I nodded quickly.

"You do know what—"

"Yes," I cut her off. "My mother informed me."

"Good. Well, try to put it from your mind for now." A slight flush rose in her cheeks. "Some women enjoy it."

"So I am told," I said. "I should like to speak to one such woman."

Clarice's lips curved into a knowing smile. "Come see me tomorrow, Simonetta, and we will talk. It would not do for married ladies to share such secrets with virgins, now, would it?"

I smiled, but a part of me wished she would not be so coy. I had been prepared for pain and discomfort and endurance, yet so, too, was pleasure hinted at. No doubt there is pleasure to be had—a great deal of it—or this act would not contain such potential for sin, I thought. Surely there is more to men and women making fools of themselves over love than chaste words and staring into each other's eyes—and beauty. Surely there is something else.

Yet I began to feel afraid again. My mother had told me I must think only of my husband's pleasure. But how would I know how to see to such a thing? I glanced at Clarice again. "But . . . what must I do? What if I cannot . . . make him happy?"

Clarice laughed, then quickly looked contrite. "I am sorry, Simonetta. I do not mean to laugh. But trust me, you need not do much of anything at all to ensure his pleasure. Especially not you, beautiful as you are."

"What are two such lovely ladies whispering about so intently?" Lorenzo interrupted, and we glanced up to see both of our husbands—yes, I had a husband now—looking at us curiously.

Clarice laughed in her throat, a low, alluring sound I had not heard from her before. "Just the idle talk of married women," she said, winking at me. "Nothing you illustrious men need concern yourselves with."

"Indeed," Lorenzo said, and I saw the look he and his wife exchanged. I knew their marriage was a political one, and I had not wanted to ask Clarice whether love had grown between them as well. In public they were fastidious and proper, as befit their station. Yet here was the first time I had seen a glimmer of something more.

We arrived at the villa before too long, and with my mind whirring I scarcely took in the picturesque setting, the charming buildings set against the lush Tuscan hills. Servants came out to greet us and to show Marco and me to the chamber that had been prepared for our wedding night. Our own servants followed us in from the cart where they had been riding, along with the light baggage we had brought with us: a few personal items and changes of clothes for our trip back to the city the following day. They brought these things into the chamber and then left us alone.

Marco turned to me, taking my hands in his. "Alone at last, as husband and wife."

I smiled. "Yes."

"It would not do to not appear at our own wedding feast, especially one that has been so generously provided for us by our friends," he said, his voice low. He stepped closer and stroked my cheek, his fingers trailing down my neck. "But by God, Simonetta, I am tempted to consummate our marriage this very moment."

My heart pounded faster, though from fear or excitement, I could not tell. "As you said, it would hardly be right," I murmured, glancing up at him.

He groaned. "Do not look at me that way. My resolve is tested enough as it is." Quickly, he leaned down and kissed me, gently but insistently, his tongue slipping into my mouth.

I gasped in surprise, but my mouth opened beneath his and I

began, tentatively, to respond. Marco groaned against my mouth and pulled me tightly against him. As the kiss went on, he took my hand and placed it on the hardness beneath his hose.

Startled, I quickly drew back, only to regret it as I saw the shock and disappointment on Marco's face. "I am sorry," I said quickly. "I just—this is—should we not . . ."

Marco took a deep breath. "You are quite right. As I said, it would not do to be late to our wedding feast. . . ." he trailed off, regarding me in silence for a moment. "Do you fear me, Simonetta?"

"Fear you? No, of course not," I assured him. "It is just that . . . I am not sure how . . . that is, I . . ." I trailed off, sounding a very fool even to my own ears. What did I even mean to say? I was not sure; I did not know how to explain to Marco, a man, all the ways in which a woman's value was tied to what was between her legs, when I was only beginning to understand it myself. When I knew barely what was expected of me in the physical sense, and nothing beyond that.

Why was there no book that spoke of such things?

I felt my love for him grow a bit more when he smiled at me then. "I understand," he said. "At least, I think I do." He stepped closer to me again, this time kissing me chastely on the forehead. "As difficult as it is, I shall wait until tonight, so that our first bedding might be a proper one. And please, Simonetta," he said, his expression growing serious, "do not be afraid of me, or of what will take place between us as husband and wife. I will be gentle, I promise. I want only to make you happy."

Relieved, I smiled up at him and let him lead me from the room and down to the hall where the banquet was being laid out and our guests were assembling.

Downstairs, Marco and I greeted our guests, starting of course with our hosts, Lorenzo and Clarice, followed by Lucrezia dei Tornabuoni.

Giuliano came behind his mother. "Ah!" he said as he approached, his hands over his heart. "Your beauty, Signora Vespucci, serves only to accentuate that this is the unhappiest day of my life. Perish the thought that a man must see his lady love wed to another!"

I laughed, uncertain how else to react to such a speech—especially since Marco seemed amused, nothing more. I remember Clarice's words when she had brought me Giuliano's love note, that this was all a game in which I was both player and prize. "You are a most devoted cavalier, Signor Giuliano."

He closed his eyes as though in ecstasy. "Such kind words from my goddess will sustain me better than all the food of this magnificent feast."

Marco clapped his friend on the shoulder. "Away with you," he said. "Go drown your sorrows in wine."

"So I shall," Giuliano said dramatically, "that I may fall into a drunken slumber and dream of my dear Simonetta's lips."

"He is almost too ridiculous, is he not?" I asked Marco, who only chuckled in reply as the next person in line stepped forward.

The overwhelming majority of the guests were not known to me, so I did my best to smile pleasantly at each person presented to me, accepting their compliments on my gown and hair, on my beauty and grace, with what I hoped was an easy and gracious charm.

"I shall never remember all of these people," I murmured to Marco during a pause. "I barely remember everyone Lorenzo introduced me to when we dined with him!"

Marco smiled. "Do not worry your pretty head about that, darling. They are all so awed by you, and thrilled simply to have a word or two from you. They should all die of delight were you to remember their names as well, and it would never do for you to slay our wedding guests."

I laughed at this, but Marco was only partially correct, I noticed. The men appeared quite thrilled to make my acquaintance, true, but the women—their wives—seemed, for the most part, cool and suspicious.

To my surprise, at the end of the long line of guests was Signor Botticelli.

"Ah," Marco said, when he spotted him. I felt his body grow slightly tense beside me. "Signor . . . Botticelli, was it not?"

He bowed to the two of us. "Indeed, Signor Vespucci. An honor that you should remember me."

It was just what he was required to say, but I was surprised by the lack of feeling and sincerity behind it. It was obvious enough to Marco as well, for he only nodded tightly in acknowledgment.

"Ah, Sandro," Lorenzo de' Medici said, turning back to us from where he had been talking with some friends. "Signor and Signora Vespucci, you remember Sandro Botticelli, do you not? He is here at my invitation."

"Indeed," Marco said, a barely discernible edge to his voice.

"I remember you well, signore," I said, smiling.

"Since meeting you, Signora Vespucci, Sandro has spoken of little else, not in my hearing, anyway," Lorenzo said. "He wishes to paint you, as I believe he mentioned when you were introduced, and I confess I invited him in the hope that you might favor him with a commission. For what better inspiration could an artist have than this most beautiful of brides on her wedding day?"

"Indeed," Marco said again. "Well, then we must follow your advice, Lorenzo, for if you recommend him, then he must be an artist of the utmost skill." If anyone but me noted the lack of enthusiasm in Marco's voice, no one remarked upon it. Still, I felt a thrill at his agreement that this talented man might paint me.

"I should be honored if such a distinguished gentleman as yourself found me so," Botticelli said.

"So it is your art that brings you here, Signor Botticelli," I said.

"Indeed. It is my art that brings me most places," he said, and a hint of a smile appeared on his handsome face. "But I do want to take this opportunity to wish both of you much joy and happiness in your marriage."

"We thank you, signore," Marco said. "Now I pray you enjoy the feast, and we shall perhaps talk in more detail about your proposed portrait of Signora Vespucci at a later date."

Thus dismissed, Botticelli bowed and left us to find his seat.

I turned to Marco, excited. "Will we truly have him paint me?" Botticelli's painting of Judith lingered in my mind's eye, and I felt that same surge of longing, of curiosity, to see how he might portray me. To see how he saw me, in ways that perhaps I had never seen myself.

Marco's face relaxed into a smile. "When you look at me so, I think I will give you anything you ask for," he said. "Yes, if you wish it, we can have this Signor Botticelli paint your portrait. It would no doubt please Lorenzo, as well."

Having thus exchanged a word with all our guests, we were shown to our place of honor at the head table with our hosts. Servants brought in the first course of what would be many: some greens and the rather bland Tuscan bread.

I was engaged in conversation by Lucrezia dei Tornabuoni, who was seated on my left, and who had heard that I enjoyed reading. I spent the first two courses happily chatting about books with her, and came away with a mental list of new titles that I was eager to read—all of which, she assured me, could be found in the library at the Medici *palazzo*. She told me that she would be presenting a volume of her own verse to me and Marco as a wedding gift, one I told her I was most honored and excited to receive.

As the main course—a tender and flavorful beef—was served, Marco claimed my attention again. "Are you enjoying our wedding feast, wife?" he asked.

Wife. The word startled me, in a way I had not been startled even when Lorenzo had addressed me by my new surname. I was Marco's wife, and he was my husband. "I am, husband," I said, testing out the word. "Everything has been as wonderful as I could have wanted."

He grinned at me, waving over a servant to refill my glass of Sangiovese. "Good," he said. He leaned forward and kissed me quickly on the lips, as if he could not restrain himself. I blushed as some of the guests noticed and let out bawdy whoops and whistles.

"I could not resist," he said, voice low, his head inclined toward mine. "And, as you are now my wife, I need not resist ever again." He kissed me once more, then leaned back.

My entire body seemed warm, flushed; and I felt as though I were short of breath. To be so unequivocally, unabashedly adored—why, it felt like more than I deserved. As if sensing my thoughts, Marco took my hand beneath the table and squeezed it, then began gently caressing my fingers with his.

As the pastries and dessert wine were served, Lorenzo rose from his seat. "I would like to sincerely welcome all of you to our villa, and to say thank you for attending the marriage feast of two dear friends of mine and of the Medici family." He indicated Marco and I, seated beside him, and the crowd applauded us. "It is an honor to host the nuptials of such a beautiful and happy young couple, who will no doubt do much to enhance this Florence of ours with their joy and intelligence. I wish them nothing but the most sublime wedded bliss." The guests cheered again. "There shall be music commencing shortly," he finished, "and if you have not yet personally extended your congratulations to the bride and groom, I pray you do so at once, as no doubt they will be retiring soon—and I am sure no one can blame the groom for wishing to take such a beautiful bride to bed without delay."

Everyone laughed and cheered at his words, and I felt myself blushing again. We rose from our seats, and the guests followed us into the next room, where musicians were assembled and began playing. I danced first with Marco, of course, then with Lorenzo, then with Giuliano, who whispered in my ear that I must let him take me away before my husband could claim me as his own. I laughed through my discomfort at his words, teasing him that though his offer was most tempting, I must decline. Botticelli, too, caught my eye more than once, and I glowed, knowing he would paint me soon.

Marco and I were pulled into conversation with a few more guests, whose names I still could not recall even upon being told a second time. I began to feel weary: weary of everyone's eyes upon me, of dancing, of standing, of being charming, of fearing what would happen once Marco and I were alone.

As the couple to whom we had been speaking wandered away, Marco turned to look down at me. "What do you say, my darling?" he asked. "Shall we retire?"

My heartbeat tripled. "As you wish, husband."

He took my hand again and tucked it into his arm. He led me across the room to the doorway and, as our guests noticed our direction, they began applauding, whistling, and calling out bits of rather explicit advice. I tried to smile, tried to laugh, take joy in their merriment, and judging by Marco's approving glance, I succeeded.

I caught Clarice's eye as we left the room, and only just remembered that she and I had scarcely been able to speak since arriving at the villa. She gave me a big smile and nodded encouragingly.

We left the noisy, crowded room behind us and climbed the stairs to our suite of rooms on the third floor. Marco left me at the door to my dressing room before moving on to his. "I shall see you in a few minutes," he said softly.

I nodded, suddenly almost too embarrassed to look at him, and stepped into my dressing room. Chiara immediately rose from her mending upon seeing me. "Madonna," she said, curtseying briefly. She stepped toward me and began unpinning my hair. I sighed with relief as the heavy pins and strands of pearls were removed. With my hair loose, Chiara unlaced my gown and helped me step out of it and my underdress, carefully folding them to be put away. Now wearing only my shift, I shivered.

Chiara noticed. "Are you well, Madonna?" she asked softly. "Are you ready?"

Again I nodded but could not speak.

A soft knock came at the door, and I started, but relaxed slightly when the door opened and my mother came in. "Ah, Simonetta," she said. "Ready for the marriage bed, I see." Her face glowed with pride.

I tried to smile back, but my face seemed frozen.

"Do not worry, my daughter," she said. She crossed the room to me and patted my cheek. "All will be well. Remember, all you need do is please your husband, and you shall have a happy and blessed life together."

"I shall try," I said.

She embraced me briefly. "All will be well. I promise," she whispered into my ear again. Then she withdrew, closing the door behind her.

There was no further way to delay. But did I want to, truly? Was it not better to have it over with?

Chiara followed me through the door into the adjoining bedchamber and drew back the covers for me. I obediently got into the bed and lay back, fanning my long hair about me.

"Is there anything else you need, Madonna?" Chiara asked me.

"No," I managed, past my dry throat. "You are dismissed, Chiara."

She curtsied again and left me without a word.

I lay alone in the semidarkness—Chiara had left a small branch of candles burning on the bedside table—and stared up at the canopy of the bed. I took several deep breaths, trying to calm my furiously beating heart.

Yet Marco's soft knock on the door just moments later, from his own adjoining dressing room, made all such efforts moot. My breathing quickened again as he stepped inside, closing the door behind him. "Simonetta," he said, my name half spoken, half sighed.

"*Si,*" I said, finding my voice. "It is I, your wife."

He slowly approached the bed, dressed only in a nightshirt. I could see the dark hair on his chest where the neckline dipped down into a V; could see the outline of his body beneath the thin linen.

"You are not afraid, are you, Simonetta?" he asked.

I opened my mouth to say no, that I was well, but I did not want to begin our time together as husband and wife with a lie. "Not afraid," I said, "but perhaps a bit nervous."

He smiled. "I can understand that, I think. But, as I told you before, my dearest, darling Simonetta, I will be gentle, and I will try to bring you joy."

He got into the bed, sliding beneath the covers beside me. I willed myself not to shrink away as he took me in his arms. He kissed me, his lips parting mine as they had before, and I did my best to lose myself in the kiss. My breathing came quicker now, but for different reasons.

Marco began to kiss his way down my neck, and I gasped aloud. The heat within me rose to my skin, and I could feel beads of sweat beginning to form.

He groaned as we drew apart. "I cannot wait any longer, Simonetta," he murmured. "You are too beautiful." He shifted himself so that he was atop me, pulling up my shift, one hand insistently reaching between my legs to gently push them apart.

I tightened the muscles of my legs instinctively, then forced myself to yield to him and relaxed them. He lowered his hips onto mine, and I felt something large and hard pushing between my legs now. I forced myself to relax as he found the entry to my body and thrust himself inside me.

There was a sharp pain, as though something had torn within me, and I cried out, though my mother had told me to expect this.

"I am sorry," Marco murmured. Then he began to move within me, and I clenched my teeth against the pain that still radiated up from that space within me, the space that he now occupied. He pushed farther and farther into me, and I bit down on my lip to stop myself from crying out—from the pain, from the weight of him, from the feeling of certainty that there must be something more I should be doing.

His breathing began to come faster, and as the pain faded he gave one last sharp thrust and cried out, a sound halfway between agony and ecstasy, his eyes closed. I felt him shudder within me, then he lay his head against my shoulder, spent.

We remained like that for a moment, Marco still inside me, and it felt almost pleasant to have him there, so close. As if he were a part of me. Then he lifted himself up, withdrew, and rolled over onto his back. "Oh, Simonetta," he murmured, eyes still closed.

Tentatively I reached between my legs, and my fingers came away sticky with blood. This, too, my mother had prepared me for. I glanced back at Marco to see him watching me. "You are bleeding, yes?" he asked.

"*Si.*"

He smiled. "Ah, Simonetta." He reached over and drew me into his arms. "You are mine," he whispered into my ear. "Mine and only mine."

After a few moments, I asked, "And did I . . . did I please you, husband?"

He chuckled. "*Dio mio,*" he said. "You have pleased me, indeed." He studied my face, suddenly concerned. "I did not hurt you too much, did I?"

I cast my eyes down so he would not see the tears forming in them—though why I should cry, I did not know. "There was pain," I confessed, "but I was prepared for it."

"Oh, my Simonetta," he said, kissing the top of my head. "I am sorry. But it is necessary. And soon it will not hurt."

"I hope you are right," I said. Almost immediately, he drifted off to sleep.

12

I was awoken at dawn by Marco stirring beside me. I wondered that he had not woken me sooner, unused as I was to having someone else in my bed. I opened my eyes to find him smiling at me. "Good morning, *moglie*," he said.

I returned the smile, feeling warmth blossom in me anew at the word. "Good morning, *marito*."

He took my face between his hands and kissed me, deeply. "We will not be expected downstairs for some time yet," he said when he drew away. "Shall we make the most of our time?" His hand moved beneath my shift to caress my breast.

I wanted to refuse due to the very present soreness between my legs, as well as the punishing headache that had developed overnight—too much wine, perhaps? But my mother's words about duty and pleasing my husband and God's will chased themselves around my head. "I suppose we may as well," I said, trying to make my voice light, flirtatious.

This time the act was less foreign to me. I had to bite my lip to stop from crying out in pain again when he entered me, but the pain was less sharp this time, just a lingering dull ache from the loss of my maidenhead. The pain subsided as he moved within me, and though I did not experience whatever pleasure it was that made him moan and sigh, nor was the experience entirely unpleasant.

Afterward, Marco dozed off again, but I found that I could not. My mind was busy with all of the things I had learned, and with beginning to accept all of the changes that were imminent in my life.

I was a wife. Marco was my husband, and never would we be parted as long as we should live. I would live in his house and be always at his side, to serve and please him. And possibly, last night or even just this very morning, we had made a child whom I would raise to make him proud.

Perhaps two hours later, Marco awoke again and sat up. "I could spend the rest of my life in bed with you," he said, "but I suppose we must do our duty as guests and appear downstairs soon."

"I think you are right," I said.

He got out of the bed and stretched. "Did you sleep any more, my darling?" he asked. "We must journey back to Florence again today."

"I did not," I said. "Too much excitement, I fear."

He smiled. "Let us pray that God grants us much more excitement and happiness in our life together."

"Amen," I said.

He leaned across the bed and kissed me. "I shall leave you to dress, then, and will go do the same. When you are ready, we shall go downstairs to break our fast."

With that, he left, retreating back into the same dressing room from which he had emerged the night before.

I lay back against the pillows for a moment, stretching languidly. I felt as though now I could fall right back to sleep, and sleep the day away. Yet Marco was right: we must be gracious guests, especially after all the expense the Medici family had gone to on our behalf.

I got out of bed and padded into the maid's room that adjoined the dressing room, rousing a still sleeping Chiara. "*Mi scusi,*

Madonna!" she cried, tumbling out of bed. "I did not know what time—"

"Do not worry," I interrupted her. "It is of no consequence. It is a strange day, I think. As soon as you are ready, I must dress."

I wandered back into the dressing room and sat before the dressing table. My reflection looked wan, tired. It was indeed a strange day, preceded by a strange night. I studied myself carefully, wondering if becoming a married woman evoked some sort of change in my visage. Yet other than weariness, I looked the same as I always had.

Chiara bustled in, more apologies tumbling from her lips, which I waved aside. She helped me change into fresh underthings and then into a soft, simple country gown that would be appropriate for the morning and for the journey back to the city. She then braided my hair and pinned it up. Already it was becoming another hot Tuscan summer day.

I wondered, idly, if Signor Botticelli had also stayed the night. Perhaps he had, as a particular favorite of the Medici family? But why did it even matter? I shook away the thought, the image of Marco beaming at me as we said our marriage vows overtaking me. I smiled to myself, remembering.

Once I was ready, I stepped cautiously out into the hallway, only to find Marco already waiting there for me.

"Ah," I said. "I did not mean to keep you, husband."

He took my hand and kissed it chivalrously. "A man could wait forever for beauty such as yours, and consider himself lucky to do so."

"I had best treasure such compliments now," I teased, "for soon we shall be a disgruntled old married couple who do naught but disagree."

I had thought to make him laugh, but his smiling brown eyes turned serious. "Never," he said, with all the solemnity of one swearing a most sacred oath. "That shall never be us, my Simonetta. I promise."

Even in the summer heat, I felt as though someone had brushed a cold finger down my spine. I shivered slightly, but I ignored it as I took Marco's arm and let him lead me downstairs.

We found our parents already at table downstairs, as well as the Medici family. No Signor Botticelli, I noted, and I pushed away my nonsensical pang of disappointment. Everyone rose and applauded when they saw us.

"Sit, sit," Lorenzo said, showing us to our seats beside his own. I sat directly across from Clarice, and she gave me a broad smile.

"I trust you both had a . . . pleasant evening?" Lorenzo asked, his polite tone belied by the wicked grin on his face.

"The most pleasant one I have yet known," Marco said, causing everyone to laugh pointedly and me to blush. I did not like to hear something so private mentioned in public, yet I knew I must get used to it.

Once we had broken our fast, Lorenzo invited us all to follow him outside for a tour of the grounds. The sun only served to sharpen my headache, but I did my best to pay it no mind. Lorenzo, Marco, and Giuliano walked on ahead through the extensive gardens, while Marco's and my parents and Lucrezia dei Tornabuoni followed behind, exchanging chatter and gossip. Clarice slipped her arm through mine, and we brought up the rear.

"So?" Clarice murmured to me, when the rest of the party was out of earshot. "How did it go?"

I must have made a face, for she laughed softly. "Not that badly, surely?"

"It was not bad," I said quickly. "Just . . . strange."

She smiled. "I thought the same as a new bride. I am sure every woman does, the first few times. I can promise you it will get easier—and more enjoyable—with practice."

I wrinkled my nose. "Practice?" I repeated. "I just . . . I do not know, Clarice. Marco told me I pleased him enormously, but I did not do anything, and I felt as though there was something I should be doing."

"That is where the practice comes in," Clarice said, her smile widening.

"But how am I to know—"

"Answer me this, Simonetta," she interrupted. "Do you love your husband?"

"Of course," I answered.

"There is no of course about it. Many women are not so fortunate as to love their husbands. But very well. You love him, and you find him handsome, yes?"

I smiled. "Yes."

"Then that is all you need. When he comes to your bed, do not think—quiet that active mind of yours. Instead, just let yourself feel the things he makes you feel, and your body will know how to respond. You will begin to sense the things he particularly likes, and, in turn, he—if he is a good lover—will sense what brings you the most pleasure."

My entire body grew flushed at this conversation. "I shall take your words into consideration."

She laughed. "Indeed. I think you are considering them already. So much so that I think I ought to send you back to your bedchamber, and send your husband in after you."

I smiled. "The second time, it . . . was not unpleasant."

"Dear Simonetta, it can be so much better than 'not unpleasant.' I promise you."

As though somehow prompted by our words, by my thoughts, Marco turned from where he walked on ahead with the Medici brothers and gave me a smile full of warmth, love, and what I now recognized as desire.

I returned the smile, certain that mine was brimming with the very same things.

We walked to the edge of the Medici property, then turned to make our way back to the villa. The day had become almost punishingly hot, and I was sweating even in my light, simple dress.

"At least in our carriage we shall be out of the sun," Marco said, wiping his brow with a piece of cloth. He had come to the back of the group to offer me his arm, and Clarice had gone to walk with her own husband.

"Small mercies," I said, feeling rather out of breath. I did not wish to complain, though, not when our hosts had been so generous to us. I could see the villa from our path; it would not be much longer now before we could step into the cool rooms.

Just then, I began to feel quite faint—a result of the heat or something else, I was not quite sure. I stumbled, and would have fallen to the grass had Marco not noticed and caught me.

"Simonetta!" he cried, and it sounded as though his voice was coming from very far away as everything momentarily faded to black.

It must have been only a minute that I was unconscious, for as I came to I heard Lorenzo speaking to his brother. "Giuliano, run back to the villa and have the servants bring a sedan chair for Madonna Simonetta. And some water. Hurry!"

I did not hear Giuliano's reply, if he made one; only his footsteps quickly retreating back up to the villa.

I opened my eyes and found myself half lying on the ground, Marco's arm beneath my shoulders to support me.

"Simonetta, darling," Marco said. "Are you alright?"

I took several seconds more to regain my breath before answering him. "I think so," I said. "I am not sure what happened, but I . . . I feel better now, I think."

My mother nodded. "The excitement, no doubt," she said.

"And this brutal heat cannot have helped," Lucrezia dei Tornabuoni added. "My dear, you should have told us you were feeling unwell! We would not have dragged you outdoors into this scorching morning had we known."

"I felt fine until just a few moments ago," I said. Now that the spell had passed, I was merely embarrassed to have caused such a fuss, and to have drawn everyone's attention. "Truly, you are all kind to worry, but it is nothing, I am sure. I am sorry to have ruined everyone's morning."

"None of that," Lorenzo said. "Your well-being is our primary concern, and nothing else."

"You are too kind," I said. "I am fine, I am sure of it."

Marco squeezed my hand. "We shall summon the doctor directly upon our return to Florence."

"Perhaps you should not return today at all," Clarice interjected. "You are both welcome to stay as long as you need, until Simonetta feels up to the journey."

"*Si*," Lorenzo said. "In fact, you can both stay here and I will send for our doctor to come from Florence to attend you, Madonna Simonetta."

"You are all too kind," I said again. "But please, let us make no more of a fuss than is warranted. I am feeling quite restored now, and I am sure the return journey will pose no problem at all."

"If you are sure, *moglie*," Marco said slowly. "But I shall still call for the physician once we arrive home."

"I do not believe there is any need," I said, getting to my feet despite the worried looks of the company. "But if it shall set your mind at ease, *marito*, then, by all means, send for him."

Just then Giuliano returned, with a wineskin full of fresh, clean water from the countryside. "For you, my dearest," he said, dramatically kneeling to offer it to me. "It is an honor and privilege to come to your aid, though it is abhorrent to me that any illness should dare inflict itself upon you."

I smiled and took the wineskin from him, and in spite of his chivalrous, playful words I could see the worry in his eyes as well.

"Simonetta assures us that she is well, *fratello*," Lorenzo said.

"Beauty overcomes all adversaries," Giuliano declared. "But even so, some servants are following me with a sedan chair. We shall not permit you to walk the rest of the way, Madonna."

As if summoned by his words, four male servants bearing the chair came down the path toward us.

"You are all making a ridiculous fuss over me," I said, but I obliged and climbed into the chair. Once I was seated, the servants lifted the chair and bore me back up to the villa, and in spite of my self-consciousness at having brought such a dramatic end to the morning, I was grateful not to have to walk the rest of the way.

Marco helped me back up to our suite of rooms, and directed Chiara to pack my things immediately. Scarcely an hour later, we were once again ensconced in a carriage with Lorenzo and Clarice on our way back to Florence.

By the time we returned to the city, it was quite clear that I was not as well as I'd thought, and that my fainting spell had been the precursor of something much more serious. The Medici carriage brought us directly back to our rooms at the Vespucci *palazzo*, which would be our new home. Yet we had to dispense with the Florentine custom wherein the groom would show the bride every inch of her new home, from top to bottom—I was scarcely conscious—so Marco carried me up to our bed instead.

Lorenzo sent the Medici physician to attend me, who pronounced that I had a fever, and bled me. He left Chiara with instructions to place cool cloths on my forehead and change them as necessary.

I woke up the next night, sweating through my shift, in an unfamiliar room lit only by a single candle. I began to panic at first—where was I? How had I gotten here?—but as my eyes adjusted and I saw Marco asleep in a wooden chair in the corner, I began to remember.

I was married. I had fallen ill, and now I was in my new home with my husband.

I struggled to sit up against the pillows and licked my dry lips. I was so thirsty . . . and yet I hated to wake Marco, who looked as though he was sleeping deeply, despite his uncomfortable position.

Almost as though my thoughts had roused him, Marco woke with a start, his eyes fixing on me. "Simonetta," he said, his voice hoarse. "You are awake."

"I am."

"And how do you feel?"

"Better," I said. "I do believe that this—whatever it was—has passed."

"Thanks be to God," he said, and even in the dim light I could see how haggard and wearied he looked, as though he had just woken from his first slumber in days.

"But why do you sleep in that chair, *marito?*" I asked. "There is plenty of room in our bed for you. . . ."

"I did not want to disturb you," he said. "Are you truly feeling well, Simonetta? I was so worried. . . ."

"As I said, better," I said. "I hate to trouble you, *marito,* but my throat is so dry . . . if there is anything to drink . . ."

"*Dio mio,* of course," he said, leaping to his feet. "I should have thought of that. I shall return directly." He quickly left the room, and returned moments later with a goblet of watered-down wine.

I accepted it and gulped it down greedily.

"More?" he asked when I was finished, hovering over me.

I set the goblet on the small table beside my bed. "Perhaps in a bit," I said. I patted the mattress beside me. "Sit here with me, and tell me what has happened."

Marco obliged, telling me of bringing me back and of what the doctor had said. "It is all my fault," he finished, burying his head in his hands.

At first, I stopped myself from reaching out to comfort him—old habits of propriety were difficult to be rid of, it seemed—but I was his wife now, and I could comfort him—and touch him—as much as I wanted. I placed a hand on his cheek, lifting his face so that I could see it. "What nonsense," I said gently. "How should my taking ill be your fault?"

He shook his head shamefacedly. "It was all too much, perhaps—the wedding and the feast and the journey and the heat."

"None of those things made me sick, I shouldn't think," I said. "I am just as yet not used to your Florentine air." I smiled at him. "I grew up by the sea, remember. I am used to fresh, clean breezes, not a landlocked city such as this, and its . . ."

"Stench," he finished for me, a rueful smile on his face.

I laughed. "My mother would no doubt tell me that a lady does not talk of such things," I said, "but yes."

He reached out and took my hand where it lay on the bedcovers, his face becoming quite serious. "If you wish it, Simonetta—if you think it will be better for your health—we can return to Genoa," he said. "I can find a position there, with my connections—I am sure of it. I want to do what is best for you, and nothing else."

"Oh, but we cannot!" I said. "You are to begin working with Lorenzo, and your whole life is here in Florence!"

His expression did not change. "You are my whole world," he said quietly. "None of the rest of it means anything to me without you."

I was quite at a loss for words. "You are so sweet, Marco," I said softly. "I know not what I have done, that God should have granted me such a wonderful husband." I squeezed his hand. "We shall stay," I said. "I like Florence, and your friends. I took a summer fever—what of it? Many do each year, and we are lucky that it was not worse."

He nodded slowly. "As you wish, *mia carissima* Simonetta." He rose from the bed. "I shall fetch you some more wine, and then perhaps it might be best for you to rest again."

I nodded, suddenly aware of how heavy my eyelids felt. "Yes," I said. "I think that would be best."

Marco returned with more watery wine, and once I drank it I lay back against the pillows again. Just before sleep took me, I felt Marco get into the bed beside me, his body curled protectively against mine, as though he would—or could—protect me from illness itself.

I smiled before falling back asleep. It was only the second night I had shared a bed with him, but already I did not know what I would do without him there.

13

Within a few days, I felt perfectly well again. The fever and headaches were gone, and I was itching to leave the house. Marco was finally able to take me through the entirety of the house. We had an entire wing to ourselves, and need not even see his parents if we wanted our privacy. We had a dining room and a receiving room and extra bedrooms for guests and—hopefully someday soon—children.

Marco had continued to sleep beside me during my illness, in case I should need anything in the night, but he did not seek to claim his rights as a husband—something that I was quite glad of, in my weakened state. Yet even once I recovered, he continued to sleep chastely beside me, and I began to worry. Had I done something wrong, in one of the two times that we had been together as man and wife?

I decided to take matters into my own hands. I had a sneaking suspicion that doing so was not strictly in the interest of wifely modesty, but I found I could not wait. Besides, I was curious about these "pleasures" of which I had heard so much.

One night, I lay abed in a clean shift, longing impatiently for Marco to come up to bed. Before dismissing Chiara, I had had her take down my long, heavy hair, rather than keeping it tied back as she had done when I was ill. It spilled over my shoulders, over the pillow and the bedclothes, in a way that I hoped was particularly fetching.

When Marco finally came in, I sat up quickly. "Husband," I said, pitching my voice low in what I hoped was an alluring tone. I knew nothing of seduction, truth be told, but was willing to try.

He paused upon seeing me. "Wife," he said, desire flickering across his face. "Have you been waiting for me?"

"I have," I said, keeping the same tone in my voice. "Our marriage bed is cold and lonely without you."

"Is it, indeed?" he asked, trying to keep his voice even. Yet I could detect the wanting in his voice, in his eyes.

"It is," I said. "I was hoping you could come warm it for me."

He swallowed, and my heart plummeted as I saw that he was fighting the desire to take me in his arms. "Are . . . are you sure that you are well enough, Simonetta?"

"I have been well enough for days," I said.

"Only if you are sure," he said, still not moving. "I would not want to put your health at further risk . . . or tax your strength . . ."

Slowly, I slid from the bed and impulsively lifted my shift over my head, and dropped it to the floor. Thus I stood before him, clothed only in my long hair, every inch of my pale flesh bared to his eyes. I tilted my head, raising my eyebrows.

He groaned aloud and swiftly crossed the room to me. He took my face in his hands and kissed me roughly, yet I did not mind. The fabric of his shirt and breeches chafed against my skin, and I drew back. "You are overdressed, husband," I murmured, my fingers moving to the laces of his breeches.

Once he was as naked as I, we tumbled to the bed, mouths locked, tongues exploring. His body half covered mine as he reached between my legs, his fingers exploring, stroking. I gasped, feeling a hint of the promised pleasure.

"Yes," I begged. "More." I was unable to articulate better what I wanted, yet I felt Marco smile against my mouth as his fingers increased their pressure, feeling waves beginning to build within me, aching to crash against the shore.

I cried out as a fierce pleasure that verged on pain ripped through me, causing my whole body to shudder, my head thrown back.

"Yes, my Simonetta," Marco murmured as the glorious storm subsided. "Good, *sì?*"

"Yes," I murmured. I wrapped my arms around him hungrily, and my legs twined around his waist, our bodies fitting themselves together. There was no pain this time, only the shadow of that delicious pleasure and the desire for more. I clutched him tighter to me, arching against him as he moved within me, so different, this time, from before.

Yes, I thought as he reached his pleasure, gasping as he fell against me. This, surely, is what the marriage act is meant to be.

After a moment, Marco rolled over onto his back, eyes closed, breathing hard. "Temptress," he whispered at last, opening one eye and smiling at me.

"I believe that God smiles on the wife who gives her husband a happy marriage bed," I said. I leaned over him, my hair falling around both of us, and kissed him.

"Then God shall smile upon you more than any woman, I should think," he said. "You are delicious, Simonetta." He grinned at me. "And I trust that my wife is happy in her marriage bed as well?" he asked, wrapping his arms around me so that I lay partially atop his bare chest.

"I am," I said. I giggled foolishly; I could not help it. "Perhaps . . ."

He eyed me. "Yes?"

"Perhaps we might make each other happy again soon?" I reached between his legs and hesitantly caressed him.

"You have cast a spell on me, wife," he said. He rolled me over onto my back in one motion, causing me to squeal with delight.

Once my illness was behind us, we spent an idyllic honeymoon period together. My parents took their leave of us once I was well again, and returned to Genoa. I had thought I would miss them terribly, yet I had other things to distract me. For a week, neither of us left the *palazzo* if we did not have to; we dined alone, retired early, and lingered in bed long into the morning. I began to learn that the joys of the marriage bed extended beyond that first wonderful night we had spent together, and I was eager to discover them all, as well as find new ways that I might please my husband. Sometimes, after we had made love, I would reach for the book of poetry Lorenzo had given us—which I had taken to keeping on our bedside table, in lieu of a Bible—and read my favorite verses aloud, Marco's head leaning contentedly against my shoulder. Every so often, he would ask me to go back and repeat a line that had particularly struck him, and we would say it over and over together until we both had it memorized.

Married life, so far, was suiting me quite well.

One morning I lingered in bed after Marco had risen. I knew my deliberate laziness could not last much longer, but the Florentine summer dragged on so hot and oppressive, and I was finding I much preferred to remain in bed wearing nothing at all.

Yet soon Marco came back in, still only partially dressed. "A messenger has come," he said, showing me a bit of parchment. "One of the servants brought this up. We are invited to dine at the Medici *palazzo* tomorrow evening."

"Oh, how lovely," I said. "It will be nice to see our friends again." I giggled. "They will think us quite rude indeed, to have ignored them for so long."

"We are newlyweds, wife," Marco said, his eyes devouring me. "It is to be expected that we ignore the world for a time."

"I am sure they shall forgive us, then."

The following day, I bathed in preparation for dinner that evening. Chiara dressed me and pinned up my hair, ensuring that I looked my best. Yet I was much more relaxed this time; I had already been judged by the Medici and their circle and not been found wanting, and I thought of them—especially Clarice—as my friends.

Marco and I arrived at the Medici *palazzo* at the appointed time, and were shown to the garden again.

"Ah, there are the newlyweds!" Lorenzo cried. "I am surprised we managed to rouse you from your lovers' nest! I knew that nothing short of a direct invitation would suffice to return you to your friends' company again." He came to greet us, clapping Marco on the back, and kissing my hand. "But who can blame you, Marco, to stay shut away from the world with such a bride," he said, though his eyes were on me. "You look as beautiful as ever, Madonna Simonetta—more so, even. I daresay that marriage agrees with you."

I did my best not to blush. "I believe that it does, my good signore."

"Do not tell my brother that," Lorenzo said in a stage whisper. "He has been most eager to see you pale and wasting, that he might steal you from your ungrateful husband."

"Alas!" Giuliano said, coming to greet us. "I shall never forgive my friend Marco for treating you so well!" He swept me a deep bow. "You break my heart again by being so happy in your marriage, *mia bella* Simonetta."

I laughed. "I am sorry to disappoint you, Signor Giuliano, for you are a most devoted chevalier," I said. My newfound happiness with my life and my husband had given me a confidence I did not have before, a confidence that I could play this game. "But my lord and husband is a most worthy man, I find, and so you have a long, hard road before you, indeed, if you seek to steal me away from him."

The assembled company laughed, and I knew from the quick look of approval from Marco that I had done well, and was playing the game just as it was supposed to be played.

"You perhaps remember my friend Tomaso Soderini?" Lorenzo said, indicating a slightly portly man who looked to be in his thirties, who bowed to me with his hand over his heart. "He was a guest at your wedding, and is another great lover of the arts."

I smiled at the man. "You'll have to forgive me, signore. My wedding was a most overwhelming day."

"No apologies needed, Madonna Vespucci," he said, taking my hand and kissing it. "I am merely delighted to renew our acquaintance."

Lorenzo nodded at the artist to whom Signor Soderini had been speaking. "And Signor Botticelli, of course."

I straightened immediately at the sight of the handsome blond painter. "Of course. A true pleasure to see you again, signore."

The painter bowed and kissed my hand, but before I could indulge in discourse with him as I longed to, Lorenzo had steered me away again.

"Some dear friends of mine whom you perhaps do not know—may I present Niccolo Ardenghelli and his wife, the lovely Lucrezia Donati Ardenghelli. *Amici,* this is Signora Simonetta Vespucci, of whom you have heard me speak, and her husband, Marco."

"Why, Lucrezia Donati," Marco said. "Excuse me, Signora Ardenghelli. It has been some time since I have seen you!"

"It has, indeed," murmured the dark-haired beauty in a low, throaty voice, extending her hand for Marco to kiss. "Both of us married and respectable now, I see."

My stomach curdled as I watched Marco converse animatedly with this Lucrezia and her husband. Who was this woman, with her flashing dark eyes and seductive voice, to speak in so familiar a manner to my husband?

"Lucrezia has been a friend of my brother's and mine since we were children," Lorenzo explained for my benefit, as Marco continued speaking to the pair. "As such Marco has known her for some time as well."

"Indeed," was all I could manage to say. I glared at this Lucrezia. She was beautiful, that much was certain. Did Marco prefer her darkness to my pale skin and blond hair? Did he think she was beautiful? As beautiful as me?

Suddenly I realized what this feeling must be. Jealousy. I was jealous. Long had I been the target of such an emotion, but never before had I experienced it myself.

It was dreadful.

"Come," Lorenzo said, steering me away from the trio. "I would introduce you to my esteemed father."

My surprise at these words erased my instant enmity for Lucrezia Ardenghelli. Lorenzo led me to a man seated in a chair beside a fountain at one end of the garden, no doubt placed there for its proximity to the cool mists in this August heat.

Piero de' Medici looked much older than he could have been—no doubt his long battles with illness accounted for that. His legs were swollen by gout, and his face—a somewhat weaker blend of his sons' very different features—was twisted in a permanent grimace of pain. Lucrezia dei Tornabuoni hovered by his side in case he should need anything, the very picture of a dutiful wife.

"Ah," Piero said as I approached on Lorenzo's arm. "This must be the famous Simonetta Vespucci."

"That I am, signore," I said. "It is an honor to make your acquaintance."

"I am sorry that I was too ill to attend your wedding," he said. "I am told it was a most lovely affair—though with my son and wife at the helm, I should expect nothing less."

"It was indeed, signore, and I must thank your family again for their kindness and generosity."

"Think nothing of it." A smile split his face, and I could see that he had no doubt been handsome, once. "You are as beautiful as they say. That husband of yours is a lucky man."

"You are too kind," I replied. "And I am most lucky in my husband."

"Beautiful *and* a loving wife," Piero said. "Dear Marco is doubly blessed."

"Beg pardon, father-in-law, husband." Just then, Clarice appeared at my side. "Might I beg your indulgence to steal my friend away for a time?"

"Why, of course, my dear," Piero said, smiling indulgently at his daughter-in-law. "You young ladies talk, enjoy yourselves, have some wine. Dinner will be served soon."

"An honor to meet you, signore," I said again, over my shoulder this time, as Clarice dragged me away to an as-yet-unoccupied corner of the garden.

"Whatever is the matter?" I asked. Now that I had a moment to study her, Clarice looked quite out of sorts, as though she could not decide whether to weep or fly into a rage. "Clarice?" I prompted, when she did not speak.

She still did not answer; instead, she waved over a servant, who brought us two glasses of fine Tuscan red wine. She took a long, fortifying sip before speaking. "That woman," she growled, her eyes narrowed at the cluster of party guests a few paces away. "I cannot believe he had the audacity to invite her here."

"Who?" I asked.

"Lucrezia Donati," she snapped. "Do not let her husband's name fool you. That marriage is all a ruse of respectability, one my most revered husband helped arrange."

"Clarice, whatever do you mean?"

Her eyes met mine, and this time I was shocked by the depth

of the pain within them. "She is his mistress," she whispered. "Lorenzo's."

Relief flooded me, that I need not worry that this Lucrezia had any designs on my husband—with a husband and lover of her own already, she surely had no time to contend with one more man. This relief was quickly replaced by guilt, however—that my release should be my friend's sorrow.

"Oh, Clarice," I said, reaching out to take her hand. "Are you certain?"

"Of course I am certain," she said harshly. "Lorenzo has been in love with her for years, before he ever met me. But he could not marry her because it was not politically expedient. I was the most advantageous match that could be found." She took another long sip of wine. "Do you know," she continued, "that he threw a joust here in Florence to celebrate our betrothal, back before I came from Rome? And at this very joust in celebration of our upcoming marriage, he named *her*," she sneered in Lucrezia Donati's direction, "the Queen of Love and Beauty." She shook her head, as if bewildered. "And he has the gall to invite her here. To our house. To *my* home."

My guilt gave way to heartbreak and anger on my friend's behalf. "Oh, Clarice," I said again. In truth I could not think what else to say. I had long wondered about Clarice's feelings toward her husband, this man brought to her by politics and family alliances. Yet it seemed that she must feel at least something for him, to be so enraged by this woman's presence. "And that she should have the nerve to accept the invitation, and be presented to you as his wife."

"Why should she mind about that?" Clarice said. "They have been friends since childhood. She is friendly with his parents, with Giuliano. Lorenzo was hers first. In her eyes, it is I who am the interloper."

"It does not matter how you look in her eyes," I said firmly. "You are Lorenzo's wife, not she. And they will need to answer for their sins someday."

She turned her gaze back to me. "Oh, Simonetta," she said. "You beautiful, innocent fool. You are happy in your marriage now, but just you wait. Someday you will find that even Marco is not what he seems." She closed her eyes and turned away. "Forgive me. I did not mean that."

"You did," I said, feeling as though I had been slapped. "You did, or you would not have said it." I began to move away from her, but Clarice quickly reached out to grasp my arm and prevent me.

"I am sorry, Simonetta. Truly I am," she said. "I am hurt and so all I can think to do is hurt those around me. I did not mean it, I swear." She bit her lip. "You are my one true friend in all of Florence, I think. I should be lost without you."

I relaxed somewhat. "Of course I shall always be your friend," I said.

"Please forgive me."

I shook my head. "There is nothing to forgive. You are upset, as you say, and rightfully so."

She sighed. "Thank you. I do not know how I shall endure this evening, though. Watching her and her knowing smile. The pity in her eyes when she looks at me."

"We shall not give her the pleasure of our discourse," I said.

"Lorenzo would not be happy with me if I was rude—"

"Oh, he would not?" I demanded, arching an eyebrow. "And does he expect his wife to make pleasant conversation with his mistress?"

"I suppose he could not, in truth, expect such a thing," she said, with a small smile.

"No, indeed. And so you must make certain I am seated beside you at dinner, and we shall converse, and not pay any attention to her whatsoever."

Clarice leaned forward and hugged me around the shoulders. "Thank you, Simonetta," she whispered in my ear. "You are indeed a good friend."

"As are you," I replied. I gestured toward where Lorenzo stood, still talking with his father. "Now go. Claim your place beside your husband so that she might see it, and mark it well."

She smiled at me. "Thank you," she said softly. She crossed the garden to Lorenzo, and I saw her smile, saw the coquettish tilt of her head as she slipped her arm through her husband's, neatly inserting herself into his conversation.

I was not alone in my corner for long, however. I was just about to rejoin the party—and keep an eye on my husband and Lucrezia Donati, just in case—when I heard a familiar voice. "Madonna Vespucci." I looked around to find Sandro Botticelli standing there, the setting sunlight creating a golden halo of his blond hair. "I confess I hoped to have the chance to speak with you this evening. May I join you?"

The smile on my face was genuine. "Why, of course," I said. "I confess that I hoped we might be able to converse as well."

"You honor me, Madonna. And now we have both made our confessions for the week."

I laughed. "Indeed. And my confessions to my priest of late have not been much more interesting, I'm afraid. This business of adjusting to married life has left me very little time or opportunity to sin."

"Brava, Madonna. Spoken like a true debauched Florentine."

I smiled. "In truth, I was a bit shocked when I first arrived here, at what seemed to me then to be rather bawdy and impious speech. Yet I have come to see it is not that at all. The people of Florence—those I have met, anyway—simply wish to enjoy life, and this world God has fashioned and that mankind has fashioned with His help. And so I cannot imagine that He shall fault us for that."

"Well said," Botticelli said, the natural intensity of his gaze seeming to focus on me more sharply. "You embody the spirit of this new age of ours well, I think."

"What new age might this be, signore?"

"An age where there is room for all wisdom, not just that of the Church," he said. "We have much to learn from the ancients, the great thinkers of Greece and Rome who, though they did not know Christ, still devoted themselves to enlightenment and learning."

"Indeed," I said. "But does the Church not censure those who wish to partake of such wisdom?"

"Holy Mother Church does indeed, though soon, we hope, she will not," he said. "It is part of the work Lorenzo is doing here, in gathering so many scholars and writers and artists about him. Great men like him seek to change the world."

"And these Greek and Roman thinkers you speak of, signore," I said. "If one wished to learn from their wisdom, where would one begin?"

He smiled at me, and the expression transformed his face. "In the Medici library, of course."

"Indeed." I considered this. What Signor Botticelli spoke of sounded dangerous, and yet exciting. "Perhaps I will soon have more exciting sins for the confessional, after all."

"And perhaps, as you say, God would not fault you for making use of the mind He has given you."

"I hope you are right, signore. Though if you are, it may be that we mistake the nature of sin altogether."

"It would not surprise me to learn that we do," Botticelli said. "For must God and His ways, by His very nature, be beyond the comprehension of mere humans?"

This was heresy, and I knew it, but I could not bring myself to pull away from these words, dancing like a beautiful flame before me, warming me even as it threatened to burn me. "A churchman would say that you are wrong; that God has revealed His ways to us through Holy Scripture, and there can be no mistaking them," I said.

"Certainly. But you are not a churchman, Madonna Vespucci," he said. "So what do you say?"

"And how can what I say possibly matter against the teachings of Holy Mother Church?"

He met my eyes unflinchingly. "It matters to me."

I held his gaze, feeling another strange moment of understanding pass between us, just as I had on that evening when we were first introduced. "I agree with you, Signor Botticelli. Or at least, I hope that you are right."

He did not look away. "I have always thought that it is important for one to know one's own heart," he said quietly, leaning forward. "And not have it be simply what others would make it."

I found myself drawing closer, spellbound by his words. They were so contrary to everything I had ever been taught—that one should learn, yes, but accept the wisdom and teachings of those who had gone before, and especially that of the Church. Yet what Signor Botticelli advocated here was making up one's own mind, deciding for oneself what to believe, taking what you had learned and thinking on it, rather than merely accepting it.

I shivered slightly. "You must mind in what company you say such things, signore," I said. "There are many who would take issue with such ideas."

"It is ever thus," he said. "And that is why I say such things here, in the company of like-minded people."

I warmed at the thought that this man, who was clearly intelligent and learned in a way I was not, considered me to be "like-minded."

"Perhaps beauty is the only truth we need," he went on. "And it is to be found everywhere: in nature, in learning, in the Church, and in the accomplishments of man: the written word, the painted canvas."

"Beauty means something very different to me, signore," I said. "I have always been told that beauty is the means to an end, not the end in and of itself."

"But that is wrong," he said earnestly. "The creation of beauty *can* be the end, the goal. For what other purpose did Dante write his verses?"

I smiled. "There you have me. I fear I cannot mount a defense against such a point, though you will devalue my whole life."

"Never say that," he said. "You add to the beauty of the world, Madonna Vespucci. And you can help me do the same."

"Oh, I can?" I said. "How?"

"Pose for me."

"Aha," I said, my smile hardening slightly. "I see what is happening here, signore. You have engaged with me and flattered me so as to obtain a commission."

"I am not so mercenary as that," he said. "I engage with you because you have a clever and agile mind, and it pleases me to converse with you. And how have I flattered you?"

"By—by doing just that," I sputtered, beginning to feel off-balance. "By acting as though my intellect is worthy."

"It is worthy, and treating you as an intelligent woman is not flattery. I am merely stating facts." He stepped closer to me. "It is a fact that your mind is as beautiful as your face, Madonna. I recall saying something similar to you when first we were introduced."

I was silent for a moment as I struggled beneath the onslaught of his words, beneath the torrent of feelings they unleashed in me. "Forgive me," I said at last. "I am hardly used to such frank speech, I find."

"You are used to accepting statements of your beauty as fact, but not those of the worthiness of your mind," he said. "It is what the world expects of you."

"You have quite flustered me, signore," I said, startled even as I spoke the words that I would admit such a thing. "You have given me more to think about than I have had in some time."

"The basis of a good friendship, I think."

"Are we friends?"

"I should very much like us to be."

I smiled, warming to the open, inviting look on his face. "I should like that as well. And I . . . I would be most happy to sit for you. You must seek my husband's permission, of course."

"*Per che?* No disrespect to your husband, but it is not he whom I wish to paint."

The hint of mischief in his eyes made me laugh. "I will ensure that he is agreeable all the same," I said.

"I appreciate it." He took my hand and kissed it. "Had Dante had you as his muse instead of Beatrice, he would have been an even greater poet," he said. "And that, Madonna Simonetta, is both fact and flattery."

With that, he took his leave of me, leaving me to dwell on his words, and the way that his lips had shaped my given name.

14

Dinner passed in a mostly congenial manner, much like the first we had spent at the Medici *palazzo*. The only difference was the heightened tension due to the presence of Lucrezia Donati, though it was possible that I, seated next to Clarice, was one of the only ones who noticed it. If anyone else marked it, they most expertly pretended they had not. Even so, Clarice and I adhered to my plan and spent most of the meal in conversation with each other, ignoring the troublesome woman altogether. Still, I did not like the self-satisfied smirk that played about her lips; it seemed to be her habitual expression. I itched to slap it off of her face.

Yet once the meal ended and everyone rose from the table, continuing to mill about the garden and the courtyard, I saw Lorenzo draw Lucrezia discreetly to one side. It was not obvious enough to draw untoward attention, yet they were far enough apart from the rest of the company that none of us could overhear their words—neither her husband nor his wife.

Well, this would never do. I squared my shoulders and moved toward them. I would accomplish two objectives simultaneously.

"Lorenzo," I said sweetly. "And Signora . . . Ardenghelli, was it not?" I asked, pointedly using her married name. "I beg your pardon; I did not mean to interrupt your conversation."

The look Lucrezia tossed me told me that I had done just that, but Lorenzo's answering smile was genuine. "Not at all, Simonetta," he said familiarly. "I am so happy that you and your husband were able to attend."

"It was so kind of you to invite us," I said. "Yet I fear I must impose on your kindness a bit further. I should like to take you up on your offer to make use of your library, if I may."

"Why, of course," Lorenzo said. "You need not even ask."

"You are an exemplary host and friend," I said. "Might I trouble one of your servants to show me the way?"

"We are all servants in the face of such beauty as yours," he said gallantly. "I shall escort you myself, if that is agreeable to you."

"You are too kind," I said, taking the arm he offered.

"Do excuse us, Signora Ardenghelli," Lorenzo said, giving her a quick smile.

God forgive me for my vanity, but I gave her a swift, triumphant look over my shoulder as I allowed Lorenzo to lead me from the garden. I could hardly stop Lorenzo from carrying on with his mistress, but at least I could stop him from so blatantly seeking her company in front of his wife and my friend.

"Is there a particular book you are seeking?" Lorenzo asked as we made our way through the maze of hallways.

"In a way," I said. "I had the pleasure of conversing with Signor Botticelli at some length before dinner. He referred me to the writings of some of the ancient Greek and Roman thinkers."

"Ah," Lorenzo said. "I am not surprised that Sandro spoke of them to you, nor that you are eager to seek out such works. Do you read Greek, Simonetta?"

"I do not," I said. "My education was a bit more limited. I am fluent only in my native tongue and in Latin, I'm afraid."

"Not to worry," he said. "My own Greek is not what it ought to be, and so I rely upon translations—such as those done by my friend and teacher Poliziano—of the original Greek into Latin. We shall find you one such."

"Do you think such works might even be translated into Tuscan?" I asked.

"It is my dream that it should be so," Lorenzo said. "The more who have access to such wisdom, the better. We shall never cease to need the wisdom and teachings of the Church, of course, but it behooves us all to learn as much as we can in our lives, I think."

"I agree wholeheartedly."

By this time we had reached the library, and Lorenzo opened the door for me. "If you will permit me to make a recommendation, Madonna," he said, following me and striding quickly toward one of the shelves, "I believe I know just the book for you to begin with." He withdrew a volume from the shelf, and I flipped it open to the title page. "Plato," I said aloud, examining the Latin title. "*The Republic.*"

Lorenzo smiled. "You may read it at your leisure, Madonna Simonetta, and I look forward to discussing it with you."

I closed the book, my face alight with excitement. "I shall look forward to that as well."

As Marco and I made our way home that evening, he himself brought up the topic I had been struggling to broach. "I saw you in conversation with that painter, Botticelli," he said. "What did he want?"

"He wished to speak to me about sitting for him, as we discussed at our wedding," I said. "But it was not just that. He and I had a most interesting conversation, and he recommended some reading material to me." I held up the book Lorenzo had lent me.

"Hmph," Marco said. "We did say you would sit for him, did we not?"

"We did," I said. "It would not do to go back on our word now."

I turned my most winning smile on to him. "And I would so enjoy it, Marco. To sit for such an artist. It would be most thrilling, *caro*."

He sighed, not unhappily. "I think I can deny you nothing when you smile at me like that, Simonetta. Very well. I shall arrange it. I trust Lorenzo knows where the man can be found."

I leaned back in my seat. "No doubt he does," I agreed, my calm words belying the thrumming of my heart. I had never had my portrait painted before, and I had the irresistible suspicion that Signor Botticelli would paint me in such a way as I had never before seen myself. I would see myself as he saw me, and I could not say why such a thought excited me so.

15

Marco was true to his word, and arranged everything within the next few days. Lorenzo passed along his enthusiasm for the commission, and sent us directions to Signor Botticelli's fledgling studio. We then wrote directly to the painter, inquiring as to when would be most convenient for me to come and sit for him.

His response was almost instantaneous; he sent our messenger back with a reply that I could come to his workshop on Monday, in just five days.

"He is extremely eager to have you sit for him," Marco said, frowning at the hastily scrawled reply. "'Tis almost unseemly."

I smiled at my husband. "He just has exquisite taste in models, it seems," I teased.

Marco smiled. "He does at that," he relented. "And I can hardly blame him."

As it happened, Botticelli's house—with his living space above his studio—was not far from my new home at the Vespucci *palazzo*; so close was it, in fact, that I told Marco he was being silly for insisting

I take the carriage. He agreed reluctantly, only insisting that I take Chiara to accompany me.

A part of me had been a bit surprised that he had not wanted to accompany me himself, even supervise the painter's work. But despite his earlier surliness regarding Botticelli, he had not felt it necessary.

"You are a married woman now, Simonetta," he said. "You do not need a chaperone to move about the city. I am not some jealous husband who does not trust his wife."

I was glad to hear him say so and, in truth, some of the realities—and freedoms—of my new status had been slow to make themselves real to me. Yet I had been surprised all the same, knowing all too well that strangely tense undertone in his voice whenever Signor Botticelli was mentioned. It seemed that my husband could sense whatever accord it was that had grown between the painter and myself, yet since there had been no untoward nor improper actions on anyone's part, there was little he could do or say on the matter. But it eased my mind that Marco trusted me so.

The painter's studio was on the ground floor of a somewhat ramshackle building, with a weaver's shop on one side and a silversmith's on the other. I bade Chiara run along to the market and do some shopping for the household—no point in having her waiting about for me all day—and then went in without knocking, as I knew Signor Botticelli was expecting me.

I found the inside to be rather chaotic. Splotches of paint covered many of the surfaces of the front room into which I stepped, and brushes and pieces of canvas were strewn about everywhere. Empty easels stood here and there about the floor, looking like skeletons awaiting a new graft of skin to give them life.

I heard male voices coming from a room toward the back, out of sight. "Please, maestro," one said, sounding like a young boy. "It was a mistake. I did not know."

"You would have known, had you paused long enough to listen

to my instructions," another voice replied sternly, one that I recognized as Botticelli's.

"It is a mistake only, maestro. I will try again."

Botticelli sighed. "No. I will do it myself. You will go out into the streets and find Luca, the lazy loafer. And when you do find him, tell him that the next time he does not appear here when he is meant to, I shall find myself another apprentice."

"*Si*, signore." With that, the boy emerged from the back room—he was perhaps twelve or thirteen. He bolted for the door, nearly knocking into me in his haste. "*Mi scusi*, signora," he said, pushing past me with barely a glance.

Having heard the boy's words, Signor Botticelli appeared as well. "Madonna Simonetta," he said, stopping short at the sight of me. "I—You are early."

"Am I?" I asked, feeling disappointment leach into my stomach. I had to admit—if only to myself—that I had expected him to be more excited upon my arrival. "Perhaps. My apologies."

"No, no," he said hurriedly, stepping farther into the room and collecting a handful of paintbrushes. "You mistake my meaning; I am delighted to see you, at any hour of the day or night." He smiled ruefully. "It is just that I had hoped to clean up some of this mess before you arrived."

"I think it is lovely," I said. I blushed as he turned his questioning gaze on me. "That is . . . this space. Your space. It is so full of life."

He smiled again, that same wide, relaxed grin that made his face so beautiful to behold. "I thank you for saying so." His smile faded as he sighed and ran his fingers through his tousled blond hair. "As you no doubt heard, one of my apprentices has been most derelict in his duties, and I have only the other boy at the moment. I set him to mixing some of the paint I mean to use today, but he is not used to the task, and so I will have to remedy the error myself. If you do not mind waiting, that is. If you wish to return another day, I—"

"Not at all," I interrupted. "But I confess I thought you might begin by sketching me, and not by beginning the painting so soon? But then I am most ignorant of the artistic process."

He glanced at me, amused, still moving about the room, collecting stray items and returning them to their proper places—or at least somewhere out of the way. "I shall begin by sketching you, yes, but I confess that I already have an idea of how to pose you, and how to begin, and what I think the portrait shall look like. So it may be a very brief sketch, indeed."

"Whatever you think best," I said.

"It has been difficult, establishing my own studio, and then finding promising apprentices," he went on. "Without the patronage of Lorenzo and his family, I should have a much harder time of it still." He shook his head. "My apologies, Madonna. You no doubt do not care about such things as the difficulties of a humble artist."

"Why should I not?" I asked. "We are friends, or so you told me when last we met."

He stopped and faced me, a slight smile tugging at his lips. "I did say that," he said. "I have hoped ever since that you did not find me too forward."

"Not at all," I said, even though I knew I should say that he had been. More than that, I should feel that he had been too forward as well, but I did not, and so I could not bring myself to say it. For every part of me wanted to be friends with this strange, intense man so set on painting me.

"Then," he said, drawing up a plain wooden chair to the center of the room, "as one friend to another, I must thank you for agreeing to sit for me."

"And I must thank you for wishing me to sit for you," I said. "I have been looking forward to it so." I flushed slightly as I thought of the ways in which he might construe my words. "I say so not out of vanity, I assure you. Only that I might contribute to art in some small way, if you deem me worthy."

He chuckled. "I think you more than know my feelings on that subject." He gestured to the chair. "Please, do sit, Madonna Simonetta. Make yourself comfortable."

I did as he said, perching myself on the edge of the roughly hewn chair.

He raised an eyebrow as he drew up a chair of his own, facing me. "Is that 'comfortable,' Madonna?"

I laughed, feeling my body relax. "I suppose not, no. But my mother would say, 'A lady always sits with perfect and straight posture.'"

"Far be it from me to contradict so noble a lady as your mother," he said, a leather-bound notebook and a bit of charcoal in his hand as he sat. "But you shall be sitting here for some time, and so it is best to sit comfortably. Let your back rest against the chair."

I did as he said, albeit hesitatingly. "Will it not . . . be the wrong pose for a portrait?" I regretted the words as soon as they left my mouth. "Forgive me. I should not ask you such questions, not when I know nothing of what I speak."

"Never apologize for asking questions, Madonna, and certainly not to me," he said. "You may ask me whatever you wish within these walls, and I shall always answer honestly. I will begin by addressing this very question: for your portrait, I wish to capture you in a natural way, such as you might look while relaxed, or in the company of a friend." A hint of a smile came to his lips again. "Such as you are at this moment."

I smiled, feeling more than my body relax now: my mind, it seemed, was letting go of some of its tension as well. "Thank you, signore. I see your aim, and I applaud it."

"Now," he said, his sketchbook propped up on one knee. "Let us begin."

It was a strange experience at first, being sketched. Signor Botticelli—or, more rightly, Maestro Botticelli, as he was the master of his own studio—stared at me with those penetrating eyes of his, letting them roam over my face, the curve of my jaw, the line of my neck, the tumbling tendrils of my hair, which I had asked Chiara to leave mostly loose. Then his gaze would flick down to the paper before him, his hand moving rapidly before glancing back up to take me in anew. In the beginning it was all I could do not to fidget under his scrutiny, and for a moment I dropped my eyes to the floor.

"No, Madonna." I started slightly at his voice, gentle though it was. "No. You must keep your chin up, your eyes up. Look right back at me. *Si,*" he said enthusiastically as I met his gaze again. He paused, gazing at me, then continued, more gruffly, quieter. "*Si.* Just like that, *per favore.*"

Soon, once the initial awkwardness had passed, I felt myself reveling in his gaze, enjoying it. But I could not quite say why. Surely there was no shortage of men who wished to—and did—look at me. Yet there was something very different about this. Botticelli did not wish to possess me, as men who looked upon me with desire might. His study of me went deeper than that, deeper than flesh and skin and beauty and even desire; his gaze went right to my soul, as if only in rendering me on the page—and later the canvas—in perfect accuracy could he come to understand what was within. And, perhaps, reveal it to me.

This was, I realized, the very same way he had studied me across the Medici dinner table the night I had first met him. He had been sketching me in his mind.

And I, boldly staring back at him, was given ample opportunity to study him in turn. He really was quite handsome, I realized, yet in a different way from Marco's dark yet buoyant charm, or Giuliano de' Medici's gilded, godlike perfection. His features were strong, chiseled, as though they'd been cut from marble; his blond hair tumbled in unruly waves about his face, threatening to curl at the ends. Several times as he drew, he would lift his other hand to push his hair off of his face, only to have it fall back again. And his eyes, his eyes that saw and sought to reproduce so much truth and beauty, were of a lovely light color. Green, perhaps? Or hazel? They seemed to change with the light, with his emotions, with his thoughts.

So hypnotized was I by this strange give-and-take, the studying and being studied, that I jumped slightly when he spoke again. "I am going to reposition you slightly, if I may, Madonna. I have completed my sketch of you straight on, and now I would sketch you in profile, which is how I am thinking of painting you."

"Of course," I said, trying not to let him see how flustered I was.

He moved toward me and I rose, allowing him to shift the position of the chair. "Sit once more," he said. I obeyed, and he hesitated for a moment. "If I may . . . touch you?" he asked. I nodded quickly, and he placed one hand softly on my chin, bringing it up and forward just slightly. "*Si,*" he murmured. "Just there. Hold that pose, Madonna, if you please."

He retreated to his chair, seized a fresh bit of paper, and resumed sketching. I could still feel the warmth of his fingers where he had touched me. It was awhile before the sensation faded.

The light coming in through the windows of the studio shifted and changed a bit as Botticelli sketched. He seemed to be endowing this sketch with much more detail than he had the first. I wanted to ask him about it, ask him why that was, as he had encouraged me to ask him anything and everything, but did not want to break the spell that had fallen over the room.

Finally, he stopped and leaned back in his chair. "I realize now that I quite forgot to remix those paints my assistant botched," he said, his voice sounding oddly loud after so long a period of silence. "But no matter. I have kept you long enough for one day. When next you return, I shall paint. I may be able to start in the meantime."

"Indeed?" I said, struggling to pull myself back into the world—the world of conversation and practical considerations. "And when should I return?"

He met my eyes. "The day after tomorrow, if you can," he said. "And if you would wear that same dress, that would be most helpful."

I looked quickly down at my gown, having forgotten which one I was wearing. Had it truly only been this morning that Chiara had dressed me? "Certainly," I said. "That is perfectly agreeable."

He rose from his chair, and I did the same. "Until then, Madonna," he said. "I shall look forward to it." His voice betrayed an earnestness that went beyond mere politeness.

"As do I, already," I said, wondering if he could hear the sincerity in my own voice as well.

The way he lingered as he took my hand and kissed it told me that he did.

16

I returned home that afternoon feeling buoyant, elated; yet also sad that the day was over. The day after tomorrow, I consoled myself, I would return.

Marco was home already when I arrived. "Simonetta, *moglie mia,*" he said, rising from his chair in our sitting room and greeting me with a deep kiss on the mouth.

"My, husband," I said when we broke apart. "Pray, do not kiss me so this early in the evening, or I shall want to retire before we've eaten our supper."

His eyes sparkled at my words. "I could be persuaded to feast on you, and you alone," he said. "But you are right. And we are invited to dine with my parents this evening."

"Ah." Marco's parents were certainly kind enough, but usually on the occasions when we all dined together, Marco and his father discussed Marco's work at the Medici bank at length, leaving his mother and me to eat in silence. I would much rather have enjoyed Marco's company on my own, or better yet, been invited to dine with the Medici family again. Perhaps next time they invited us to dine I would contrive an invitation from Clarice. She would not mind if I dropped by unannounced.

Marco released me and stepped back, and we both sat down. "But how have you spent your day, wife?" His eyes darkened slightly. "You have not been at Botticelli's workshop all this time, have you?"

"I have."

"*Dio mio,*" Marco said, his tone a bit sharper than I thought strictly necessary. "Has he completed your portrait by this time, then?"

"No," I said. "He merely took some sketches today. I am to return the day after tomorrow."

"An awfully long time to be sketching one woman."

"And yet that is what he was doing," I said. Unbidden, I recalled Botticelli's eyes studying me so intently, how I had gloried in his gaze. And how I, in turn, had delighted in studying his handsome face. Guilt sharpened my tone and made it more defensive than perhaps was warranted. "I am confused, Marco. Did you not tell me that you are not a jealous husband who does not trust his wife?"

"I did. But—"

"Then why are your words, and their tone, reminiscent of a jealous husband?" I inquired innocently. "I cannot be sure, of course, having never before been possessed of a jealous husband—or am I?"

"I do not mean anything by it, Simonetta. It just seems like a longer stretch of time than is necessary to sketch someone."

"Are you an artist now, Marco? Do you know how it is done?"

"No. But I—"

Yet I was becoming angry now. Why had he agreed to let me sit for Botticelli, only to then behave this way? "Are you trying to ask me something, Marco? To accuse me of something, perhaps?"

"No," he said, a response that was gratifyingly swift. "I would never."

"Good. Then stop giving lie to your own words."

"For the love of God, Simonetta!" he burst out. "How can you accuse me of being jealous? I let you go there alone, did I not? Giuliano de' Medici flirts with you with his every breath, and I say nothing. I do not even mind, not truly. I know how the game is played. Yet I am a man, mortal and flawed. I know how beautiful my wife is, and I know that other men notice."

I rose to my feet. "You had best get used to other men noticing me, husband," I said. "Artists, lechers, noblemen, what have you. It has been happening since I was a child, and will no doubt keep on until I age and my beauty fades." I stalked from the room, only pausing briefly in the doorway to glance at him over my shoulder. "And remember that it is you whom I married."

It was our first argument as a married couple—or ever. I was glad that we were dining with his parents, as it gave me an excuse to ignore him. Yet the lack of conversation around the dinner table in which I could participate meant that I found my mind wandering back to the light touch of Sandro's hand on my face as he adjusted my position, the warmth his fingers had left behind. It was almost as though I could feel his touch again; and, after a moment, when I remembered where I was and glanced up again, I was relieved to see that no one seemed to notice my blush.

That night, when Marco and I went to bed, I turned my back to him and stayed that way. It was the first night since my illness—save for the days when I was suffering my monthly courses—that we did not make love. I lay awake most of the night, anger and guilt churning in my gut.

The next morning, as though in acknowledgment of how silly we'd been and of his desire that we return to normal, Marco reached for me in bed, and I went to him willingly. He took me hungrily, bringing me to pleasure with such force that it left me gasping. Maybe a little jealousy was good for a man, after all. I found myself feeling quite bereft when he had to rise and make ready to leave.

Yet even so, I spent the day happily engrossed in the book of Plato's writings that Lorenzo had lent me. In a way, it felt rather like studying with Padre Valerio again: I found myself making mental notes of certain points or lines that I wished to discuss later—either with Lorenzo or with Maestro Botticelli, whom I was sure had read this book as well. I would ask him the next day, I resolved.

Eager to discuss the book even further, I suggested to Marco that night over dinner that he might read it as well, and we could exchange our views. "I wish that I could, Simonetta," he said, "but I think that I shall be far too busy in the coming days. You must read it and tell me of it."

I did my best not to allow my disappointment to show.

The following day, I had Chiara dress me in the same gown I had worn to my first sitting, and returned to Maestro Botticelli's studio. I was even more eager than I had been the first time, and a part of me could not help but continue to wonder why.

Maestro Botticelli and I are friends, I told myself. I wished to discuss Plato's writing with him. And it would be lying to say I wasn't excited for this portrait, and to see the finished product when it was ready. That was all.

When I arrived at the studio I let myself in, and found a bit more activity than two days ago. Two apprentices bustled about the room: the boy who had dashed past me last time, and a somewhat older boy whom I assumed must be the recalcitrant Luca. Both looked up as I came in, and both stopped dead in the midst of their activities and stared at me.

I laughed. They made quite a picture: one carting an armload of rolled canvases, and the other holding a pot of yellow paint, which was smeared on his hands and arms; yet both looked at me with the same comically shocked, open-mouthed expression.

"Do not let me distract you from your work, gentlemen," I said sweetly. "What, have neither of you seen a woman before?"

"They have, but never one such as you, Madonna Simonetta," Botticelli said, emerging from the back room and coming toward me. "And that is not quite fair, for you to use that tone on them." He took my hand and kissed it. "Welcome back."

"It is good to be back," I said.

He turned around and cuffed Luca on the back of the head as he did so. "Enough of that. Back to work."

With a mumbled, "*Mi scusi*, maestro," the boy did just that, and his younger counterpart followed suit without a word.

"Over here, if you please, Madonna Simonetta," Botticelli said, gesturing me toward where a chair and easel had been set up right in front of the window. "The light is best here, I find. I have everything ready, so we can begin as soon as you are settled."

"I am ready when you are, maestro," I said, sitting in the chair.

"Very good. If I may position you, then? Turn so that you are sitting at an angle—yes, just so. Now raise your chin slightly—" Here he reached out and touched my chin lightly but firmly with his fingers, lifting it. "Yes. Just so." He retreated back behind the easel and picked up a brush. "I was able to make a start with the sketches I took last time," he told me. "I cannot say how long I shall keep you today—sometimes the muse is kind and I quite lose track of time."

I smiled. "I shall stay as long as you need."

Immediately a look of intense focus came over his face. "That expression, there. Hold it, if you can. *Per favore*." He turned back to the easel and applied himself to the canvas.

It was not hard to hold the smile, as he bade me—his excitement and enthusiasm were catching. I had hoped we might have more time for conversation before we began, but far be it from me to interrupt the muse who, it seemed, was speaking most eagerly to the painter even now.

The same spell as before seemed to fall over us again, and I embraced it fully. Even the clattering about and whispered conversations of Botticelli's apprentices could not break it, could not disturb this wordless connection being woven between us once again.

Somewhat to my dismay, the easel partially concealed him, and the way in which I was positioned left me facing away from him, so I was unable to study him as I had previously. But I could feel his eyes on me. And when I knew his eyes were trained on the canvas, I would sneak a glance at him, at his tousled blond hair, at his strong hand gripping the brush. If he noticed, he did not react at all.

After perhaps an hour, he sighed and laid down his brush. "I shall let you take a break now, Madonna," he said. "I should have done so last time, and I do apologize for the lapse."

"It is quite alright," I said, rising from my chair. Ah, but it did feel good to stand.

He rose as well, flexing the fingers of his painting hand. "Giovanni," he called, to the younger of the two apprentices. "Bring me that yellow paint you were mixing."

The boy obliged, and Botticelli looked satisfied as he examined it. "Well done," he said. "You've gotten it right this time. Do you know what you did differently?"

Young Giovanni launched into a recitation of the different proportions he had used in mixing the paint, and where he had made his mistakes the last time. Botticelli listened attentively, then clapped the boy on the back when he finished. "Good," he said. "Very good. You and Luca may go find some lunch now." The boy eagerly scampered off, and Botticelli watched him go, chuckling.

"You are a good teacher," I observed.

"I try to be," he said. "Being beaten and berated for mistakes never taught me anything, that much I know. So I take a different approach." He met my eyes and smiled. "It is a lovely day, Madonna Simonetta. Worthy of your beauty, even. Perhaps you would like to join me in a short stroll before we return to our work here?"

"That would be wonderful," I said, both surprised and elated.

Botticelli opened the door of his studio for me and allowed me to precede him outside, into the bright Tuscan sunshine. He offered me his arm, and we began to stroll through the dusty streets in the general direction of the Arno. I was beginning to learn my way about this city, a fact that filled me with pride.

"I took your advice, maestro," I told him as we walked.

"Oh?" he asked, arching an eyebrow at me. "And what advice was that?"

"To partake of certain books as I might find in the Medici library," I said. "Lorenzo was kind enough to lend me a volume by Plato. I am finding it most enlightening."

"And which volume is this?"

"*The Republic.*"

"Ah, yes," he said. "I am not surprised that you read Latin, nor that you have sought out such a worthy tome."

"So you are familiar with it? I had thought you might be." I blushed at admitting that I had been thinking about him.

"Indeed, I am. I am most eager to hear your thoughts."

"It is like nothing I have read before," I said, "which I suppose is to be expected."

"What?" Botticelli demanded, in mock surprise and outrage. "You mean your tutor did not teach you pagan philosophy?"

I laughed. "To be sure he did not, so it is a good thing I have come to Florence. That I might learn."

"And here I thought you came here to be married."

I paused, uncertain how to navigate this abrupt change in topic. "I did, of course. But I must confess, Marco's description made me all the more eager, for he told me of all that Florence has to recommend her."

The painter went silent, and I could tell there were words poised on his tongue that he wished to speak, but was holding back.

"What is it you wish to say?" I asked him. "Are we not friends, my dear Maestro Botticelli?"

"We are," he said.

"Then why can you not ask me anything you wish, when you have extended the same courtesy to me?"

He gave me a half-hearted smile. "You are kind to make me such an offer," he said. "But the difference in our stations dictates that such a reversal is not always appropriate."

I waved his words aside. "I care not for such things," I said. "What difference is there between us at this moment, maestro? We are two friends out for a stroll through Florence's streets. That is all anyone who looks at us shall see, and all that I wish for either of us to see as well."

His smile widened. "I should say that most people, looking at us, are seeing only you, Madonna Simonetta."

"Maybe so, but I am used to it, and so I take no note of such things," I said. "Now, I shall say it again: you may speak as freely to me as I do to you."

"Very well," he said, chuckling. "Yet now that you have talked me 'round, I find that I have quite forgotten what I meant to say."

"Liar," I teased. "You have forgotten nothing."

"I should know by now that your beauty and your wits are equally matched."

"Stop trying to distract me with flattery."

"Very well," he said again. His face grew serious before he spoke. "You said that your husband's description of Florence, and all to be found here, persuaded you to leave your home. But what of Marco himself? Did you not marry him because you love him?"

I drew in a breath sharply. I had been expecting such a question, since he had been so reluctant to voice it. So why had I prodded him into asking it anyway?

The painter did not speak, only watched me as I considered what to say next.

"You must understand," I said. "Many women are not so lucky in marriage as I am: to be offered for by a man for whom they feel affection. Marco came to me, speaking of Dante and poetry, and he seemed the romantic hero. Then he spoke of this city, this Florence, and the Medici and the artists and poets and all there was to be learned. It seemed that he was offering me everything I had ever wanted, but had never dared to hope for. I did not know him well enough to love him, at first."

Botticelli was silent for a moment before speaking again. "So you are happy?"

"I am," I said. "And I do love him now. As I understand love."

Even as I spoke, though, I began to regret telling him such things, and having urged him to be so frank with me in the first place. Was it not unseemly for me to be discussing my husband and my marriage with another man? It was no sin that I could name, yet it felt wrong all the same. Guilt began to gnaw at the edges of my mind; for while I had said nothing that was not true, it felt somehow like a betrayal of Marco, like I had spoken of some secret of marriage that I should not have spoken about.

He did not speak again for a few paces, and when he did, his tone was slightly guarded. "Then I am happy for you, Madonna Simonetta. I want for you to be happy. Know that to be true."

"Thank you."

"And now, I think, we must return to Plato, for we have neglected him for far too long. What are your thoughts on his *Republic*, Madonna?" he asked.

I brightened at his question, glad to change the subject and excited by the turn the conversation had taken. "As I said, it is very interesting. I am intrigued by the argument of some of the philosophers with whom Socrates debates—you will forgive me for forgetting their names, I hope."

He smiled. "You are forgiven, for I would be hard-pressed to recall them myself. Greek names have an odd sound to the Tuscan ear, methinks."

"Indeed. I am intrigued by their argument that justice is only a result of the fear of punishment and censure, essentially. That any man—or woman—only behaves justly because they fear being caught out doing otherwise."

"And do you think these philosophers are correct?" he asked.

"I like to think that they are not," I said. "I know that there are some in this world about whom that is true, but I like to think there are those who will act on the side of right, of justice, no matter what. Even if there is no one to applaud their actions, or to condemn them for doing wrong."

"I agree wholeheartedly," Botticelli said. "The right or just course is not always the easiest, and we well know that there are those in this world who prefer the easy route, whatever it may be."

"Indeed," I said. I lowered my voice slightly, though there did not seem to be anyone near enough to overhear us. "And I can see why the Church would object to such writings. The idea that mankind only does good to avoid the fires of hell . . . well, that seems to be a very dangerous idea."

"And yet it is true, is it not?" he said. "Priests preach sermons meant to fill us with fear of hellfire, so what else but fear can motivate us to do good? When our ears are filled with what awaits the alternative?"

"A priest would no doubt say that the reward of heaven should be the ultimate motivator," I said, "though I do see your point. Holy Mother Church may have brought such a problem upon herself, then. Though I should think that the priests would not thank anyone for pointing such out to them."

He chuckled. "I shouldn't think so, no."

"Anyway, that is quite as far as I have gotten with Signor Plato at the moment, I am afraid. I am trying to read slowly so that I may give each point my full consideration." I smiled. "I cannot tear through it quite as quickly as I do my favorite poetry."

"Ah, but is not poetry as worthy of our consideration as philosophy?" Botticelli asked, as we turned to walk along the Arno.

"I confess I have never thought about it as deeply as I am thinking about Plato's words," I said. "It is beautiful, of course, but I read it mostly as a diversion."

"And would you not say that Dante was trying to teach us something with his *Divina Commedia*?"

I smiled ruefully. "I know that he was, yet in truth it is his love for Beatrice that most captivates me."

The painter laughed. "You are a true romantic, Madonna Simonetta."

"So I have discovered. I must strive to become more pragmatic, it seems."

"No," he said, his voice suddenly taking on a sharper tone. "Never seek to eliminate that romanticism, Simonetta. There are not enough such dreamers in this world." He stopped, and I noticed, to my surprise, a blush colored his cheeks. "Forgive me. I should not address you by your Christian name alone."

"Not in company, no," I said, "for that would cause gossip. But when it is just us, you may call me Simonetta."

"I could not presume so far."

"I insist," I said firmly.

Even as I spoke, I wondered at what I was doing. Were anyone to overhear the painter addressing me so familiarly, it would cause a scandal. God forbid Marco should ever hear such. Yet I could not remember the last time I had been so comfortable in anyone else's company, and I did not want any formality standing between me and this man or our conversation. Or rather, I wanted there to be as little as was possible. And so I could not bring myself to care.

He smiled, and it was like the sun rising after a night of storms. "Very well. Then you must call me Sandro."

I returned the smile, though my own must have paled in comparison.

We paused along the riverbank, having just passed the Ponte Vecchio and its collection of shops and storefronts, selling mostly costly gold items. Beyond it, on the other side of the river, green hills rose up above the city, above the buildings of Oltrarno, keeping watch over their domain.

It occurred to me at that moment that if I was a painter, if I had even the slightest notion of how to mix these colors, this would be the scene I would paint: the muddy brown of the Arno and the reddish tile of the roofs and the emerald of the hills and the fathomless blue of the sky, blue as the Virgin's robe.

After a few moments, Maestro Botticelli turned away from the river. "I suppose it is time to return to the workshop," he said. "I must paint some more before the light changes too much."

"Very well," I said. "Lead on, Sandro." And as his name trespassed my lips, I felt that more than merely the light was about to change.

17

The next few weeks fell into a comfortable pattern. I came to Sandro's workshop as often as he needed me, and took up my place in the chair by the window so that he could continue work on my portrait. No matter how I pleaded, he would not let me have a peek at it before it was done. "You must wait until it is finished, Simonetta," he said to me one evening as we finished our session. "I would not be able to bear you judging the work when it is yet unfinished."

"I am not used to a man refusing me anything," I said, only half joking.

He made an odd motion then, as if to reach out and cup my face in his palms, but he checked himself. "It shall be a good experience for you, then," he teased, his tone light, matching mine.

Marco, for his part, made no further comments about my visits to Sandro's workshop, except to inquire how the portrait was coming along.

"Maestro Botticelli seems happy enough with its progress," I said. "I have not seen it."

"You have not?" he asked incredulously.

"No," I said. "But I have every confidence that it will be beautiful."

Marco's face softened slightly then. "And how could a painting of you be anything but?" he asked tenderly.

I smiled, though the gesture felt somewhat forced. It was at moments like this that I felt most guilty for how much I had come to look forward to the time I spent with Sandro, for how I enjoyed the feel of his eyes on me, for the free and easy conversations that we shared when we would rise and take a break from the work. I would return home to my husband and feel ashamed each time that I had not thought of him once while posing for the portrait that day.

Oh, what nonsense I worry myself over, I told myself sternly. When I spend a day with Clarice, I do not pine for and think constantly of my husband, do I? And yet I feel no guilt for that. But this felt somehow different, in a way that I could not quite articulate.

Pulling myself out of my thoughts, I leaned forward and rewarded Marco with a kiss for his sweet words, hoping all the time that he could not taste the guilt on my lips.

Once, as the portrait neared completion, Sandro painted on into the evening, lighting a plethora of candles about us so that he might keep working. I did not mind; I remained perfectly still and watched the deepening twilight cast shadows across the part of his face that was visible around the canvas.

He had barely spoken to me that day; simply positioned me upon his arrival and gotten to work, with only the briefest of pleasantries. Though usually I did not mind the silence in the least, I missed our usual conversation between sittings. So, though I had never done so while he was working before, I spoke. "You have been very quiet today, Sandro," I said, my voice low, though his apprentices had left for the evening. His eyes flicked to me. "I take it the muse is speaking to you most eloquently?"

His eyes never left my face. "You are the muse, Simonetta," he said, his voice raspy. "There is no other."

Summer had long since faded into fall as Sandro worked on my portrait, and one day in early October I arrived at his workshop to find him in a flurry of excitement such as I had never seen before. "It is done," he said when I entered, in lieu of a greeting.

"It is?" I asked, somewhat surprised. "Why, you do not need me today at all, then."

He took my hand and kissed it. "I always need you here, Simonetta," he said, his voice low. But then he released my hand and led me to a room in the back of the workshop. "I finished it yesterday; I could not stop working. And so it is good that you are here now, for you must be the first to see it."

He gestured toward the easel where it was situated, and I gasped.

It was like looking into a mirror. He had captured me, absolutely: the fabric and design of the pale gown I wore when I sat for him; the line of my long neck; the pale shade of my skin; the exact shape of my nose, my lips, my chin; the exact texture of my wavy hair, though in the portrait he had painted it into an elaborate, Grecian style. The look in my eyes was a serious one, almost studious, and I realized that this was how I had looked all along, staring back at him, studying him even as he studied me.

I was partially in profile, as he had positioned me in the chair each day, and the background was plain and dark, causing the colors of the painting to shine in sharp relief.

I must have stared at it for so long that he grew nervous. I heard him clear his throat behind me, then shuffle his feet a bit, before he finally spoke. "And so?" he asked. "What do you think?"

I turned to him, and the look on my face must have answered his question, for a relieved smile spread across his face. "It is beautiful," I said. "It is me—exactly. I do not think a better likeness could have been captured!" I turned to look at it—at myself—again. "I was here the entire time you painted it," I said softly. "I watched you do it, and yet I cannot fathom how such a thing is possible."

He moved closer to me, so that I could feel the whisper of his shirt against my back. "I am so glad you like it," he said. "I do not know how I would have borne it if you did not."

I turned to look at him, and the expression on his face was earnest. "It is beautiful, perfect," I said, glancing at his mouth. My breath caught, and I shifted, looking away. "Perhaps I sound immodest, praising a painting of myself so, but it is only your skill I mean to compliment."

"But you and your beauty have everything to do with it," he said. "I have never painted better, I do not think, for I have never had such a model."

I began to protest, but he cut me off with a shake of his head. "I mean it, Simonetta." He moved ever so slightly closer to me and placed his hands lightly on my shoulders. "You have inspired me as no one else has. Ever."

I felt myself swaying slightly where I stood. The urge to let myself fall against him, to feel him take me in his arms, was, suddenly, almost overwhelming.

And he would, I knew. He would crush me to him so that there was no space left between us, no room to breathe, to speak nor protest nor question. Yet I sensed that he would not come toward me any further. If someone was to take the step that would push us over the edge, it would have to be me.

And I could not do it. I was afraid, afraid of the things I was feeling. I am a married woman, and I love my husband. What wickedness now overtakes me? I wondered.

I stepped back quickly. It took a moment for me to collect myself, and a part of me cursed him for remaining silent, for not saying something that would take us back from this strange, frightening brink and back into the world in which we both belonged. "I thank you for showing it to me," I managed at last. "I . . . it is everything I dreamed it would be, and more."

He nodded, his eyes dropping from mine. "Of course," he replied. "As I said, it is only right that you should be the first to lay eyes on it." He cleared his throat. "Will Marco—Signor Vespucci, that is—like it as well, do you suppose?"

I took another step back, as though Marco's name in the space between us was a reprimand of some sort. "I am certain he will," I said.

"I am glad," Sandro said. "I was thinking of perhaps unveiling it at the Medici *palazzo*—I know Lorenzo is most eager to see it, and I am sure I can convince him to give a dinner in honor of my new work, and of its subject."

"That would be lovely," I said. "It is a nice thought."

He nodded. "Very good. I shall arrange it with Lorenzo and Clarice."

"And I shall await my invitation."

We both stood there in silence for a moment.

"I suppose I had best return home, then," I said finally. "It would seem that our work here is complete."

My own words brought the truth home to me: the painting was complete, and I would not be returning to Sandro's workshop again. There would be no more delighting in the feel of his eyes upon me, of surreptitiously studying him behind his canvas, no more intellectual debate or invigorating walks by the Arno. I would still see him at the Medici *palazzo,* of course, and no doubt quite often; yet it would always be in the company of others, not in this world of ours that we had carved out for just the two of us. It would be back to *Madonna Simonetta,* and *Maestro Botticelli.*

The days seemed to stretch out before me in an unending, meaningless march, and I did not know how I could bear it.

For shame, I reprimanded myself. You shall use your extra time to better devote yourself to your husband, of course.

Yet as though Sandro had heard my thoughts and sought to

reassure me, he took my hand and kissed it, his eyes never leaving mine. "For now," he said. "Our work is complete for now."

I was both excited and saddened when I returned home that day. "The painting is done," I informed Marco when he arrived home and came into the sitting room, where I was reading.

His expression lit up. "Is it? And? How does it look?"

I smiled slowly, remembering, wishing I had it here to show him. "It is wonderful. A very flattering likeness. San—Maestro Botticelli has skill beyond anything I had dreamed."

Marco's lips twitched slightly at my slip, but thankfully he did not comment upon it. "That sounds wonderful, indeed," he said. "And when might I expect it to be delivered to us?"

I told him about Sandro's plans for the painting to be revealed at the Medici *palazzo*. "If I know Lorenzo, it may become a very grand affair indeed," I said.

"And why should it not be, to celebrate a painting of so beautiful a model as yourself?" Marco said. "And to celebrate the painter as well, for being so fortunate as to have you sit for him."

I had to bite back a retort at that. It is nothing to do with me, I wanted to say. If only you could see Sandro's skill, his talent, his gift. He could make any model look beautiful simply for being alive.

"You flatter me, husband," I said instead, lightly. "Now, shall we dine? I have had the cook prepare your favorite beef."

"Indeed?" he asked as he followed me into the dining room. "Is it a special occasion, that we should have beef for supper?"

"It is always a special occasion when I dine with my beloved husband," I said, smiling. "So I bade Chiara find the choicest cut she could at the market. Here, sit," I said, "and I shall serve you."

Marco did as I bade, and I cut him a fine piece of beef and poured his wine myself. I banished the pernicious thought that the looks of happiness and approval my husband gave me were not enough.

That night, when Marco took me in his arms in our bed, I went to him willingly, enjoying the feel of him moving within me. Yet true pleasure eluded me, and Marco—attentive lover though he was—did not seem to notice.

18

Within the week, a messenger came to our house with an invitation for a dinner at the Medici *palazzo*, to "celebrate the newest work by Maestro Sandro Botticelli, and his beautiful subject, Signora Simonetta Vespucci," so the wording went. It would take place in a week's time.

"Your painter wastes no time," Marco commented to me, handing me the letter to read over dinner.

"He is hardly *my* painter," I said quickly. "He is just eager to show off such an exceptional work, as he should be. I am proud of it as well, for my own small contribution."

After that our talk turned to other matters, though Marco sent a reply the very next morning stating that we would, of course, attend.

Time, which had flown by at an exceptional pace when I was sitting for the painting, slowed to the pace of the oldest, most broken-down horse in the week before the unveiling *festa*. I finished reading *The Republic*, though since my first urge was to discuss it with Sandro, it hardly served as a distraction. For that, too, I would have to wait until the party. I tried to implore Marco to read it yet again, and again he told me that he was too busy. "Perhaps in a few months, if business should slow down," he told me.

So I went back to my copy of Dante, and the book of Petrarch that Lorenzo had given me, and tried to read the poetry with the same critical mind with which I had read Plato. Truly the purpose of the language, especially in Dante's *Divina Commedia*, I found, was threefold: to tell a story; to create a beautiful, pleasing phrase; and to enfold within it another, more subtle meaning. Of course this, too, I wished to discuss with Sandro, and so my plans for distraction were once again foiled.

Fortunately, one day that week Clarice invited me to take a midday meal with herself and her mother-in-law, so I passed a happy afternoon with the Medici women, discussing plans for the upcoming party, as well as matters of fashion.

"I do not know if you noticed, Simonetta," Clarice said, her eyes bright with mischief, "but half the women at Mass last week were wearing gowns just like the one you wore to dinner here last."

My eyes opened wide, shocked. "I did not notice," I said. "Surely you are mistaken. Why would anyone have copied my gown?"

Clarice and Lucrezia exchanged knowing looks, united, for once, in their teasing of me. "Why, can it be that you do not know, my dear?" Lucrezia asked. "You are the reigning beauty of Florence. You are the one who decides the trends, the fashions."

"Surely not," I protested. "Why, what silliness! I have not even met many people in Florence, save your friends and acquaintances, and Marco's—"

"Simonetta, those are all the people that matter," Lucrezia interjected. "And just because you have not met the rest of Florentine society does not mean they do not know who you are."

"Why, surely you notice how everyone—men and women—stares at you in the street," Clarice said.

I blushed. "I had not noticed. Not to sound vain, but . . . it has ever been so. I am stared at wherever I go, and always have been. So I do not even take note anymore."

Lucrezia sighed. "Ah, to be young, and so beautiful."

"I shall never know what that is like," Clarice said, laughing.

"Nor I," said Lucrezia. "But come, we are embarrassing poor Simonetta. See how red her face grows?"

Thankfully, Clarice changed the subject, asking her mother-in-law what she had thought of the sermon from Sunday. I chimed in as needed, though I confess that most of my mind was devoted to considering this new information I had learned.

Before leaving, I asked Clarice if I might borrow a new book from the library. "Not more of my husband's pagan philosophers, I hope?" she asked, lips pursed. "He had best hope Holy Mother Church does not take an interest in the contents of that library any time soon."

I smiled tightly but did not respond, nor did I show her the title I eventually selected: a book of stories of the old Greek gods. Pagan, indeed.

I passed the rest of the week happily enough between my poetry and the new book, which contained some stories with which I was familiar, and others with which I was not. At the rate at which I was reading, I would need to begin paying much more regular visits to the Medici library.

Finally, the appointed day arrived, and in a fit of showmanship I had Chiara dress me in the same gown I had worn when posing for the portrait. I also had her put up my hair in an elaborate braided style; I could not recall the exact details of how Sandro had painted my hair in the portrait, but Chiara's finished product would be an echo of it, certainly. I would look as though I had just stepped from the canvas itself.

Today, as always, everyone would be looking at me, but today I was ready for them. I would be artwork made flesh; would show everyone the masterful resemblance Sandro had created.

Even Marco looked slightly taken aback when he saw me. "Simonetta," he said, as he came to escort me down to the carriage. "You look . . . beyond words. An artist could have no worthier muse, in truth."

I smiled serenely at him. "You are too kind, husband," I said, placing my hand on his arm. "Shall we go?"

As we made the familiar journey to the Medici *palazzo,* I considered seriously why I was so eagerly anticipating this evening. I craved it. Never had I been possessed of the type of vanity that would allow me to revel in a room full of people looking at a portrait of me. It was not that; no, I was *proud* of the painting, almost as proud as if I myself had created it.

And why should that be? Nothing of skill or talent had been required from me; all that was needed was to sit still as Sandro worked. No, the truth had lain somewhere in my words to Marco the day we had received our invitation. I was proud of Sandro, proud of what he had accomplished with the portrait, and eager for everyone to see it and marvel at his skill and give him the praise he so richly deserved.

Marco was right—somehow, Sandro was *my* painter, and I wanted the rest of the world to respect his talent—and him—as I did. I had tried not to think about it, to avoid it, but it was true.

And, of course, I had been looking forward to seeing him all week. That could not be denied, not even to myself. Perhaps least of all to myself.

I miss the company of my friend, that is all, I told myself. I am allowed to enjoy the company of others than my husband.

"Are you ready?" Marco asked, jolting me from my reverie, and I looked up to see that we had arrived. "You have been quite lost in your thoughts."

I pushed aside my musings and smiled at him. "I have been, indeed," I said. "My apologies, husband. I am ready."

We went inside and were led up to a receiving room on one of the upper floors that I had never been in before. The ceiling was carved with elaborate gilded moldings, and rich, vibrant tapestries hung on the walls. Gilt chairs lined the perimeter of the room, and to my left tall, elegant windows let in the autumn light.

"There she is! Signora Simonetta Vespucci, our own Maestro Botticelli's great muse!" Giuliano de' Medici said, immediately coming toward us. He swept me a deep bow and kissed my hand. "Your beauty shall now be preserved throughout the ages, as it should be." He gestured to the back of the room, where my portrait was displayed upon an easel for all to see. "I have written you a poem in honor of this occasion, that I may make my own small artistic offering to your beauty," he went on. "Shall I read it to you?"

"Honestly, Giuliano," Lorenzo said, approaching us. "Let Simonetta come in and gather herself first, I pray you." He offered me his arm, and I took it, my hand slipping from Marco's grasp as I did so. "The portrait is as beautiful as its subject," he said, leading me toward the easel. "Sandro has outdone himself, truly, yet how could he do otherwise, with you as a model?"

As we approached, Marco behind us, I felt rather than saw Sandro's gaze on me, and turned to see him off to one side of the room, accepting congratulations—and no doubt commissions—from other members of the Medici circle. Among them, I noticed, was Lucrezia Donati Ardenghelli and her husband. "You must paint my likeness, Maestro Botticelli," she purred, laying a hand on his arm. "Mustn't he, *marito*?" she asked of her husband.

"Whatever you want, my dear," Signor Ardenghelli said tolerantly.

Jealousy, hot and thick, exploded within me and dripped down my insides, giving the feeling that my innards were coated in hot wax. How dare she? Look at her preening in front of him. Who did she think she was? And would Sandro truly paint her?

Of course, I told myself, startled slightly at my own reaction. He would paint whoever gave him a commission, and I must wish that he received many of them, that he might flourish and prosper.

I took a deep, steadying breath and turned my attention back to my portrait. It was even more beautiful than I remembered. I had forgotten certain details: the brilliant texture of my hair and gown, the vividness of the pendant about my neck, which had been a wedding gift from Lorenzo and Clarice.

I turned to Marco, who had come up on my other side. "What say you, *marito*?" I asked him.

"It is masterful, as you said," he replied, smiling down at me. "A perfect likeness."

I was happy that he liked it, happy that he saw all its merit. "I am so glad you think so," I said. "It is a true testament to the talent of its creator, is it not?" I glanced in Sandro's direction to be sure he had heard my words, and the smile he threw my way gave me every assurance that he had.

"Indeed, it is," Lorenzo said. "And so we must persuade you to sit for him again soon."

"I would like nothing better," I said. I could not resist glancing at Sandro again, and his smile had grown even brighter. He beamed.

Before the evening was over, I resolved, I would try to steal him away for a private word. It would not be long enough, I knew. It could never be long enough.

In the meantime, Lorenzo was steering me to a table filled with refreshments. I quite lost track of Marco. "Wine?" Lorenzo asked. I nodded, and he handed me a goblet. "I shall take some as well. Come, *amici*," he said, turning to address the room at large, and everyone ceased in their conversations and looked to him—to us. "A toast! To our brilliant Maestro Botticelli, and to his muse—*la bella* Simonetta!"

The gathered company echoed him, raising their glasses in my direction. "To Maestro Botticelli, and *la bella* Simonetta! To *la bella* Simonetta!"

"Now," Lorenzo said, once the toast had been drunk, "I see that my copy of Plato's *Republic* has been returned to my library. Pray tell me, Simonetta, what were your thoughts on it?"

Truly, I would never tire of this wonderful Florence of mine.

19

Though we knew winter could not be far to seek, November favored us with some lovely mild weather. Bored and listless now that my sessions with Sandro were at an end, I insisted upon accompanying Chiara to the Mercato Vecchio one day, if only to leave the house and stretch my legs. She agreed after a bit of persuasion and so, dressed in a simple wool gown and cloak and leaving my jewels and adornments at home, I joined her in the streets of Florence.

We made our way through the busy, dirty streets, pressing close against walls of stone and stucco in the narrow alleyways as carts and wagons passed us by. Chiara knew the way well, of course, yet I allowed myself to pretend that she was not with me, that I must find my own way. I kept my eyes on the great dome of Santa Maria del Fiore when it appeared between the buildings, as I knew the Mercato Vecchio was not far from the Piazza del Duomo, and that I must continue in that direction. I imagined that everyone in Florence must navigate by the great cathedral, at least until they learned their way.

Soon, due more to Chiara than to my fancied attempts, we arrived at the bustling Mercato Vecchio, which, I remembered hearing—from either Marco or Sandro—had been the site of the forum in the days of the pagan Romans. The great open piazza—one of the larger ones in Florence—was crowded with wooden stalls arranged in tight rows, lengths of coarse cloth stretched between the wooden poles to offer some protection to the merchandise from sun and weather. The stalls sold everything from fresh fruits and vegetables from the countryside to recently slaughtered meat to live animals to bolts of cloth. I looked about keenly for a stall that sold books, but did not see one. Not such a loss, perhaps, I consoled myself, for I do have Lorenzo de' Medici's entire library at my disposal.

We were pressed close by our fellow shoppers in the narrow aisles between stalls, and the noise was incredible: people talking, shouting, laughing, arguing; merchants hawking their wares and buyers bargaining and haggling over prices. I took it all in, quite glad that Chiara was with me to do the actual shopping; every last thing distracted me, and so I was not much use.

Vaguely I realized that the people around us were staring, but I paid it no heed. I could see from Chiara's nervous glances that she had taken note as well, but she, too, was well used to such attention when in public with me and she did not remark upon it, either. "If you see anything you would like me to bring back for the kitchens, Madonna, just say the word," she said.

I smiled; perhaps I had misinterpreted her nervousness and she was simply uncomfortable at having the lady of the house accompany her to market. "The kitchen girl does a fine enough job keeping us fed," I said. "You need not worry about that, today. I am happy to simply be out."

Chiara nodded, and I trailed happily behind her as she looked for herbs to mix into remedies, and a bit of ribbon to mend a gown of mine.

As we looked over the ribbon and cloth spread across a wooden board at one stall, I was certain I heard my name. "*Che?*" I asked, glancing at Chiara beside me. "I did not hear you, Chiara."

She looked puzzled. "I did not say anything, Madonna."

"Oh. I thought you had said my name." Yet even as I spoke I realized that Chiara would never address me by my Christian name in public—she scarcely did so in private.

Just as I thought that I had imagined it, or misheard, it came again. *Simonetta.* I turned around, scanning the crowd of people around me for a familiar face—someone I had met at the Medici *palazzo,* perhaps. Yet it was only then that I realized there *was* a crowd around me, and not the usual market crowd: men and women alike openly gawked at me, and I heard my name being whispered among them: *Simonetta. Simonetta Vespucci. La bella Simonetta.*

I placed a hand on Chiara's arm; fortunately, she had just completed her purchase. "Come, let us go," I said, a bit nervous now.

She glanced up and saw everyone gathered around us, and nodded quickly. We pushed our way through the crowd, which, thankfully, parted to let us pass.

In an unspoken agreement, Chiara and I made our way to the end of the aisle to leave the market. I tugged off my silk gloves, growing warm from our hurried walking.

We had nearly reached the edge of the piazza when I heard a scuffle break out behind us. Chiara turned before I did, and I heard her draw in her breath sharply. "Oh, for the love of all the saints," she huffed, a bit scornfully.

I turned to see two young men—richly dressed young men, at that—shouting at each other. I looked closer and saw that each was holding on for dear life to a bit of blue silk. In fact, it looked just like . . .

I looked down and saw that I held only one of my gloves in my hand. I must have dropped the other without noticing it.

"She meant for me to pick it up, I am sure of it!" the fair-haired young man declared.

The other man, who had flowing brown hair beneath his feathered cap, scoffed. "And why would *la bella* Simonetta give her favor to a dolt like you? You flatter yourself far too much, you—"

He broke off with a squawk as the other man reached out and knocked the cap clean off his head. "How dare you, you cur," the brown-haired man hissed, releasing my glove and taking a swing at his opponent.

I could not believe my eyes, especially not as they began to engage in fisticuffs in earnest over my dropped glove. Part of me wanted to walk away and not trouble myself further, but the rest of me was upset at the thought of any injury occurring on my behalf—even if these grown men *were* behaving like fools. Briskly, I headed for them. "Madonna!" Chiara called after me to no avail.

As they saw me draw nearer, they ceased their brawling and tried to straighten their clothing, now very much askew. "Madonna," the fair-haired man said. "You approach like a very goddess."

"Your beauty would make the Virgin herself jealous," the other man interjected, not to be outdone. I heard gasps from the crowd around us at the blasphemy.

I stretched out my hand and let my other glove fall to the ground at their feet. "There," I said. "Now you shall have no more need for violence." I turned my back on them and strode away. "Come, Chiara. Let us go."

Of course, by the next day the story was all over Florence, with each of the young men—I never did learn either of their names—claiming to be the hand-selected chevalier of *la bella* Simonetta. If Marco heard the tale—and I cannot imagine that he did not—he said nothing of it to me.

I wondered, fleetingly, if Sandro had heard the story, and what he made of it if he had.

20

I sat somberly beside Marco in the church pew, both of us dressed in our most understated clothing—dark, sober colors; of fine cloth but boasting no beading nor lace nor any other kind of adornment. The rather simple church of San Lorenzo rang with the sounds of muffled weeping, carrying over and above the priest's intoning of the Requiem Mass.

One of those weeping was Clarice, though she tried to hide it, tried to appear dignified as she must, now that she was the first lady of Florence—though part of me doubted that, even as a widow, Lucrezia dei Tornabuoni would simply step aside. She sat on Lorenzo's other side, still and controlled as a statue, though I would wager that there were tears on her face as well, if I could but see it.

The fall and early winter days had seen a further decline in the health of Lorenzo and Giuliano's father, Piero. He had not been truly healthy in many years, so I gathered—I had only met him myself the one time, as his health often had not permitted his attendance at social gatherings—yet in November it had become apparent that he had passed the point of no return. In December, as Christendom prepared for the coming of the Savior, he died.

The funeral was a small affair—even if everyone else treated them like royalty, the Medici must not be seen to think of themselves that way, not in republican Florence. The coffin had made its unobtrusive way through the streets to San Lorenzo, the Medici family church, for the funeral Mass and burial in the tomb that Lorenzo and Giuliano would be commissioning for their father.

Clarice had been most distraught upon her father-in-law's passing; she had been most fond of him, and he had always been kind to her. I had gone to visit her after we'd been told of the news, and I had held her hand tightly and let her cry and reminisce.

The only bright spot amid her grief—and Lorenzo's as well, I imagined—was the fact that she was expecting their first child, which would arrive in the summer. She had told me the news during that same visit when she had wept for her father-in-law.

"The Lord giveth, and the Lord taketh away, so Scripture says," she cried, full of both sorrow and happiness.

I tried not to scan the gathered mourners for Sandro, but I could not help myself. However, I did not see him.

Once the Mass ended, we rose from the pews and waited to give our condolences to the family members one more time. "It is very sad, to be sure," Marco whispered to me as we waited. "Piero was a kind soul, and always treated me well, from the time I was a boy. And he loved his family and his city like no other." He paused for a moment before lowering his voice further. "And yet even so, I cannot help but feel that Florence is in better hands with Lorenzo. He is a more capable leader than his father by far, and will bring the city fully into this new age."

"Hush," I said. "Do you want someone to overhear you? The poor man is not even buried yet."

"I mean no disrespect, Simonetta," Marco said. "I merely speak the truth, and you know it."

I did, yet it seemed wrong to admit it—or to speak of it at all—in this time and place. From the first time I had met Marco, he had spoken of the wondrous things that Lorenzo de' Medici would achieve in Florence and, by extension, in Italy as a whole. He had not mentioned Piero at all in those early days when he had told me of his home, and since coming here I could see why. Lorenzo had taken over much of the governmental work for his ailing father, and all the improvements in the city's culture, and in its relations with other city-states, were attributed to the charming and politically savvy Lorenzo, and rightfully so.

Yet now he was alone at the helm of the ship of state in Florence. I observed him, standing by one of the great columns that lined the nave and receiving the condolences and well wishes of what seemed to be everyone of note in Florence. Tears glittered in his eyes, yet he held his head high and had a kind and grateful word for everyone who approached him. Even now, even in his grief for the death of his beloved father, he was the consummate politician, and it was a mantle he would never be able to shed so long as he lived.

I was watching the dawn of a new age.

PART II

VENUS

Florence, September 1474–April 1475

21

I had flung open the window of the bedroom to let in the fresh September air. Now I could hear bits of song floating into my dressing room; a chorus of men singing.

"*La bella* Simonetta, come to the window, please! *La bella* Simonetta, let us see your fair face, please!"

Chiara, who was pinning up my hair, rolled her eyes at me in the mirror. "This is the third time this week."

I sighed. "I know. If ever I should meet the composer of that song—if indeed he can be called a composer—I think I shall slap him."

Chiara giggled. "Slap him twice, the second time on my behalf."

I laughed. "I certainly shall."

She slid the last pin into my hair. "There you are, Madonna," she said. "That should do. Now best go let your admirers catch a glimpse, so that we may have some peace and quiet around here."

I smiled. "Marco and I are leaving for the Medici *palazzo* soon," I teased. "It is nothing to me if there is peace and quiet here or not."

Chiara groaned. "For my sake then, Madonna, that I might have peace and quiet while you are gone."

"Very well, then." I rose and went to the window, peering down. The men below cheered at the sight of me. "Here I am!" I called to them. "Now, away with you!" I blew them a kiss and closed the window.

"Now they shall be happy until their dying day, and tell their grandchildren on their knee that once, *la bella* Simonetta blew them a kiss," Chiara said.

Now it was my turn to roll my eyes. "Honestly. It is all quite ridiculous. You would think none of these Florentine men had seen a woman before."

Chiara smiled. "There is no help for it now, Madonna. You've become a legend."

The sad truth was that she was right. I should have heeded the words of Lucrezia dei Tornabuoni and Clarice de' Medici more closely on that day—almost five years ago now—when they had told me that I was the reigning beauty of Florence.

Their words had been accurate in more ways than I could have foreseen. Ever since that day in the market when the two young swains had fought over my glove, my popularity had only increased. Women continued to copy my dresses—the style and cut and fabric and color, everything. And the young men of the city began passing by the Vespucci house, hoping to catch a glimpse of me. Passing by soon turned to congregating on the street outside, waiting for me to emerge. Gifts would appear on the doorstep for me: flowers; poetry; glass beads; and sometimes finer items such as gloves, small paintings, books, and silver hairpins.

Soon they began to serenade me, pledging to me their eternal love and fealty, begging to be my lover, my cavalier. It had all been amusing enough at the beginning, but soon such antics had begun to wear on the patience of everyone in the house.

We had escaped the noise this summer, as we had in years past, by spending a couple months at the Medici villa at Careggi with Clarice, Lucrezia, and Giuliano. Lorenzo would join us from the city when he could spare the time, and we had spent many a pleasant summer day and evening there in the last few years.

This year, however, we had had to come home early, as I had taken ill. I had spent most of the last month in bed with a cough, and a fever that came and went. Despite the assurances, after I'd fallen ill after my wedding, that I simply had yet to adjust to the warm, dry Florentine climate, I continued to take sick fairly regularly. The first few years, whenever I became unwell, Marco would repeat his offer to return with me to Genoa, where the air seemed more conducive to my health. Each time I refused him, and so he no longer offered.

Florence was my home now, and nothing could persuade me to leave it. Despite such occasional bouts of illness, I had felt myself blossom within Florentine society, amidst the books and conversation and artwork and beauty. My life had become exactly what I'd always hoped and dreamed it would be, and if now and then some notes of discontent would slip in, well, was not the same true of everybody?

So, now that I was recovered, we were joining Lorenzo and Clarice for dinner. It would be a small affair; just their usual circle of friends. I found myself wondering, as I did every time we went to their home, if Sandro would be there.

More often than not I was disappointed. He had become ever busier in the years since he'd painted my portrait. He received some commissions from Lorenzo himself, and many others from other prominent Florentine men and families. When he did appear at one of the Medici dinners, the two of us would always converse, but never for long, and never in private. Never again like those long afternoons in his studio, or when we would go out for walks along the Arno during a break. I missed the unexpected intimacy we had found.

I had never stopped yearning for those days, though my yearning had cooled over time, more for my own sanity than anything else. If he so missed my company, would he not seek me out more often? Invite me to sit for him again, perhaps? Would he not have come to call on me, as a friend would do? Perhaps it was not quite appropriate for him to do so; even in republican Florence, the difference in our stations was considerable. But would he not do it anyway, if he truly wished to see me?

But perhaps he no longer needed me, I thought now, staring glumly at my reflection in the mirror. There was a rumor going about that Maestro Botticelli had painted a small portrait of Lucrezia Donati Ardenghelli at the behest of Lorenzo de' Medici. It was said to be a most scandalous painting, one of the supposedly respectable matron as Eve—or, another tale said, as Salome, dancing naked before Herod—and one that il Magnifico kept in his private chambers and permitted no one else to set eyes upon. Where the rumors had come from if no one else had seen the painting I was not sure, and so most of the time I was able to dismiss it as yet another fabrication of Florentine society. Yet, whether it was true or not, I found it gave me another reason to quite dislike Donna Ardenghelli.

Perhaps our friendship had always meant more to me than to him. I was a fool for putting so much stock by it.

So while I always hoped to see Maestro Botticelli, I had long since stopped hoping for anything more.

Of course, he was there that evening.

Even as Lorenzo drew me into a conversation with some of his friends about another work of Plato's—one recently translated by Lorenzo's friend, Angelo Poliziano, and which I had read eagerly as soon as I could get my hands on it—I was constantly aware of where Sandro was in the room, of who he was speaking to. At times I fancied I could feel his eyes on me, but I always—though barely—resisted the temptation to turn and see if my suspicions were correct.

Almost as though he could sense my thoughts, Lorenzo soon waved Sandro over. "Sandro," he called, and the painter made his excuses to Donna Ardenghelli, with whom he had been speaking—the very sight caused jealousy to prickle my skin like a nasty rash—and came to join our circle. "You must tell our friends here about the newest commission you have accepted. I do not believe they have heard."

Sandro nodded briefly at those gathered around—did I imagine it, or did his eyes settle for just a moment too long on my hand where it was tucked into Marco's arm?—before answering. "Indeed, it is a very great honor, and a commission I was most pleased and grateful to accept," he said. "I am to paint a work for one of the chapels in Santa Maria Novella."

There was a chorus of congratulations. "And what is to be the subject of the painting?" Marco asked. He seemed relieved by the change of topic, as he had not read the book we had all been discussing previously.

"It is to depict the adoration of the Magi," Sandro replied. He inclined his head toward Lorenzo. "My most noble friend suggested it."

"That I did," Lorenzo said. "It is a favorite theme of mine, having grown up with the marvelous frescoes in our chapel here on the same theme."

"Indeed," Sandro said, a slight smile playing about his lips.

It occurred to me that the Three Kings were the only rich men in the Bible who entered into heaven, or were indeed spoken well of in the Good Book. No doubt that had more to do with the Medici family's preference of the theme than anything else. I bent my head slightly to hide the sudden smile that spread across my face, yet when I looked up again Sandro caught my eye and flashed me a quick smile in return, as though he knew my thoughts.

"You have become quite successful, Maestro Botticelli," said Tomaso Soderini, who had also bestowed a commission upon the painter not too long ago. "As we all knew you would. Why, no doubt you have a suitable income now to take a wife, and to settle down."

The smile I had been fighting back drained from my face.

"I suppose that I do, signore," Sandro said, his smile now looking a bit forced. "But I have no plans to take a wife anytime soon. My work is a jealous mistress, indeed."

"But do not the Good Lord and his apostles tell us that marriage is a most desirable state?" Signor Soderini pressed. "Would it not be helpful for your work to have a woman to keep house for you?"

"Since you press me, signore," Botticelli said, his smile widening as he spoke, "let me tell you what befell me one night. I dreamt that I did indeed have a wife, and my anguish and despair awoke me. I so feared dreaming such again that I spent the rest of the night roaming Florence like one possessed to stop myself from falling back into sleep!"

The group of men roared with laughter at this, even Signor Soderini. I laughed as well, more with relief than anything else. Just then Sandro's eyes caught and held mine, for a moment longer than was seemly, and there was naught but sincerity in them. I shivered.

"Ah, there is my boy!" Lorenzo proclaimed proudly, interrupting the laughter. He bent down to scoop up a small boy who had toddled over and was grasping at the hem of his father's tunic—Piero, who was two years old. Perhaps jealous of the attention being paid her younger brother, four-year-old Lucrezia followed, crying, "Papa!"

Lorenzo leaned down to ruffle her pale curls. "And my *principessina*," he said affectionately.

Clarice appeared at her husband's elbow. "They wished to say good night before they go to bed," she said. "Come, children. Time to say your prayers and go to sleep."

Lucrezia had left her father's side and come to mine, wrapping her arms around my waist in a childish hug. "Someday, Signora Simonetta," she said, looking up at me, her dark eyes serious, "I shall be a grown-up lady and wear beautiful dresses like you, and stay at parties all night!"

I laughed and leaned down to hug her, releasing Marco's arm.

"You certainly shall," I said. "And you shall be the most beautiful lady at any party."

Clarice had often brought Lucrezia to visit me in the four years since her birth, and as the girl had grown older, I had become something of a favorite with her. With a child yet to come for Marco and myself, I loved spending time with Lorenzo and Clarice's children, even though—especially lately—it only served to underscore all that I had not achieved.

"Come, Lucrezia," Clarice said again. "Until you are a grown lady, you must keep to your bedtime."

"Can Signora Simonetta tuck me in?" Lucrezia asked.

I laughed again. "I certainly can if you wish it."

I waited as Lucrezia bid her father good night, then I let her lead me to the nursery. Clarice tossed me a grateful look over her shoulder.

Clarice settled young Piero into his little bed as the children's nursemaid helped Lucrezia change into a clean shift. The youngest Medici child, one-year-old Maria Maddalena, was already in bed and clapped with pleasure at seeing her siblings.

"Now, come, Madonna Lucrezia," I said as the little girl climbed into her bed. She giggled at being addressed like a grown-up lady, even as she allowed me to draw the covers over her. "To sleep, and you shall have dreams about attending parties wearing beautiful gowns."

"I will?" she asked.

"I am certain of it."

Within seconds, it seemed, she had nodded off to sleep, and I rose and tiptoed from the nursery. Clarice had been watching from the door.

"Thank you," she said. "You are so wonderful with her."

"She is a joy, truly," I said. "If only I . . ." I trailed off, unable to meet my friend's eyes.

"Surely there is still hope," Clarice said. "Why, you are only, what, twenty-one?"

I lowered my voice, though there was no one around to overhear. "In truth, I am beginning to lose hope," I said. "Five years I have been married, and no sign of conception."

"Perhaps the fault lies with him," she suggested. "Some sin on his soul, perhaps."

I shook my head. "I do not know if God works that way, despite what the priests say," I said. "And you know as well as I do that the fault always lies with the woman. Even if it does not."

Clarice pursed her lips; she had never abandoned her conservative Roman upbringing in favor of her husband's liberal view of the world, though Lorenzo, too, was pious enough. "Well, whatever the case," she said at last, deciding not to argue the point, "never lose hope, Simonetta. God may bless you in time."

"I hope you are right," I said, casting one last look back at the nursery door as we returned to the party. Then there was the thing I could never bring myself to confess to Clarice, with her nursery full of children and her husband keeping a mistress: I had begun to feel that Marco was upset with me for not providing him with children, with a son and heir. He had never said such to me, of course; but despite my words to my friend, he had come to my bed less frequently of late, and what other reason could there be but his dissatisfaction with me? Of course, I had been ill recently, but that excuse rang hollow within my heart. The night before had been the first time we had made love since my illness, and even as he moved within me he felt somehow removed, distant, as though he performed the act more for duty than for pleasure.

Yet Clarice, too, had known sorrow in childbearing. There had been a set of twins born the year after Lucrezia who had died mere hours after their birth, and just a few weeks past she had given birth to a daughter who had survived only days. This party was her first public appearance since her lying-in, and though I could still see traces of the sadness in her eyes, both her faith and her practical manner allowed her to go on.

Perhaps she was right. I could not give up hope just yet.

I pushed aside such melancholy thoughts as best I could. I was at a party given by my dearest friends, and whatever problems existed in my marriage—real or imagined—could be dealt with another time.

22

I had just found myself a fresh glass of wine and was going to join Clarice and some other women friends of hers when I heard an unmistakable voice behind me. "Madonna Simonetta."

I turned to see Sandro sweeping me a bow. "Maestro Botticelli," I said, forcing his Christian name back from the tip of my tongue, as I always did. As I still did, even after all this time. "I did not get a chance to properly greet you earlier. You are looking well."

"And you are looking as beautiful as ever," he said, "though you do not need me to tell you that. Yet I do think you are more beautiful now than when I painted your portrait."

In spite of myself, I enjoyed the compliment, which would always mean more coming from him than from anyone else. "I am like a fine wine, perhaps," I said. "I improve with age."

"I would say so."

When the conversation seemed to end there, I felt my annoyance grow. *Why seek me out at all, if you merely wish to exchange trivial pleasantries and nothing more?* I wanted to ask him, but of course I did not. "Well, if you will excuse me."

"No," he said quickly. "That is, I had hoped to have a word. Alone."

His last word made my pulse spike even as he continued. "As alone as we can be in this crowded room, at least."

"Perhaps we stand a better chance of not being overheard in a crowded room," I said. "Although I wonder what you can possibly have to say that warrants so much secrecy."

He drew me into a corner. "It is a delicate matter."

"Indeed?" I asked. My heart was hammering foolishly at his nearness. "Then perhaps it is an inappropriate subject to discuss with a lady."

He gave me a frustrated look. "Please, Simonetta, I pray you. Do not play the high society lady with me now."

I should have reprimanded him for speaking to me so familiarly in public, but I did not—whether because he finally used only my given name, or because I had longed to hear him speak familiarly to me for so long, I could not say. "Very well," I said at last. "What is this delicate matter, then?"

"I wish you to pose for me."

"Ah," I said. "Since I have done so once before, I cannot quite comprehend why it should be such a private matter now. And I see that you only seek me out when you want something from me."

"You have not let me explain," he said. "And that is not true, Simonetta. We converse every time we see each other. If we could do so more, no one would be happier than I."

"Then, why—" But I stopped abruptly, knowing I could not go on. He was right; we conversed and interacted exactly as much as was proper for two people of our different stations. If it was some further intimacy I wanted—like when he had painted my portrait—well then, I had no right to long for any such thing. And therefore I could hardly take its lack out on him.

When I remained silent, he went on. "It is a very different sort of painting that I have in mind this time," he said. "That is why it is delicate."

"What is it?" I asked, almost breathless with anticipation.

He lowered his voice. "A depiction of Venus, being born from the sea," he said. "I can envision it all, the whole thing in its entirety. And the only woman I can picture as Venus is you."

For a moment I was quite speechless at these words. Unbidden, I remembered what he had said to me one night as he worked on my portrait: *You are the muse, Simonetta. There is no other.*

Had his words meant more than I had dared to dream?

"I see," I said, struggling to regain my composure. "And is it delicate because the Church would, no doubt, not approve of such a work if they were to learn of it?"

He waved this aside. "Perhaps they would not, but that is not the point. No, I . . . you see, in my vision, Venus is being born anew from the waves, greeting the world for the first time. She must be . . ." He paused, glancing at me. "Nude."

Again I fought to speak, but for very different reasons. "And so," I managed finally, "you ask me to pose for you without a shred of clothing on, in your studio, before your assistants and apprentices—"

"No, no," he interrupted. "I would not ask you to . . . no. There would be no one there but me."

"That may be even worse," I said. "In my husband's eyes, anyway. Surely you cannot think Marco would approve?"

"Perhaps not," he said. "But it is not Marco I am asking."

I laughed, and the sound was brassy with bitterness. "You spoke similarly to me once before, if I recall. Perhaps it is that you do not know how the world works for women, Maestro Botticelli."

"Please, Simonetta," he said. "At least think about it. I know it is a strange thing I am asking, and entirely improper, but—I cannot rid myself of this vision with you at its center."

"I . . . I can think about it if you wish, but—"

He interrupted me again. "This painting—this work—if it ends up as I envision it, it may be something great. Something new. Something the world has never seen before." He paused. "And I cannot do it without your help."

"Surely there are other women . . . artists' models who . . ."

"No," he said. "It can only be you."

I was silent, hypnotized by the intensity in his eyes. I felt that if I did not look away, I would agree to anything he asked me, absolutely anything. The doubts I had felt and wrestled with over the past few years since I had posed for him began to melt away. Is it possible that we have both been waiting and yearning and dreaming and hoping for the same thing all this time? For the restoration of that connection we once had? "I will consider it," I said softly, looking down.

A hesitant yet relieved smile broke out on his face. "*Grazie mille,* Simonetta," he said. "Take as much time as you need to think, to accustom yourself to the idea. We can go about it in whatever way makes you the most comfortable."

"I can make you no promises, maestro."

"I understand," he said. He took my hand and kissed it. "And, Simonetta," he added, "though we have not been often in each other's company, do not doubt that not a day goes by when I do not think of you."

And with that extraordinary pronouncement, he walked away.

That night, I lay awake in bed after Marco and I had made love—a short affair, due to the wine he had consumed that night. I had given up trying to take any pleasure in his short, jerky thrusts and simply waited for him to finish. Even the thought that perhaps tonight we might conceive a child brought me no joy, nor any true hope.

No, I could not sleep because my mind was still turning over Sandro's words, his offer, his plea.

What was I to do? It would be completely improper for me to go along with his request. Paintings of the female nude were not unheard of, but I did not think high-born ladies posed for them. And Marco would never allow it. He had never quite lost his animosity toward Maestro Botticelli, as though he could sense the intimacy that had existed between the painter and me, once.

Therefore, if I was to do this, I would need to do it without my husband's knowledge or consent. I would need to keep it a secret. Could I do that? What sort of wife kept such a secret from her husband? And would that not be much more trouble than it was worth? What if he found out? I decided that I did not care to imagine that. Marco had never been cruel to me, in deed or in word, but this—this would be a transgression of the sort I had never before even contemplated. He would be furious, and rightfully so.

He would be furious to know that Maestro Botticelli had even asked such a thing of me.

The guilt I used to feel at my enjoyment of my sessions with Sandro came flooding back, having laid untouched and unconsidered for many years now. Even then, the painter and I had always seemed on the verge of something inappropriate, something that felt unfair to Marco. How could I now contemplate such a venture, and the lying that it would involve?

Yet I tried, for just a moment, to leave Marco and his feelings aside. What did I want?

I wanted to do it. I wanted to pose—nude or otherwise—for this great, thrilling work that Sandro envisioned, that he saw when he closed his eyes. I wanted to be a part of it. I wanted to help him bring it to life. And if a part of that had to do with reclaiming the same fellowship we had had the first time he'd painted me, well then, so be it. I could admit that much to myself, at least. That I missed him and wanted to spend more time in his company than was proper.

But like this? Could I do it, what he was asking? Could I remove all of my clothing before him, let his eyes take in all of me, every last inch of my body? Could I let him see what only my husband had ever seen, or had any right to see?

Heat seeped through my body. I not only could, but I wanted to.

I tossed and turned much of the night; Marco, in his alcohol-induced slumber, did not stir. At some point I fell into a troubled sleep and dreamed strange dreams, of which I could only remember fragments: canvases coming to life and colors whirling before my eyes and Sandro beckoning and myself running. Yet I could not tell if I was running away from something, or toward it.

23

The following day dragged by as I rattled about the house, alone. I wished Marco were there, that I might have some distraction from my thoughts and my endless, cyclical wonderings and questions and justifications and fears. But he was at the Medici bank with Lorenzo, as he was nearly every day. Whether they actually engaged in any banking business there or whether it was all politics and plotting I could not say. Even when I asked, Marco insisted he did not want to "bore" me with his work. Eventually I had stopped asking.

I read a little, and consulted with the family cook about the evening's meal: fish and fresh greens, along with the tasteless Tuscan bread to which I had never managed to grow accustomed. I was looking forward to dining with Marco, having in a sense been apart from him for much of my illness.

Yet as the dinner hour neared, still there was no sign of Marco. The cook came into the sitting room where I waited, glancing up from my book to peek out the window every so often. "Beg pardon, Madonna," she said, "but should I proceed with the meal? Even though the master is not yet home?"

"Yes," I said, after only a moment of hesitation. "And have the table laid when everything is ready, as usual. No doubt he will be here soon."

But time dragged by, the table was laid, the sun began to set, and still Marco did not appear.

"Everything is ready, Madonna, as it please you," the kitchen maid said, tiptoeing into the sitting room.

I sighed and rose. "Very well. I still must eat, so I will do so."

Yet despite my outward calm, I was worried. Marco had never not come home before. And without so much as a word! If he had been detained, no doubt he would have sent a messenger.

I ate alone in the dining room, trying to ignore the worry gnawing at my insides. Surely it was nothing. No doubt he had simply lost track of the time.

Yet as the night wore on, as I finished eating what little I could and the remnants of the meal had been cleared away, as I went upstairs and began to ready myself for bed, still there was no sign of Marco.

Perhaps I should send word to Lorenzo and Clarice, and ask if either of them has seen him, I thought as Chiara unpinned my hair. Perhaps Marco had an engagement this evening that he forgot to mention to me, and if so, Lorenzo may know.

I did not send a message, though. I did not wish to seem an anxious, overly worried wife. Surely there was some explanation.

At least, there had better be, I thought, feeling a bit of anger begin to creep in alongside the worry. God help him if this was merely some nonsense, some silly party or some such that he forgot to tell me about, when I'd been beside myself all evening. And all that food that went to waste as well; if he wasn't going to be home, the least he could have done was told me so. I might have invited Clarice and the children for dinner, perhaps, and had some company and someone to eat the meal I had prepared.

Even so, I must have fallen asleep—no doubt exhausted from

poor sleep the previous night—for the next thing I remember is being awoken by shouts from the street below.

I jerked upright in bed. Surely it was not some silly Florentine swains, come to pay me court at this hour of night, and wake the whole house in the process. Yet as I groped about on the bed next to me in the darkness, I found that Marco was not beside me. Still he had not come home.

Leaping from bed, I pulled on a dressing gown and went downstairs, where I could now hear a pounding on the door. Dear God, it must be to do with Marco. My heart wedged in my throat. Perhaps something has happened . . . should I wake his parents? But I could not stand not knowing any longer, so I went right to the door and opened it.

Before me stood my husband and Giuliano de' Medici—though perhaps "stood" was too generous a word. Giuliano had his arm looped around Marco's waist to help him stand, and Marco had an arm draped around his companion's shoulders—though Giuliano was none too steady on his feet himself. He was swaying, eyes half closed, a sloppy, drunken grin on his face.

His eyes flickered twice and opened wider as he saw me standing before him. "Simonetta," he said. He drove his shoulder into Marco. "Wake up, Vespucci. Is—your wife," he slurred.

Marco's eyes fluttered open. "Simonetta?" he asked, his voice thick with drink. "Can you—open the door?"

"I've opened it," I said. "How do you think I came to be standing here?"

Rather than make them realize their folly, my words instead sent both men into a fit of laughter.

"Come inside," I hissed, reaching out and grabbing Giuliano's arm to pull him into the house. "You fools will wake the whole neighborhood." He stumbled over the threshold, pulling my husband behind him. "You, Marco, might have a care to not wake your parents."

Marco shrugged, and the simple gesture nearly sent him toppling over.

"Madonna? I heard voices—" I turned to see Chiara behind me, rubbing sleep from her eyes even as she took in the scene.

"Run and fetch my husband's manservant," I bade her, "and make up one of the extra bedrooms. I don't suppose the gallant Giuliano will be able to make his own way home tonight."

Silently, Chiara left to do as I bade her.

"Honestly, Marco," I said, knowing he was in no condition to pay heed to my words, but unable to stop myself. "I have been beside myself all evening, worrying because you had not come home. And all this time you've been out carousing with him?" I gestured angrily at Giuliano. "You both should know better!"

"God's thumbs, Marco," Giuliano slurred, "but she is beautiful, Simonetta, isn't she? If she wasn't your wife, I'd take her right here in this hallway—"

I reached out and slapped him, causing him to stumble back a step, though otherwise he seemed to scarcely notice. Unfortunately, though, it did not stop his tongue.

"Tell me, *amico,*" Giuliano went on, draping an arm around Marco's shoulders where he leaned against the wall, "is your wife as heavenly a fuck as she looks? Is she as good as—What's her name, your favorite whore, that Frenchwoman—"

Yet what the Frenchwoman's name was, I could not hear over the roaring in my ears, the echo—over and over again—of Giuliano's words. *Your favorite whore. Your favorite whore. Favorite. Whore.*

Whore.

I turned away from the two men and almost bumped right into Chiara and Giovanni, Marco's manservant. "Get them out of here and into bed," I managed. "I have had my fill of this nonsense." I started to walk away, but stopped and turned back. "And see that wherever my husband sleeps tonight, it is not in my bed."

"But, Madonna," Chiara protested, "I only readied one of the extra rooms."

"Then ready another," I snapped, "or else put them both in the same bed, if you will. It is no matter to me."

With that I climbed the stairs and returned to my bedchamber, where I barred the door and prepared for another sleepless night.

Shortly after dawn I awoke—after what little sleep I had managed to get—with a ghastly headache and with dry, red-rimmed eyes, as though I had been the one who had overindulged in drink. My whole night had been laced with repeats of Giuliano's words, the words uttered carelessly, thoughtlessly, in a drunken stupor but that nevertheless had the power to upend my entire life. *Your favorite whore, that Frenchwoman . . .*

I had assumed—like a fool, apparently—that Marco was a faithful husband to me. After all, why should he not be? Why should I have had any reason to think otherwise? He professed his love for me, often; we made love regularly and certainly with gusto; I ran a proper, efficient home and played hostess whenever he needed me to; I had become accepted among his circle. What could he possibly find lacking in me as a wife? What could be missing? What more did I need to do?

And was I not hailed as the most beautiful woman in Florence? No one in this house knew a day's peace because of the men calling to me from the street outside, singing to me, begging me for a glimpse or a token. Could this Frenchwoman—this whore—be more beautiful than me? I thought not, for I had not heard of crowds clogging the streets outside *her* door, whoever she was, to pay her homage.

What more could Marco want in a woman than what he already had?

And thus I came to the crux of it: what was the use of being the most beautiful woman in Florence if I could not keep my own husband faithful to me?

I began to cry.

At some point, I decided I had best rise and dress and eat something. I would need to face my husband sooner or later—we did live in the same house, after all.

I unbarred the door to my bedchamber and called for Chiara. She came in and dressed me and pinned up my hair, all as if it were a normal day. She did not speak, though; she only cast worried glances at me in the mirror until I felt as if I might scream at her. Yet none of this was her fault, and so I bit my tongue and did not allow myself to take my frustrations out on her.

Why, she was my most loyal friend in the house. Perhaps my only friend.

I went down to the dining room and saw that the kitchen maid had already laid out some bread and cheese and cold meats for me to break my fast. Judging by the amount of food, it seemed the kitchen staff had been told we had a guest as well.

I sank down into a chair and closed my eyes for a moment. I was angry at Giuliano, as well—for speaking of me in such a crude, disrespectful manner, and for letting slip something I would rather not have known.

Yet maybe I ought to be thanking him: for showing me the truth, that I might see my husband clearly, and without any naïveté coloring my gaze. Apparently I had been very naïve where Marco was concerned. But no more.

And yet there was nothing I could do. We were married in the sight of God, and if a husband's infidelity was cause for an annulment, then there were surely no valid marriages anywhere in the world.

Perhaps blissful ignorance would have been better, after all.

I sighed, opened my eyes, and took some food for my plate, eating in silence.

It was not long before I heard footsteps at the doorway, and the clearing of a throat. I looked up to see Giuliano de' Medici standing before me—still in his rumpled doublet and hose from the night before—wearing a very sheepish expression on his tired, haggard face.

"Signora Vespucci," he said, inclining his head to me.

I did not rise. "Signor Medici."

I let the moment stretch out, just long enough for it to begin to be uncomfortable, before inviting him to sit. "Please, do be seated," I said, "and help yourself. This food is nothing extravagant, but it will serve to break your fast."

He came and took a seat, leaving one chair between him and me. He pulled a plate toward himself and began filling it with food. His nighttime debauchery, it seemed, had left him with quite an appetite. "I must thank you for your kind hospitality last night, and this morning as well," he said. "You are a saint among women, truly."

"Well," I said, "you were hardly in any condition to get home." I knew I was not being gracious, yet I could not help myself.

As if reading my thoughts, he spoke. "I wish to apologize to you, Simonetta. Most profusely. Our behavior—my behavior—was most inappropriate last night, and I realize that I said some things that were most offensive to you."

"You did, yes," I said. "I would have thought Lucrezia dei Tornabuoni raised her son better than to speak so about the wife of a friend."

He flushed. "Yes. She would have thought so, too, and she would be deeply ashamed by my conduct last night. As am I. It was not worthy of me and my name, nor of you and yours. And so I must beg your forgiveness most humbly. It is no excuse, of course, but drink—well, you know what it can do to a man. That was not me, not truly."

I felt myself relent somewhat under his pleading gaze, his

handsome face. "You are forgiven," I said, "though I pray we do not have a repeat incident."

He looked visibly relieved. "I can assure you that we will not," he said.

"Very well, then," I said. "Now please, eat. I would be a poor hostess, indeed, if I sent you away hungry."

He gave me his usual charming, winning smile and began to eat.

Giuliano was easy enough to forgive. My husband was another matter entirely.

He appeared in the doorway not long after, dressed in clean, simple clothes, and looking much worse for the wear. Someone who had not seen the two men the night before would have had no trouble discerning that Marco had been the deepest in his cups of them both.

"Simonetta," he said, not quite meeting my eye. "Giuliano. I trust you slept well?"

"Very well indeed, thanks to your wife's generous hospitality," Giuliano said.

"And how did you sleep, Marco?" I asked, my voice sweet but barely concealing the barb within. "Very well, no doubt, thanks to the alcohol. Much better than your wife, I'm sure."

There was an awkward silence—or at least I presume it was awkward for Marco. I continued with my meal as though he wasn't there at all.

After a moment, he came and took the empty chair between Giuliano and myself. He took a bit of bread, but nothing else.

"Is the meal not to your liking, husband?" I asked. "Shall I have the cook prepare something else for you?"

Marco grimaced and shook his head. "No, thank you. I find I am not so hungry."

"Indeed," I said, unable to stop myself from smirking.

As soon as Giuliano had finished wolfing down his food, he rose. "Thank you again, Signora Vespucci, for opening your home to me, and for the meal." He kissed my hand. "I trust I shall see you again soon, under . . . more pleasant circumstances."

I smiled. "Indeed. It is all in the past, good signore."

With that, he bowed and took his leave, no doubt anxious to be clear of the storm brewing between my husband and myself. Yet I would be damned if I would speak first.

It was a few moments before Marco spoke. Clearing his throat, he said, "Simonetta . . ."

"Yes?" I asked expectantly. "Do you have something to say to me, husband? I rather think you do. Or you should." I laughed. "Yes, I can think of a whole host of things you should be saying to me right now."

"Well . . . yes." He looked away. "I am sorry."

"Sorry for what, exactly, Marco?"

"Sorry that we came home in such a state, that we behaved so. That we disturbed your sleep."

"Indeed?" I asked. "And what of the French whore you were with before returning home? Are you sorry for her as well?"

Marco's face reddened. "I am sorry you had to hear that. Giuliano was drunk—obviously, we both were—and he did not realize what he was saying, nor in front of whom."

"Oh, so *that* is what you are sorry for?" I said, my voice becoming louder, harder. "That I had to hear something so indelicate? That I found out you are an adulterer?" I barked out a laugh. "Yes, no doubt you are sorry that I know that now."

"Simonetta," he said. He reached for my hand where it lay on the table, but I angrily pulled it back. "I did not mean to hurt you. This is nothing to do with you."

"Oh, is it not?" I asked.

"You do not understand," he said, his voice low.

"You are right, I do not," I said. "I do not understand at all. Am I not enough for you? Do I not please you enough? Apparently I do not."

"That is not it at all, Simonetta," Marco said. "I swear to you."

"What is it, then?" I demanded.

"What do you expect me to say?" he burst out. "It began when you were ill. Giuliano would come to get me out of the house, and he took me to a house owned by a woman he knows. I met a courtesan there, and I took my pleasure as I saw fit. What was I to do? You were ill. A man has needs, Simonetta."

"Oh, indeed," I said scornfully. "Are men no better than animals, then? That when your wife, whom you profess to love, is ill at home you must go out and fuck the first harlot who—"

"How dare you speak to me so!" Marco said, pounding his fist on the table. "I will not tolerate it!"

"And I am expected to tolerate you going out to visit your whore, and expected to welcome you back into my bed when you return?"

"Yes!" he all but shouted. "Because you are my wife and that is the way of the world. I am a man and the master of this household and I shall do as I see fit."

Silence fell over the room. I was certain the servants were listening just beyond the doors, but I could not bring myself to care. I pushed my chair away from the table and rose, determined not to let Marco see that I was trembling—with fury, with despair, with sadness, with jealousy.

"As you wish," I said. "You are an interesting man, Marco Vespucci. The most beautiful woman in Florence is not enough for you. What am I to make of that?"

I turned and stormed from the room before he could reply. In my haste to leave, I almost knocked over Marco's mother in the hallway just outside. "Simonetta!" she cried, startled. "I heard yelling—whatever is the matter?"

"Ask your son," I said curtly, stalking past her.

24

Because I could not think where else to go, I barricaded myself in my chambers again. Let Marco leave the house again, or stay, for all I cared. It would be some time before he would find himself back in my bedroom again, let alone in my bed.

The horrible part was I knew that he was right. This was the way of the world. Men went out and took their pleasure where they found it, and we wives were expected to look the other way, to never notice nor speak of it, and remain at their beck and call as though nothing had happened. As though nothing had changed.

I remembered, with a sickening twist of guilt, the way I had pitied Clarice that night when her husband had invited his mistress to dinner. The way I felt sorry for her, angry on her behalf yet confident in the knowledge that what was happening to her would never happen to me. She had called me a fool that day, and she had been right.

What, then, is beauty good for, if it cannot protect me from feeling like this? I wondered. What good is being desired by every man who sets eyes on me when even my own husband cannot remain faithful?

What does this cursed beauty mean? What has it brought me in my life other than despair?

Suddenly I remembered what had haunted my thoughts all the day before, in that other life when I was a different woman from the one I was now.

Maestro Botticelli wanted me to help him. He had had a vision, he said, of a great work of art, with me at its center.

This, then, was my answer. This was what beauty was good for. To create a masterpiece.

A slow smile slid across my lips. I would do it. I would pose for him, naked as the day I was born. If Marco felt no guilt for fornicating with a whore, then why should I feel any guilt for a far lesser infraction?

I would not even give him the chance to object. I would simply do it; I would not hide my actions from him nor volunteer any information. He might never know. And if he did, well, was that not the way of the world? That beautiful women should inspire great artists?

I found a bit of parchment in my dressing room and penned a simple note: *I will do it. Just tell me when we begin.* I signed it simply *Simonetta,* and bade Chiara take it to Maestro Botticelli's workshop. She cast me a quizzical look, but she did as she was told.

To my surprise and pleasure, Chiara returned almost immediately, bearing a sealed reply. I took it and thanked her; she nodded and left without a word.

I eagerly opened the letter and found that it was just as brief as my own message had been: Grazie mille, *Simonetta. I am eternally in your debt. Come tomorrow afternoon, and we shall begin.*

It was signed just as I had signed mine, with simply his Christian name: *Sandro.*

I clutched the parchment to my chest, feeling a wide smile stretch across my face and a curious, wild joy bubble up within me. I sensed that when I stepped into his workshop the next day, I would be passing a point from which there could be no return. And yet I did not care. More than that: I would welcome it.

Marco wisely slept in one of the extra bedrooms again that night, and I did not even see him the next morning. Just as well. I had nothing to say to him at the moment. I knew that soon I would need to find a way to put this behind me, a way to move forward with our marriage, a way to continue to be a wife to him in every sense of the word. But I could not and would not do it yet.

At just before one o'clock, I set out for Maestro Botticelli's workshop. I casually told Chiara where I was going, though no doubt she knew. She seemed prepared to keep my venture a secret without being told to do so, yet I did not care. Let her tell Marco. Let there be no secrets in our marriage.

As I approached, though, I found myself feeling a nervousness I thought I'd banished. In my defiance and rebellion and determination to do what I wanted to do, I had let the details of this venture become hazy in my mind. In a manner of moments, I would be removing all of my clothes in front of a man who was not my husband. A man who was a friend—but still. It was contrary to everything I had been taught, to how I had been raised. To the strictures of the Church and of society.

Yet I wanted to do it anyway, and that was what frightened me most. I wanted to, even though and perhaps because it scared me, and now I must learn if I could go through with it.

I hesitated as I reached the door, and I knocked, though I knew Maestro Botticelli was expecting me. In those moments after knocking I became vividly aware that, if I so chose, I could leave now. This would be my last chance.

I remained where I was until he opened the door.

His eyes widened upon seeing me, as though he was surprised, as though he hadn't been expecting me. "Simonetta," he breathed, and my name was a greeting and a prayer and an invocation.

"Maestro Botticelli," I said, stepping inside. Yet even as I spoke I realized that if I was to go through with this, there could be no more formalities between us. "Sandro," I amended.

The workshop was even more littered with canvases and sketches and brushes than it had been when I was here before—no doubt a sign of the maestro's popularity. He had lit a fire in the grate, perhaps unnecessary for what was a warm autumn day, yet I could see that he would need the light: lengths of cloth had been pinned over the windows so that no passersby would be able to see in. This, no doubt, was to preserve my modesty. And the room was empty of any other living soul. It was, I realized, the first time he and I had been truly alone together.

I turned back to face him, and he must have read the question in my eyes. "I dismissed my assistants for the rest of the day," he said, locking the door behind me. "As promised. I am asking enough of you as is; there is no call to have you disrobe before other men as well."

"I thank you for that," I said. I wondered if my nervousness could be heard in my voice.

"Simonetta," he said softly, stepping close to me and placing his hands on my shoulders. "You are certain, *sì*? You do not have to do this. If you have changed your mind . . ."

Drawing in a deep breath, I met his eyes and shook my head. "I have not changed my mind. I want to do it."

He smiled, relieved. "Very well. I cannot thank you enough, Simonetta. Truly."

He led me over to the center of the room, where an overturned wooden box, covered with a length of cloth, had been placed. The worktables and benches had, I saw, been shoved back to make space. "This is where I will have you stand, if that is agreeable," he said, gesturing to the box. "The light will be right, and I will have you in the center of my vision. Let me know if you get cold, and I can build up the fire."

So the fire served a dual purpose. I was surprised by his thoughtfulness, though I knew I should not be.

I knew, of course, that Sandro lived above his studio, yet at just that moment I found myself very conscious that his bed was only just upstairs. I was about to undress, and so very close to his own intimate space.

He studied me again for a moment. "We shall wait until you are ready," he said. "There is no need to rush. We shall not be disturbed all afternoon; I have seen to it."

I took one more deep, shuddering breath, and bent down to remove my shoes. "No," I said. "We can begin now. I am ready."

"Very well," Sandro said, situating a chair a few paces away from my pedestal—or so I had begun to think of it—fetching his sketchbook from one of the tables.

I kicked my shoes beneath a nearby chair and removed my cloak, draping it over the back of the same chair. I had taken care to keep myself shrouded in my cloak on my way here, despite the warmth of the day; I had purposely worn only a simple gown and shift that I would be able to remove myself; not anything I could be seen wearing in public. There was no lady's maid to help me, and I would not ask Sandro to help me undress.

"Wait," Sandro said, standing beside his chair. "If you could—would you unbind your hair?"

My throat was dry as I tried to respond. "You mean . . . leave it loose?"

"Yes," he said. "If you do not mind."

My hands reached up and fumbled for the pins. "Whatever you wish, maestro." I found the courage to flash him a smile, and his answering smile warmed me and gave me the courage to proceed.

Once released from its pins, my wavy, yellow-gold hair tumbled down my back, ending just below my knees. I shook my head once, letting the front strands fall over my shoulders and frame my face.

"*Perfetto,*" he murmured. His face flushed slightly as he nodded at my dress. "Do you need . . . that is, should I . . . ?"

"No," I cut him off. "No. I shall do it myself."

Slowly, looking away from him, I reached back and unlaced my dress, draping it over the back of the same chair as my cloak. I slid my shift down my shoulders and pushed it down to my feet. I stepped out of it and dropped it next to my other things before stepping up onto the overturned box. The air of the room felt chilled against my flushed, bare skin, and I closed my eyes for a moment. Yet I knew I could not continue to look away. I must do this with my whole heart. Boldly, I looked up and let my eyes find his.

His mouth was open partway as he beheld me and, in that moment—just for that moment—he was naught but a man looking on a woman: his eyes took in my shoulders; my round, firm breasts; my waist and belly and hips; the thatch of pale hair between my legs; my thighs and knees and calves. Every inch of me.

"Simonetta," he breathed, and the reverence I heard in his voice made me flush deeper.

I lifted my chin haughtily, about to ask him whether he meant to gape at me or to sketch, and in that instant he became wholly the artist again. "*Si, si,*" he said excitedly, though his voice was low. "Just so. Hold that position." With that, he bent his head over his paper and began to sketch.

This, now, was familiar to me: holding a pose, sinking into time and letting it envelop me so that he may capture me and, in so doing, capture time itself. Never again would I be just as I was at this moment, yet it would be one that would be preserved through the alchemy of Sandro's hand and eye and pencil.

But it was foreign as well. I had expected it would be so, even as I hoped that soon it would come to feel the same, and I would forget entirely that I was naked.

Yet I could not. I was aware of every inch of my bare self, on display for Sandro to see and study; could feel each breath—his and mine—as it stirred the air around me, causing the strands of my hair to move ever so slightly, whispering against my skin. And I could feel his eyes on me like a physical touch, could feel every place that they studied as though they were hot coals brushing against my skin. His gaze was a caress, one of heat and light and warmth on a body which was always hidden away from the world; and far from feeling exposed, as I had been anticipating, I felt free and strong and uninhibited. I leaned into his gaze as one would lean into a lover's embrace.

Every so often he would look up and meet my eyes, and neither of us would look away for a long moment. Then he would return to his sketching, his eyes continuing their beautiful dance over my body.

My heartbeat and breath began to quicken. Despite my initial chill as I had disrobed, the room now felt quite warm, almost too much so. Yet I did not speak, did not move, could not have if I wanted to. I did not want to break this spell, did not want this delicious enchantment to end. Did not want to go back to hiding myself from him, now that he had seen all of me, body and soul.

I could not have said how long it was before Sandro rose from his chair. "We should stop here for today, perhaps," he said gently.

I blinked twice, like one awakening from a deep sleep. "Very well," I said, wondering if he could hear the reluctance in my voice, and what he made of it if he did.

"Do you need any help dressing?"

In my imagination, I said that yes, I did, and just the thought of his hands on my body was almost too much to bear. Could that simple act be wrong after the intimacy of what had just occurred? "No," I said aloud, resisting the temptation. "I . . . I believe I can manage on my own."

"As you wish," he said. He stepped closer, picked up my shift off of the chair, and handed it to me. I shivered as his fingers brushed mine.

I stepped into my shift quickly, suddenly as eager to cover myself as I had been reluctant to do so a moment ago. I pulled on my dress as well, then donned my shoes, and when I was finished I looked up to find Sandro studying me as though he had never stopped.

The air between us felt heavy, laden with so very many words that we could not say, that we wanted to say but knew we must not.

It was he who looked away first, clearing his throat and running a hand through his tousled blond hair. "And are you . . . would you be able to return the day after tomorrow?"

"Yes," I said.

"Very good. I . . ." he faced me again. "I cannot say how long this will take, Simonetta. To fully execute the vision that I have. It may take some time, and with these other commissions—"

"It is of no matter," I said, cutting him off. "I shall be here as long as you need me."

"I think that I shall always need you," he said softly.

I swayed slightly where I was standing, wanting to step into his arms, to fall against him.

He walked me to the door, took my hand, and kissed it soundlessly. His lips were like a brand against my skin, as though he was marking me for his own.

25

That evening Marco sent word that he was to dine with Lorenzo and some other dignitaries in the government. I know he had been hoping to be appointed to a government post, and so naturally he would seize this opportunity. It was just as well: I still had no interest in speaking to him. I do not know what time he returned, as I had already gone to bed. He was just leaving the following morning when I went downstairs to break my fast.

"I hope that we may dine together this evening," he said, kissing my cheek.

"As you wish," I said indifferently.

I made sure that dinner was ready when he arrived home, and sat through an hour of him telling me of his engagement the night before, though I plainly did not care. Later that night he returned to our bedchamber, though he did not attempt to exert his husbandly privilege, for which I was glad.

The next afternoon I returned to Sandro's workshop again. It went much the same as the first time. I undressed and took my position, and we spoke little, save for when he had me turn to one side, then to the other, then put my back to him, so that he might sketch me from all different angles.

Even when I could not see him, I still felt his eyes on me, caressing and brushing against my flesh. My skin hummed. When I left that day, I felt somehow drained but exhilarated as well, as though we had made love without touching.

It was nearly a week before Sandro had me return; he had a commission coming due, so he needed to spend his time finishing it before he could return to our painting, as I had begun to think of it. It had not escaped my notice that this was not a work that had been commissioned; no patron was supplying him with the money (and therefore time) to create it. It would be a work of art in the truest sense, born only of Sandro's own inspiration and passion and diligence and hard work.

The third time I went it was somewhat later in the day, and so the fire burning in the hearth and the candles scattered about the room were crucial to providing light in the fading afternoon. He welcomed me, and I undressed and took my place. It was easier each time, though the feeling of his eyes on me had yet to lose its force.

This time, though, instead of taking his usual seat, he hesitated. "I have a specific pose I would like you to take today, Simonetta," he said. "If you would."

I smiled. "Whatever you need."

He took a step toward me, then stopped, looking unsure. "May I . . ." He cleared his throat. "May I touch you?"

A blush rose to my cheeks; I was sure he could see it, but there was no help for it. "Yes."

He reached up to gingerly take my face in his hands. The rough cloth of his shirt brushed against my skin, and I shivered. I knew he felt it, but, thankfully, he made no comment. He gently tilted my head to one side, then stepped back slightly. "Yes. Just like that." He reached out and placed a hand lightly on my bare left hip. The warmth burned through me. "Shift your weight into this hip—yes. Yes, exactly." As swiftly as his hand was there, it was gone, and I felt a pang of loss at its absence.

He reached up and pulled a strand of hair across my right shoulder, letting it fall across my chest. I waited for his hand to move lower, to brush against my breasts, but it did not. I told myself that I was not disappointed.

Shifting to my other side, he carefully gathered the rest of my hair in his hand as though it were something precious; truly made of gold, perhaps. "Now," he said, "if you would take your hair and bring it around your body, as though you are using it to cover . . ." For a moment his professional demeanor slipped, and he gestured silently, his mouth opening and closing as he tried to find the most delicate word.

My own blush deepening, I took pity on him and pulled my long hair from his grasp, using it to cover the area between my legs.

"Yes," he said, clearly relieved. "Just so. And now, with your other hand, partially cover your breasts—yes," he said excitedly. He reached up and moved my right hand, guiding it more precisely into the position he desired. I wondered if he could feel the heat radiating from my body as he touched me. Surely he could. What would he think it meant?

What did I think it meant?

He stepped back, his eyes once again critical as he studied me. "Yes," he said. "Just relax that right hand slightly—relax your whole body. Yes!" he said. "Remember, you are Venus as she is first being born from the sea. You cover yourself because you are unsure of this world you have come into, not because you are ashamed. You are never ashamed."

I tried to embody his words as best I could. I straightened my spine, let my hands rest casually against my body as they—and my hair—partially covered me. I felt a small hint of a smile touch my lips as I tried to become the goddess he had described. Venus was not ashamed of being nude—it was natural to her. It gave her power over those who beheld her, power over their dreams and desires. She was not exposed—she would expose those who laid eyes on her.

"*Dio mio*, yes. Yes. Perfect." Sandro scrambled for his parchment and pencil and began furiously sketching.

My lips were dry, so I licked them once before speaking. "I remember hearing a tale when I was a girl," I said, "that when Venus was born from the waves, she came ashore in Genoa."

Sandro stopped drawing and looked up at me. "You come from Genoa, *sì?*"

"I do."

"Then the tale is true. Venus was indeed born in Genoa." With that, he turned his attention back to his sketching.

That evening, when I returned home, Marco was already there, and waiting for me.

"There you are, Simonetta," he said, an edge of annoyance in his tone as I entered the sitting room.

I made sure my cloak was drawn securely around me so that he could not see the simple garments I was wearing. Thank God I remembered to bind my hair up again before leaving the workshop, I thought. I had forgotten the last time. "*Buona sera, marito,*" I said.

"*Buona sera,*" he said, frowning. "Where have you been? I asked Chiara when I did not find you home, and she said she did not know."

"Did she?" I asked. "I am certain that I told her. But it is of no consequence. I was at Maestro Botticelli's workshop. I have been posing for him again." I had said that I would not hide my doings from Marco, and so I would not. The one detail I would omit, however, was the exact nature of my posing.

Marco's eyebrows lifted nearly into his hairline. "Oh, you have been, have you?"

"*Sì.*"

"I do not remember discussing this," he said, "much less you asking my permission."

"I was not aware that I needed your permission. Maestro Botticelli asked for my help in posing for a new work, and I agreed." I was struggling to maintain my light, indifferent tone. "I see no reason why we both should not do what pleases us. I thought that was what you wanted."

"Oh, you did?" Marco said, tossing aside the book he'd been reading and rising from his chair. "I had thought that we understood each other, Simonetta. Need I remind you that you are *my* wife? No one else's. Certainly not that painter's. That means you ask my permission before you go off and do as you please."

"I am your wife, yes, but you do not own me," I said, letting the steel behind my words show through.

Marco laughed, a harsh sound. "That is what marriage is, you beautiful fool."

His words bit into me. In the eyes of the law, and of society, yes, he was right. But were there not other types of ownership over a person?

I thought about my parents' marriage: my loquacious, vain mother and my sober, taciturn father. It had certainly never seemed to me that he owned her. And yet, their marriage was no great love affair, either.

Was that what love was? To own, or desire to own, another person? Did his love give him ownership over me whether I consented or not? Whether I loved him or not?

And he does not love me, not in the real sense of the word, I realized. He loves me in his way; he loves me as he understands love. But if he really loved me, he would never go off to spend his nights in the arms of some whore, the "way the world works" be damned.

"I am my own person, wife or no," I said at last. "Our marriage vows may give you dominion over my body, yes, but not my mind."

"You read too much, Simonetta," he said, frustrated, dropping back into his chair.

"I thought that was one of the things you loved about me."

He had no answer for that; no doubt he was remembering the early days of our courtship, and of our marriage as well, when we would read love poetry in bed, whisper verses in each other's ear as we made love. Perhaps he had believed that my devotion to poetry and reading would be transferred to him when he became my husband. Yet my intelligence had made me an asset to him among the Medici circle, and he could not deny that.

Suddenly it began to come clear. He had brought me to Florence intending for me to be the jewel in his crown; hoping that I would charm and delight his friends and acquaintances and help him to rise in the world—and that I would give him a son. I instead had become the one they all flocked to. I was the one Lorenzo spent his time in discussion with, the one sought out by poets and painters, even as Marco faded into the background. Even as I remained barren, or so it seemed.

And, even as I felt disgusted with him, I pitied him, and myself, too—that a marriage that had started out with such hope could come to such disappointment. Yet was I to apologize that I had become happy in this city to which he had brought me?

In his eyes, I supposed, I should do just that. And even as I remembered fondly that handsome, somewhat naïve young man who had come, quoting poetry, to woo me, I was now able to admit to myself that what had most enthralled me about him was the glittering new life he had promised me in Florence.

I had gotten what I wanted, for the most part. He, it seemed, had not.

I felt as though I was about to cry, yet that was the last thing I could allow myself to do. I drew a deep breath and pulled myself up to my full height. "And so?" I asked, breaking the silence. "Are you to forbid me from posing further for Maestro Botticelli, then? Even though I have already given my word?"

Now that I was aware of it, I could read the calculation in his eyes as plain as if it were written on parchment. If he were to forbid me from continuing to pose, Lorenzo de' Medici would hear of it, and would no doubt take offense at this slight to one of his favorite painters. This, in turn, would not bode well for Marco's political aspirations.

"I suppose you may as well keep on, since you have already begun," he said finally. "In the future, though, mind you consult with me about such things."

"Of course, *marito*," I said. With that, I turned and left the room.

That night, Marco turned to me in bed, and though I thought to push him away, I did not. I was still upset over our quarrel earlier, true, but that had as much to do with my realization of the bleak reality of our marriage as with anything he had said. Perhaps we could repair what had gone wrong between us. Perhaps it was not too late; perhaps this strife would soon pass.

I opened my legs for him, and as he slid inside me I sighed aloud in pleasure, realizing that I had missed this, had missed him. I moved my hips against him, meeting his thrusts, and I heard his breathing quicken at my response. We moved together, slightly faster now, and we both reached our release at the same time, our voices mingling as we cried out. He let his head fall to my shoulder, and kissed my neck, my cheek, and then my lips before lifting himself off of me.

Yet afterward, and only when I was certain that Marco was asleep, I let tears slide silently down my face. My hopefulness as we had started to make love had gone, and everything now only felt wrong.

26

And so, with Marco's cooperation—however grudging, however incomplete his knowledge—I continued to go to Botticelli's workshop and pose. He did another day's worth of sketches of me in the same pose as the last time, then tried a few variations of it.

"I think I shall keep to my original vision," he said to me as I dressed at the end of one session. "I am sorry to have wasted your time by being so indecisive. But the good news is that the next time you are here, I can begin to paint."

I smiled. "Not at all. I am happy to help in whatever way you need. It is not so difficult, after all, standing up there for a time."

His expression turned serious as he regarded me. "Perhaps not," he said, "but I still thank you all the same. I know it is no small thing that I have asked."

The words I wanted to speak sprang to my tongue with such force that I was only just able to hold them back. *You could ask of me anything in the world, and I would say yes.*

As he had before—and almost as if he had read the words in my eyes—he made a small motion as though to take me in his arms, but did not.

I lowered my eyes quickly, shame flooding through me at all that I was feeling. "I should go," I said. "When would you like me to return?"

He sighed, and I noticed he took a step back from me. "I shall send word, if that suits. It shall take me a bit of time to find and prepare the proper canvas." He smiled. "It shall be a very large one."

I smiled back distractedly, barely hearing him. "Very well," I managed. "Until next time, then."

"Indeed," he said, seeing me to the door. "*Buona notte,* Simonetta."

I did not reply, afraid of the words that would tumble from my lips if I did.

It seemed so foolish, that things should change so suddenly. In truth, I had long desired him, ever since I sat for him the first time. It was the reason I had always sought him out at gatherings, the reason why I always knew where he was in a room without having to look. It was why I had wanted to pose nude for him, to let him see all of me, even as the thought frightened me. It was the fear of wanting something I could not have.

It was the reason his eyes burned me as he studied me: because I imagined they were his hands on my body, instead.

It should not have mattered that I had finally formed the words in my own mind. The feelings had been there for years. But somehow, now, just having admitted it to myself, the world around me suddenly looked both brighter and darker at once.

I thought of a section of one of Dante's poems: "*I felt a spirit of love begin to stir/Within my heart, long time unfelt till then;/And saw Love coming towards me fair and fain/(That I scarce knew him for his joyful cheer),/Saying, 'Be now indeed my worshipper!'*"

I shivered as I walked home, even though the night was not cold.

Desire was what I felt, certainly. But what I also felt—even though I should not, even though I had no right to be feeling it—was love.

27

Several days passed, and I had no word from Sandro requesting that I return. He had warned me of this, of course, but in light of my new discovery—about myself, about him—it felt painfully dire. Did he no longer need me? Had he thought better of the whole project?

It was silliness, I knew. I remained listlessly in the house, though one day I did go to the Medici *palazzo* to take the noon meal with Clarice. We had a pleasant enough time, though it was punctuated by several mild coughing fits I could not contain.

"Are you quite well, Simonetta?" she asked me. "You are not taking ill again, are you?"

I smiled. "I hope not. I have spent quite enough time being ill of late, I think."

Our talk turned to other things, and I impulsively invited her and Lorenzo to dine with us the following evening, an invitation which she gladly accepted.

"It will keep him out of that Donati woman's bed, anyway," she said irritably. "He has scarcely been home of late. How does he think to get another son if he strays from his wife's bed?"

"Men are fools," I said. "Even the ones who ought to know better."

Just then, we were interrupted by the excited arrival of little Lucrezia, who had insisted her nurse bring her in to greet me. It was just as well, for I did not wish Clarice to question me as to my words. I had not told her what I had learned of Marco, and of the strain in our marriage since. I could not bear for her to know the truth; she who had been witness to all of my early, girlish hope and happiness in those days leading up to, and immediately after, my marriage.

Friend though she was, I could not bear to admit to her that she had been right all along.

The next morning my cough seemed to have worsened, so I stayed abed that I might recover in time to host Clarice and Lorenzo later that evening. I sent Chiara to the market for everything we would need, then slept most of the afternoon. Indeed, when it became time to dress for the evening I felt much improved, and Marco and I had a lovely time with our friends. It became much easier, I found, to put aside our differences in the presence of company.

Maybe we should move in with Lorenzo and Clarice, I thought to myself with a bit of humor as we lingered over our dessert wine.

However, despite feeling well at dinner, it soon became clear that I was not truly well.

I awoke in the night to another coughing fit, yet this one showed no sign of subsiding. My hacking woke Marco, as well, who, once again in the role of attentive husband, dashed down to the kitchen to fetch me a glass of watered-down wine to soothe my throat. I was only able to take small sips in between the coughing, and soon blood was being expelled from my lungs.

"Send for the doctor," Marco barked at Chiara, who had come in to assist. "Now! Get him here at once!"

Marco sat beside me in the bed, rubbing my back, trying to get me some wine in between coughs. Yet the blood was still coming when the doctor arrived.

He examined the blood staining a bit of cloth Chiara had given me and, with Marco's permission, laid an ear against my chest, that he might listen to what was happening within. Then he laid a hand against my brow. "She is burning with fever," he informed Marco, as though I were not right there.

"She was fine at dinner this evening," Marco protested. "How can she have become so ill so quickly?"

The doctor hesitated. "She has been ill in the past, yes? Recently?"

"Here and there," Marco said. "The climate of Florence does not agree with her; I have offered to take her home to Genoa, but she does not wish to leave."

"I'm afraid the climate has not much to do with it," the doctor said. "Signor Vespucci, perhaps you and I had best step outside to discuss—"

By then my coughing had slowed enough that I could speak. "I am right here, *dottore*, and I am not deaf nor addled in the head. Whatever you wish to say to my husband should also be said to me."

The doctor hesitated again, but when Marco showed no sign of following him out of the room, he relented. "I am not certain yet," he said. "I will need to monitor your condition throughout the coming days to be sure, Signora Vespucci, but I believe that you have consumption."

Silence filled the room, broken only by a cry of anguish from Chiara.

Consumption. The wasting disease of the lungs that killed thousands every year.

"That is ridiculous," Marco said. "How can this be? Simonetta is perfectly healthy."

"Is she, signore?" the doctor said, albeit gently. "You have just told me she has been ill on and off since she has lived in Florence."

"How long do I have to live, *dottore?*" a voice I somehow recognized as mine asked.

The doctor chuckled, though somewhat uncomfortably. "Do not fret yourself overmuch, signora. If I am right, you may still live a full life. After all, you have likely had the disease for years now and not known it. Such things happen."

What he did not say was as loud as his words—louder, perhaps. I may still live a full life—but I may not, if the disease worsened, if it afflicted me at its full potential. And even if I had had the disease for the past few years, did not the fact that I was now coughing up blood mean that it was getting worse?

"I will bleed you, for now," he said, "which may make the fever come down. And then I shall return tomorrow to see what progress you have made."

I turned my head away as he got out his instruments, so that I did not need to see the silver knife enter my flesh, nor my blood dripping into the doctor's bowl. I closed my eyes and waited for it to be over.

Yet in so doing, I soon fell into a deep, fever-laced sleep. In the brief moments when I awoke in the next few days, I saw Marco's and Chiara's faces, as though from very far away; felt the dampness of the sheets and blankets from my sweat; felt a pounding ache in my head as I continued to cough. Soon even these images blended into my dreams, and I could no longer tell when I was asleep or awake, what was truth and what was illusion.

Once I thought that I awoke to find Sandro with me, beside me in the bed. His hands were on my body, hungrily, and I cried out as heat rippled through my skin, as he took me in his arms and touched me in all the ways I had wished he would touch me as I posed for him. And I touched him in return, unable to believe that this was happening, that we were finally here. He whispered my name, and I could hear all the love and desire in his voice. Yet I awoke to find only Chiara in the room with me. "Chiara," I asked, struggling to speak. "Where . . . where is he?"

"Signor Vespucci is . . . not home," she said. "May I bring you anything, Madonna? Water or wine or . . ."

I frowned. *Marco?* That was not who I had meant. But of course Sandro would not be there; he was not my husband. Yet Marco was. Where was Marco?

A memory sneaked into my head, tinged with anger. There was another woman. Was that where he was, as when I had lain ill before?

Suddenly it seemed as though I could see them, could see Marco with some dark-haired harlot, a beautiful woman who panted wantonly and cried out his name as he thrust into her. I turned my head away, yet still I could see them, still the image followed me, and I could not escape it. I closed my eyes and curled into a ball, and I heard a woman weeping raggedly, and I could only wait for it all to be over.

When I finally awoke, it seemed to be afternoon, judging by the slant of light that came in through the window. Chiara was sitting in a chair near the window, doing some mending.

My mouth was so dry it was a struggle to speak; I had to moisten my lips with my tongue twice before any words would come out. "Chiara," I said hoarsely.

She started, leaping out of her chair. "Madonna! Oh, you are awake! How do you feel?"

"Water," was all I could manage.

"Of course, of course," she said. "I will fetch you some immediately. And I will send Signor Vespucci in." Before I could question her—What day was it? How long had I been asleep? Had *il dottore* been back?—she was gone.

Perhaps a minute later, Marco came into the room, looking weary and haggard. "Simonetta," he said. "You are awake."

For an instant the image of him with the whore flashed through my brain, and I recoiled at the sight of him. But that was but a fevered dream, no more. I had not really seen such a thing. "So it would seem."

He dropped onto the bed beside me and let out a sigh.

"How long was I asleep?" I asked, fearing the answer but needing to know.

"Three days," he said.

I drew in my breath sharply, shocked.

"It . . . it was terrible." He ran his fingers through his already disheveled hair. "I thought I was going to lose you for certain."

Despite everything, I was touched by the way that thought had obviously upset him, despite all that had gone awry between us of late. He does care for me. He must. "Has the doctor been back?" I asked.

"He has. He has been here many times, though you do not remember, I am sure."

I shook my head. "I dreamt many strange things . . . and I cannot say what was real and what was a dream."

He nodded. "Well, he has been here a great deal of late. He said . . ." Marco hesitated.

"Tell me, Marco," I said, my voice as strong as I could make it. "For pity's sake, tell me what he said."

He sighed again, then finally met my gaze. "He confirmed that you have consumption."

I closed my eyes. Suddenly, I felt unimaginably weary again.

Consumption. It was not a surprise, but to hear it confirmed was another thing entirely.

"And does he know, now," I said, my voice thick with tears when I spoke again, "how long I may be expected to live?"

Marco hesitated again before speaking. "He could not say," he said. "In truth, as I said, we thought we might lose you over these past few nights. But since you have recovered—well, there is no telling."

"It might be years," I whispered. "I might live to be an old woman yet." I paused, trying to muster the strength to speak past my sobs. "Or I might die tomorrow."

"No." Marco leaned across the bed and took my hands in his. "You have recovered for now. You can be well again, and go about your life. This attack has passed. The doctor said if this attack passed, you would recover."

"For now, *marito*," I said, speaking the words he would not. "I will recover for now. Until the next attack. And then my life will hang in the balance all over again."

"Do not think like that," Marco said. "As you just said, you may yet live to be an old woman."

I laughed through my tears. And in many ways the idea was ludicrous. I was twenty-one years old. I could not fathom the idea that my life could end in a matter of months. Not then, not as I lay on that bed—still weak, still weary—but awake and very much alive. I could have risen from the bed and gone about my life right then. How was I to accept the idea that my youth, my vitality, my beauty might not save me?

"But even if I do, I shall carry this disease with me all my years, never knowing when it may strike," I said. "Perhaps it would be better not to live so long."

"Simonetta," Marco said, his voice breaking. It was then that I saw there were tears in his eyes as well. "Do not say that."

"Maybe it would be for the best," I said. "Perhaps it would be better for everyone if I did not live to have my beauty fade."

I insisted on getting up from bed that very day and walking about the house a bit. I took some broth sitting at the dining room table, then fell back into bed, exhausted but not willing to admit it.

My parents arrived from Genoa the next day, Marco having sent for them when it appeared I may not survive. It was wonderful to see them again, even if my father was stoic and silent and my mother could not set eyes upon me without bursting into tears. They stayed only a few days, long enough to assure themselves that I was well enough again, and I was not altogether sorry to see them go.

A few days after I awoke, Marco mentioned from his spot at my bedside, "Your painter wrote while you slept. Two days ago, perhaps." His worry about me dulled the scorn that would normally have been in his voice.

Suddenly I remembered. I had dreamt, too, of Sandro. My face, and then my whole body, flushed as I remembered the things I had dreamed.

"He did?" I asked. "What did he say?"

Marco's face became disapproving as he replied, sharpening my guilt. "He sought to arrange the next date for you to pose for him. I replied and told him you were ill."

"And what did he say to that?" I asked, unable to stop myself.

"Nothing," Marco said shortly. "What else would there be for him to say, Simonetta?"

My husband's words were a challenge, one that I did not take up. What, indeed, I mused. I supposed there was nothing he could have said, in the interest of propriety. But had he worried? Was he concerned for me? Did he know the true extent of what is wrong with me? And . . . would he still have me as his muse? As his Venus?

What good was being the most beautiful woman in Florence if the man I loved did not care for me?

"I shall write to him," I said, getting up from the bed, heedless of my unseemly haste. All that mattered was that I return to posing as soon as possible, for what if the worst should befall me before the painting was finished? "I shall tell him that I can return next week, if that suits him."

Marco caught my shoulders and gently pushed me back onto the bed. "Simonetta, really," he said. "Whatever this painting is, it can wait. Indeed, given your condition, it may not be wise for you to return to sitting for him, in any case."

For a moment, my guilt urged me to say what I knew Marco wanted to hear, that I would not pose for Sandro again, or even see him. I can be a good wife, can I not? I can do that for him, I tried to tell myself. Yet I knew that, truly, I could not. I had to see Sandro again, no matter what.

And did Marco deserve such devotion? What kind of man left his wife, whom he thought was dying, to visit his whore? My nightmare of her and Marco flashed again through my mind. You cannot blame your husband for an illusion of your fevered brain, Simonetta, I reprimanded myself. But it was not only a dream, not really. Such a scene had occurred, and would again.

I had loved Marco, yes, and in some ways I still did; yet I had begun to feel that my love was wasted on him.

"I will continue to pose for him," I said aloud. "I will help him finish the painting. I made a promise, after all. This . . . this disease changes nothing."

"It will need to change some things, perhaps," Marco bit out.

"Not this," I said. "And I do not think quarreling with you is helpful, given my condition. Do you, *marito*?"

With that, Marco let the matter drop, though the scowl did not leave his face for some time.

Later that day, when Marco stepped outside for a bit, I rose and went to my desk, where I penned a missive to Sandro:

> Marco tells me you wrote whilst I was ill. I have been very ill, in truth, and shall speak of it more when I see you again. I am recovering now, and I wish to help you continue the painting, if indeed you still need my help. I can return next week.

I signed it simply *Simonetta*, and sent it off with Chiara. She brought me back a response almost immediately:

Mia bellissima Simonetta,

I have been worried about you, more so than I can possibly say, but your husband's reply to my note let me know in no uncertain terms that any further inquiries by me would not be welcomed. Please, if you are feeling well enough, return to me Tuesday next at 2 of the clock. I shall be waiting for you.

He, in turn, signed it simply *Sandro.*

I read the letter twice, then tossed it into the fire. *Your husband's reply to my note let me know in no uncertain terms that any further inquiries by me would not be welcomed. . . .*

Indeed. I wanted to fly into a rage at Marco, demand by what right he carried on correspondence on my behalf, but I could not, for then he would know that Sandro had written to me directly. And, as my husband, he had every right.

Instead, I let my mind repeat to me the rest of Sandro's letter.

Mia bellissima Simonetta . . . return to me.

I shall be waiting for you.

28

On the appointed day, I appeared at Sandro's workshop. He was alone, as he always was when he arranged for me to pose. At the sight of him, my explicit dream of him from my illness flashed through my mind, and I found myself suddenly a bit short of breath.

"Simonetta," he said, clasping my hand in his as I entered. "I am so glad to see you looking well. You have no idea how worried I was."

I tried to smile; I had intended, when he inquired about my illness, to tell him that it had been nothing, a mere fever only, and that I was fine. I had not wanted to tell him the truth. Yet in the face of his genuine concern and happiness to see me, I crumbled. I began to sob, burying my face in my hands as though to hide from him.

"Simonetta," he said, bewildered. His arms came around me, and slowly, hesitantly, he pulled me against his chest. I stiffened for a moment, knowing I should pull away, but I could not bring myself to do it. Not then, not when I was so in need of comfort and wanted it only from him. I let myself melt into his body, let him clutch me tightly to him. He smelled of paint and candle wax and sweat and, despite my tears, I reveled in this moment of closeness. I thought, in that moment, that I would weep forever if it meant he would never let me go.

"Simonetta," he murmured in my ear. "What is wrong? Please tell me." To my dismay, he released me and stepped back, that he might see my face. "You can tell me, whatever it is."

"I . . . I am sorry," I managed.

"Do not be. You have nothing for which to apologize. Here, come with me, and sit," he said. He took my hand and led me to the back of the workshop, through the back room I had been in once before, and into a small kitchen. He sat me at the rough-hewn wooden table. "Some wine, perhaps?"

I nodded.

He found a glass for each of us and poured some Tuscan *vino rosso* into each. I took a long sip, taking the opportunity to collect myself.

"My illness," I said at last. "It . . . I . . ." I took a deep breath, composing myself further so that I might finish my sentence. "The doctor has said that I . . . it seems I have consumption."

I remembered well the shock and devastation on Marco's face when the doctor had first made his pronouncement, before we even knew for certain. Yet never before had I seen an expression quite like Sandro's on another human being's face. He looked as though his entire world had been shattered right before his eyes, as though he was watching the final pieces crumble into irretrievable ash and there was nothing he could do to stop it.

He looked like a man with nothing left to live for.

"No," he whispered at last. "That cannot be. You are here—and you look as healthy as ever."

"*Il dottore* said that I may have had it for some time now and not known," I said quietly. "This was simply the worst attack." I hesitated before adding, "Thus far."

"Did he say . . ." Sandro trailed off and was silent, as though he could not even bear to ask the question, let alone hear the answer.

"There is no telling," I said, knowing what he wanted to ask. "It is always so with such things. No one knows except God."

He stood up abruptly, turning his back to me, dropping his head into his hands. I watched him, paralyzed, wondering what this meant, wondering what he was thinking.

When he turned back to me, his eyes were red-rimmed. "I cannot bear to contemplate a world without you in it," he said, his voice rough. "And so I will not do it."

I smiled in spite of myself. "Perhaps if we do not contemplate it, we may prevent it from coming to pass."

We were both silent for a moment longer. Finally he spoke again. "You . . . do you still wish to pose?"

"Yes," I replied instantly. "That is why I am here. I want you to finish the painting. No matter what. If I become ill again . . ." I bit my lip and looked away. "If I become ill again, then I shall return when I am well. And we shall proceed as before."

He sighed. "Only if you are certain. If you are certain it will not tax you overmuch."

"It will not. I am going to live my life as I always have, Sandro. I am not going to become some invalid."

The pain in his eyes as he looked at me nearly caused me to cry out, as though I was bleeding. "But what if doing so would prolong your life?"

I shuddered as I drew another deep breath. "That is in the hands of God," I said. "And even if staying in bed the rest of my days would prolong my life, I do not think that would be a life worth living."

He nodded reluctantly. "I understand. And I . . ." He reached out and covered my hand with his own. "Whatever happens, I should like to think that in this painting, you will live forever. Venus is immortal, after all."

At this I began to cry anew.

"Oh, Simonetta . . . please do not cry," he whispered. "I should not have said that. I wish . . ."

But he did not finish whatever he had been about to say, and instead kept his hand on mine until my tears subsided.

"Perhaps we should not work on the painting today," he said at last. "I do not know that either of us is in the right state for it."

I smiled gratefully at him. I did not feel quite able to disrobe before him again just yet, with the weight of all that had just been said between us—and with my dreams still lingering a bit too vividly in my mind. "I agree," I said. "I doubt I would have any men writing me verse or serenading me under my window if they had ever seen me cry. I am not one of those confounding women who weeps beautifully."

Sandro's lips twitched into a smile. "No, I suppose not."

For a moment I stared at him, dumbfounded, unable to believe what I had heard. Any other man would have rushed to contradict me, told me that I look sublimely beautiful no matter what. Any other man would not have been honest with me.

That, I supposed, was one of the reasons I loved him.

I started to laugh, softly at first, then harder, until my shoulders were shaking and I could scarcely breathe. Sandro began to laugh as well, and when I looked up at him, both of us had tears of mirth running down our faces.

29

Sandro and I agreed that we would continue work on the painting, when I was feeling well enough and when his schedule allowed. I came but half a week later, after that day when our intimacy was deepened by tears and laughter. With me posing in his original, desired position, he executed two sketches of what the finished painting would look like, albeit without color.

This time, posing when I was finally fully aware of my feelings for him, I felt as though the air in the room around us had changed, grown more alive. I wondered if he could see it on my face, read it in my eyes, as he studied me so closely, as he drew me into being on a blank piece of parchment. Wearing not a scrap of clothing, I ached for him to touch me, craved his hands on my body, burned for him to help me down from my pedestal and lead me up the stairs to his bed. As I studied him and, in turn, let him study me, I imagined what it would be like to lie with him, to have him make love to me, to make love to him, to have him inside me and to move with him. Could he see all this on my face, as well? Could he see the lust etched in each soft curve of my body, see how my very being yearned for him?

Perhaps it was just as well. The Church would censure and punish me for such thoughts, for my lust, for committing adultery in my mind. Yet, sin or no, I had somehow ceased to feel guilt for such desires. And were not such thoughts, such longings, perfect for a pagan goddess? Should not Venus be painted with desire in her very form, with lust for this new world into which she was being born?

When we were finished for the day, he gave me one of the sketches for my own. I gasped when I saw it. He had only told me bits and pieces of his vision up to that point, and when I saw the whole together, even without color, I was astounded at the scope, at the grandeur, at how it retained a simple, primal beauty even so.

Venus—I—was in the center, standing in a great clamshell that bore her to shore from the waves that had conceived and given birth to her. The winds—personified—blew her in to shore, flowers tumbling about her in their wake, the breeze catching her hair and making it dance. A maid waited at the shore with a robe to cover her, both the robe and the maid's dress fluttering in the wind.

What most astounded me, perhaps, was how Sandro had been able to capture *motion,* even in so simple a sketch. The whole tableau looked as though it was moving before my eyes, as though this bit of parchment was a window into some other active, living, breathing world.

"What do you think?" Sandro asked nervously, and I realized that I had not spoken for some time as I took it all in.

I looked up at him, vaguely aware that there were tears in my eyes. "Oh, Sandro, it is beautiful beyond words," I said. "More so than I had dared to dream."

He smiled, and I could hear his relieved sigh, nearly silent though it was. "I am glad you think so," he said. "I do not think I could carry on with it if you did not." He chuckled. "And that is just a simple drawing. Wait until the painting is finished. If I can capture it in just the way I intend, that is . . ."

"Why, it shall rob me of all speech, of all reason," I said. "It shall be too incredible to take in."

His eyes bored into me as he brought one hand up to my cheek, and for a moment, I thought he was going to lean in and kiss me. "Then I will know that I have succeeded. When its beholders react in precisely that way," he said, releasing me.

After that day, we were not able to meet again for some time. He had other works to attend to—most notably his commission for the great church of Santa Maria Novella—and the shift to cold, damp winter weather brought with it a return of my cough, though thankfully nothing so severe as my last attack of illness. Nevertheless, Marco was so concerned that he begged me to remain in bed, which I did only to appease him. In reality, other than coughing, I felt quite fine, but knew that it would not be worth the trouble it would surely bring me to push the issue of my returning to Sandro's workshop. So I obeyed Marco's wishes, for the time being.

Yet even once I was recovered again to the point where Marco could no longer keep me in bed, Sandro was much occupied with another project that had most of the city's finest artists and craftsmen busy as well. The Medici family was planning a magnificent joust to be held in the Piazza Santa Croce at the end of January, in celebration of a recently signed and sealed treaty with the Republic of Venice and the duchy of Milan. As Florence's Signoria—and the Medici bank—had recently gotten into a spot of trouble with Pope Sixtus in Rome over the appointment of the new archbishop of Pisa, having the fabulously wealthy Venice and the militaristic Milan as allies was indeed something worth celebrating for all Florentines. As such, artists were needed to paint flags and banners and decorations for the event, and craftsmen were needed to build lists and viewing galleries.

December and most of January passed without my seeing Sandro once, even as he consumed most of my thoughts. Yet though this caused me to grind my teeth in frustration and impatience, somehow it was different from when we had been separated for long periods before. I knew, now, that it was not because he did not wish to see me; it was not because he did not wish me to continue posing for him. It was circumstance keeping us apart, and nothing more; I was at last confident in that knowledge.

At times I took the sketch he had given me out of the locked drawer where I kept it—I could not bring myself to burn it, or even give it back to Sandro for safekeeping, though I did not want to contemplate what would happen should Marco discover it—and studied it, marveling at it anew. Much as I wished the painting might be done quickly so that I could see the finished product, I knew that once it was, I would no longer have a reason to spend time with Sandro. And so I came to see that these delays were perhaps for the best—for me, at least.

30

The day of the joust dawned bright and clear, if cold—"What are they thinking, really, holding a joust in January?" I grumbled to myself as Chiara dressed me in my warmest fur-trimmed gown and bundled me into my thickest cloak. Marco had already left; he would be riding as a part of Giuliano's entourage. The joust was very much Giuliano's affair: Lorenzo had intended for it to be a means of formally debuting his younger brother before the Florentine people, as he had with a joust of his own some years ago. The fact that the Florentine people already knew Giuliano, and loved him well, seemed scarcely to matter.

Giuliano had—or so Marco told me—been seeing to every detail of the day, from the decorations to the costumes to the banners to the feast being served at the Medici *palazzo* afterward for the members of Florentine high society. He did love to be the center of attention—yet he understood, as his brother did, the many ways in which spectacle could win the hearts of the common people.

I frowned at my reflection in the mirror as a thought struck me. I had not even heard Marco leave this morning—he had not woken me so that I might give him a favor, which would have been customary, even though he himself was not jousting. Perhaps he had forgotten, or perhaps I might still give him a ribbon or some such thing at the field.

"Is something amiss, Madonna?" Chiara asked me.

I shook off my thoughts. Surely it was nothing. "No, everything is fine, Chiara," I said. "Are you ready to go? Will you be warm enough? Good; then let us be off."

Chiara and I made our way to Piazza Santa Croce; once there, she went off to join the crowds of common people, while I was escorted by one of the liveried Medici servants—a veritable legion of them had been hired for this day—to my privileged spot in the stands beside Clarice.

"Thank goodness you are here," Clarice said once I took my seat beside her. "Finally I shall have someone to talk to."

I stifled a laugh as I noted Lorenzo and his mother standing a few paces away from us, peering out at the field. Even as I beheld them, Lucrezia dei Tornabuoni called over one of the servants and began giving him instructions of some kind.

At the far end of the piazza stood the familiar church of Santa Croce. The Franciscan basilica stood tall and proud, dominating the square with its marble façade adorned with a simple rectangular pattern in marble, and its brown brick *campanile* and the small spires on the façade pointed the way to heaven.

The rest of the piazza, however, had been completely transformed. I could see fully the work that had gone into transforming the piazza from its usual plain, dirty self into something out of a chivalrous tale of old. Banners and pennants flew from flagpoles installed on the top of each building in the piazza, and I was astonished to see tapestries in all colors—some even glittering with gold thread—draped over the fronts of the structures. Indeed, the yellow and brown façades of the buildings could barely be seen. And everywhere—from the banners to the livery of the servants—the crest of Florence and the crest of the Medici family could be seen. And while the church itself had been spared any sort of decoration, the conversion of the square as a whole to a scene for spectacle had given it the air of an old fairy castle.

Clarice gave a much put-upon sigh. "It really is quite gaudy and overwrought, is it not?" she said.

"Oh, no," I said excitedly. "I think it is all quite wonderful. It is just like a scene out of a fairy tale!"

Clarice laughed. "You are ever the innocent, Simonetta. I admire that in you."

I was not quite certain how to reply—she had phrased it as a compliment, but I was not certain that it was meant as one—so I changed the subject. "Is Lorenzo saddened to not be riding today?" I asked.

Clarice waved a hand carelessly. "Oh, no. He is much too exalted for such sport nowadays, and quite frankly, Giuliano has always been the better horseman, and the better athlete. He is content not to be cast in the shade by his younger brother, methinks."

Just then Lorenzo and Lucrezia returned, a servant carrying goblets of mulled wine in their wake. "Madonna Simonetta, always a pleasure," Lorenzo said, sweeping me a bow. "For the ladies, please," he said, indicating that the man should serve us first. Once Clarice, Lucrezia, and myself each had a glass, Lorenzo took one and settled into his cushioned chair. "Everything looks to be in readiness," he told us. "Giuliano has outdone himself. This shall be a spectacular day, indeed."

"It all looks wonderful," I said enthusiastically. "Why, I hardly recognized *la piazza*."

Lorenzo grinned. "Giuliano will be pleased to hear it," he said, "for that was his intent."

Shortly thereafter, trumpets blared from somewhere not too far off, and a hush fell over the crowd. We all listened, straining to hear the heralds coming closer, to hear the thunder of hoofbeats. The rumbling drew nearer until a veritable cavalcade of mounted knights came streaming into the piazza from the street opposite the church, the clanking of their armor and the clomping of their horses' hooves drowned out by the cheering and screaming that greeted their entrance.

At the head of this procession was, of course, Giuliano de' Medici. His armor gleamed so in the winter sunlight that it had to be new; on his shield was an image of the head of Medusa, set in pearls, very clearly casting its bearer in the role of the heroic Perseus.

Yet it was the banner he carried that made me gasp aloud.

It flew and snapped behind him as he rode and made a circle of the piazza, fluttering so that it was not immediately easy to see the image that it bore. But after squinting at it, a strange, uncomfortable feeling hatched in my stomach. There was no mistaking it.

It was an image of me, in the guise of Pallas Athena, wearing a warrior's helmet over my long, freely streaming blond hair, and with the owl of wisdom perched on my outstretched arm. A pile of books lay stacked at my feet.

Nor, I realized, was there any mistaking the artist. None other than Sandro Botticelli had painted this image. I knew his style, would know it wherever it might appear in the world.

I stared at it, open-mouthed, my face slowly turning crimson as I felt the eyes of nearly every person present—or so it seemed—move from Giuliano to me.

Why was he doing this? What was he hoping to achieve? And why, *why* had Sandro not warned me, so that at the very least I did not look the fool? For I surely looked the world's greatest fool at that moment. Any other woman in Florence—in all of Italy, no doubt—would have been ecstatic to be singled out for such an honor. Yet I only could gape at the banner and its bearer in shock, wondering what it all meant.

Out of the corner of my eye, I caught sight of Sandro, standing at the far end of the same gallery on which I sat. He was watching Giuliano ride around the piazza, but instead of looking on his work with pride, he wore a scowl blacker than any expression I had ever seen on his face.

I was taken aback. I stared at him for a moment longer, and just as I was about to turn away he turned his head and caught my eye. The anger in his gaze melted away and was replaced with sorrow. His lips parted as though he meant to speak to me, to call out to me across the crowd, but I looked away, my mind a tumult of confusion.

His round of the piazza complete, Giuliano and his company came to a stop before the gallery where I sat. After saluting his brother, Giuliano removed his helmet and bowed deeply to me from his saddle. "Signora Simonetta Vespucci," he declared, his voice ringing out loud enough for all to hear. "I ride this day in your honor, and dedicate my joust to you, the most beautiful woman in Florence!"

His words elicited a cheer from the crowd gathered within the piazza's confines.

"I beg you, *mia dolce, bellissima donna,* to give me your favor, that I might ride with it this day," he said.

I remained frozen in my seat for a moment, my eyes seeking Marco among Giuliano's entourage. I found him quickly enough, just a few paces from his friend's side, mounted on a beautiful gray stallion. He was resplendent in yellow hose and a doublet of many bright colors, with an elaborately worked brocade pattern—a match to that worn by his brothers-in-arms. He was avoiding my eyes, studiously looking down at the ground, as though there was some action taking place in the dust from which he could not bear to look away.

One piece of the puzzle, at least, fell into place. Marco had not asked for my favor this morning because he must have known what Giuliano was planning. He must have known and did not wish to cast a pall over his friend's day, even when said friend was professing his devotion to Marco's own wife.

Surely if Marco was offended, he would not have gone along with Giuliano's plan? Surely he would have stopped his friend from carrying it out?

Yet what could any of us do when a Medici had his mind set on something, truly?

I heard Clarice's words from years ago echo in my mind. *Dear Simonetta, your role in such games is to simply be adored, and to enjoy yourself.*

It is all a game, I reminded myself, rising from my seat and pulling a ribbon from my sleeve. It is all a game, and I must continue to play it as I have ever since arriving in Florence. It is a game, nothing more.

"Take this, good signore, as a sign of my favor on your gallant deeds today," I said, projecting my voice so that the audience could hear. I leaned down and handed Giuliano the ribbon. "And may God protect you in the lists, and guide your lance and give you victory."

Giuliano smiled and bowed his head again, tucking my ribbon beneath his breastplate. Around us the crowd cheered, louder, it seemed, than they had when the company had made its entrance. With the show of chivalry over, the men rode off to the edges of the field to prepare for the jousting to begin.

"Well done, Simonetta," Lorenzo said, leaning across his wife to speak to me. "My brother is right—Florentines love a good spectacle more than anything else."

"Indeed," I said, feeling suddenly light-headed and out of breath.

"Goodness, Simonetta," Clarice said, and she could not entirely hide the note of jealousy in her voice. "Did you know what Giuliano was planning?"

"I did not," I said. "I am as astonished as you are."

Clarice gave an unladylike snort. "Well, I cannot say I am astonished, in truth. We all knew Giuliano would make some grand declaration of his love for you sooner or later." She peered at me. "And what of Marco? Did he know of this, do you suppose?"

I remembered Marco's downcast gaze, as though looking away

was the only way that he could endure what was happening before him. But nothing in his posture, in his reaction, had suggested any surprise.

"I do not know," I said, my voice coming out harder than I had intended. "You would need to ask Marco."

31

Giuliano won the day on the jousting field, to no one's surprise. I had to concede that—limited though my knowledge of jousting was—he was perhaps legitimately the best athlete on the field, as Clarice had alluded to. It made sense, after all—even among the other wealthy families of Florence, whose sons could have afforded to devote so much time to sport and leisure? It seemed likely that Giuliano would have won the day no matter what, though I did detect that some of his opponents did not tilt to the extent of their abilities. The one exception, I could see, was the young man representing the Pazzi clan—another Florentine banking family, and the bitterest rivals of the Medici, both in business and in government. Yet though Giuliano did not unseat him, he managed to win the match nonetheless, three lances to two.

I had not witnessed a joust since I was a girl in Genoa, and I had quite forgotten the suspense and excitement that accompanied watching two young men racing at each other from opposite ends of the field. I rooted for Giuliano, of course: even had I not given him my favor, he was the only participant whom I knew well. But as the day wore on and Giuliano continued to triumph over all who came against him, I began to grow weary of the spectacle—and of the cold, which had not abated as much as I had hoped.

Therefore I was glad when it all came to an end—though I was forced to again take the stage and crown Giuliano, as the victor, with a wreath woven of laurels. He beamed up at me, and then climbed up beside his brother to accept the adulation of the crowd. He motioned for me to stand beside him, which I did, and he reached down and squeezed my hand in his.

I was uncomfortable in this role I had been cast in, a role I had not asked for and in which I did not know what was required of me. I was glad when it came time to adjourn to the Medici *palazzo* for the banquet. I looked forward to seeing Marco, as well; for as strained as our marriage had been of late, at least when I stood by his side I knew what my place was. I knew what was expected of me, even if I did not always like it.

I went to the *palazzo* in the company of Lorenzo, Clarice, and Lucrezia; Marco would meet us there, with the rest of Giuliano's entourage. Upon entering, one of the servants took my heavy cloak; I almost wished I could keep it on, as the chill that had settled into my bones at the jousting field had yet to leave me.

I was then shown into the now-familiar receiving room, where a veritable army of servants waited to tend to the needs of the exalted guests who would soon be arriving. I was handed a glass of mulled wine as soon as I entered, and Lorenzo and Clarice immediately drew me into their circle.

"Did you enjoy the day, Simonetta?" Lorenzo asked me.

The smile that stretched across my face felt false. "Very much," I said, hoping the words did not sound as stiff as they felt.

"Good," he said. "I know it will mean much to Giuliano that you should say so. I did not know what he had planned—he managed to keep it a secret even from me!" He chuckled and shook his head. "And

I must commend Sandro Botticelli on his painting of you—what a perfect choice, to depict you as Pallas Athena! Beautiful and wise and fierce—just like our Simonetta."

"You do flatter me, signore, as always," I said.

"It is no flattery to speak the truth," Lorenzo said. "But you must excuse us now, *amica mia*—we must begin to greet the rest of the guests." With that, he and Clarice stepped away toward the door, where the rest of the guests had begun to enter. One of the first among them, I noted, was Lucrezia Donati Ardenghelli and her husband. I could see the stiffness in Clarice's spine as she greeted the pair. Lorenzo's affair with Lucrezia had continued unabated for the past few years—when his duties in the bank and government permitted him to spend time with her, in any case. Clarice had become more accustomed to it, even if she did not like it and never would.

Lucrezia dei Tornabuoni soon engaged me in conversation. "I always knew Giuliano was quite taken with you, but I had not expected such a grand, courtly gesture," she said. "He is a true romantic, my son, and a truly chivalrous gentleman."

I had to bite back a sardonic smile, remembering his crude words the night he had stumbled drunkenly into my house. "Indeed he is," I said aloud. "I was not expecting so much to be made of me, this day or any other."

Lucrezia smiled. "A woman as beautiful as you shall always have much made of her," she said. "Indeed, I wonder that you do not expect it yet."

I returned her smile, though irritation was pricking at me. Is this what everyone thinks of me? I wondered. Even the people who know me well? That because I am beautiful, I expect to be the center of everyone's attention, at all times?

Or perhaps it does not matter what I do, what I say or how I act. Perhaps people see what they expect to see, what they wish to see when they look at me, and that is all. That is all they have ever seen.

Just then, a commotion drew my attention to the doorway of the now-crowded room as Giuliano and his entourage burst in triumphantly. Everyone present ceased their conversations and began to applaud. Giuliano and the young men with him bowed in appreciation, all of them smiling widely, all of them looking as though this was the happiest moment of their lives.

Their ovation ended, the youths began to mingle through the crowd, finding their wives, parents, friends, and being given glasses of wine.

Marco drifted rather aimlessly through the room, until he saw me. I excused myself from Lucrezia and went to his side at once. "Marco, *marito,*" I said, kissing him on the cheek. "I am glad to see you."

He smiled. "And I you, Simonetta. Did you enjoy yourself?"

Here, at last, was one person I could be honest with. "Well enough," I said. I rolled my eyes. "The whole thing was rather overwrought. And I did not expect so much to be made of me."

There it was again—the same glance at the floor, the same avoidance of my eyes. "Giuliano thought only to please you," he mumbled.

"It was a lovely gesture, but I wish I had known, so that I might not have been so taken aback," I said. "Why did you not warn me, Marco?"

He shrugged, still not looking at me. "Giuliano told me not to," he said. "He wished it to be a surprise."

That same uncomfortable feeling that had come upon me when I first beheld the banner with my likeness slithered through my stomach once again. Something was wrong here, and no one would tell me what it was. "Does he not know there are no secrets between husband and wife?" I asked lightly.

Yet I knew by the look Marco gave me that this was the wrong thing to say. He finally met my eyes again, his expression heavy with warning and reproach and guilt—for the secrets he had kept from me in the past, for the ones he seemed to know I was keeping, and for whatever this was, now, in the air between us.

I should no doubt have apologized for not choosing my words more carefully, but I could not just then. "What is it, Marco?" I whispered. "What is wrong?"

He shook his head and pasted a false smile on his face. "Nothing at all," he said. "This is naught but a joyous day, Simonetta. All is well." He took a glass of wine from the tray of a passing servant and downed half of it in one gulp.

I decided not to press the issue. Whatever was troubling Marco was not something he was going to speak of just then, if ever, and it would do me no good to beg my own husband to confide in me.

Despite the celebratory feel of the whole day, I found that I could not wait for it to be over. Once dinner commenced, I was seated beside Giuliano, as though I were the guest of honor, and before the meal began he proposed a toast to me, saying that my beauty and grace had blessed his joust that day. I smiled as though I was pleased beyond anything to accept such a tribute, but my sense of discomfort and wariness only increased.

When finally—*finally*—dinner was at an end, everyone adjourned back to the receiving room, and I began to look about for Marco, to let him know that I was ready to leave. Somehow we had become separated in the short trip from the dining room to the receiving room, and I could not see him.

As I was peering about for him, I heard a familiar deep voice speak my name. "Simonetta."

I turned to see Giuliano, still wearing the costume he had worn beneath his armor, similar to those his entourage had worn, but with a different brocade pattern still, to set him apart. "Giuliano," I said, smiling. "My congratulations on your triumph this day."

"Ahh, but it was all due to your favor, dear lady," he said.

I laughed, warming up slightly as I always did when he and I spoke—and were not observed by a crowd of thousands, anyway. "I think your own skill in the lists was of more use to you than my favor."

He smiled but did not respond. "I crave a word with you," he said.

"You are having one now."

He laughed. "As witty as you are beautiful. I meant a private word." He lowered his voice slightly. "Alone."

"Now?" I asked. My wariness returned.

"I insist, *mia bella donna*."

"Very well," I said. If he heard the reluctance in my voice, it did not deter him. He led me from the receiving room and down the hall, to a small, private parlor where I had visited with Clarice and Lucrezia many times in the past.

"Please, be seated," he said, closing the door behind us.

I did as he said, albeit uneasily. "This is most irregular," I said. "And, dare I say, improper."

He laughed, and in one bound had crossed the room to me, kneeling at my feet and taking my hand in his. "Ahh, but it need not be, Simonetta *mia*," he said. "It need be neither of those things."

I remained motionless, neither pulling my hand away from his nor clasping it in return. "Whatever do you mean?"

"It is why I wished to speak to you," he said. "Why I have arranged this day so much in your honor. That you might know the high esteem and regard in which I hold you."

"You are too kind, signore," I said. "And you know that I hold you in the utmost regard as well, as a friend of mine and of my husband's. But this, surely, you could have said to me in the presence of others."

"Indeed I could have," he said. "But that is not all that I wish to say." His fingers tightened around mine.

"Then what more do you wish to say?" I said, unable to disguise the nervousness in my voice. "Speak plainly, I beg of you."

"Your wish is my command, *mia donna dell'amore*," he said.

His words caused an unpleasant twist in my stomach. *My lady love.*

"My feelings for you can come as no surprise," he said. "You know that my love for you has only blossomed over these past years of our acquaintance. And so the time has come when I must ask you—nay, beg you—to allow that love to be consummated."

A part of me had managed to remain in denial as to what he was really asking until that last word. *Consummated.*

This, then, was what it had all been about. He had created an entire spectacle—beginning with the banner with my image and ending here, in this room—to seduce me. And while a part of me could only be astonished at the lengths to which he had gone, the rest of me was disgusted.

He had planned all along to seduce me. And Sandro had helped him.

"You . . ." I found that I could barely speak from shock and betrayal. Shock that he had the gall to ask for it so plainly, so unashamedly. And the betrayal, ah, God, it was as great as when I had learned of Marco's whore. Greater. "You wish for me to be your mistress."

He looked somewhat uncomfortable now—at my choice of words or at my tone, or both. "I ask for you to be my one and only love," he said, recovering somewhat and retreating again into the language of courtly love. Flowery language that I had once thought masked a lack of meaning. A courtship I had always believed was a game.

Yet it appeared that neither of those things was true where Giuliano de' Medici and I were concerned.

"I beg you," he went on, "to end my torment, and to allow us to be together. I beg you to allow me to worship you as a goddess should be worshipped."

"You flatter me," I said—and indeed, a small, disgraceful part of me *was* flattered, that Giuliano should have gone to so much trouble to please me this day, that he desired me enough to make a cuckold of one of his friends. I did not like this part of myself, but it was there all the same. "But, as you well know, I am a married woman."

"I do know it well," he said. "Otherwise this would be a very different kind of proposal."

"So because you cannot have me honorably, you would have me dishonorably?" I asked. "Perhaps it is all the same to you, signore, but what of *my* honor?"

He did not speak, yet I could hear the words as loudly as if he had spoken them: *A woman has no honor.*

Perhaps not. Perhaps not in the way that men did, but I would be damned if I would not live my life as seemed best to me, to the extent that I could. If that was not honor, then I did not know what to call it.

"You . . . flatter me with your offer," I said again, trying not to let anger seep into my tone. "But I could not cast aside my marriage in such a way, not when my vows were sworn before God." I paused. "And not when my husband is a good friend of yours, signore—or so I thought. It would be wrong."

His grip on my hand tightened further. "Is not love the holiest of gifts God can give us?" he asked. "God forgives worse sinners all the time, and when a couple loves one another . . ."

I wrenched my hand from his grasp. "You presume too much, signore," I said. "I have not spoken words of love to you, nor will I. I do not speak what I do not feel."

"Simonetta," he said, and there was a touch of a whine in his wheedling tone—that of a spoiled young man who had never been denied anything he asked for. "Please. I am besotted with you. My every thought is of you. My loins ache for you. I can make love to you such as—"

I rose from my chair. "This interview is at an end," I said. "I do not wish to cause you pain, Giuliano. Truly. As I said, I consider you a friend, and a fine man, but that is all. That is all that can be between us."

He remained motionless on his knees, then slowly rose to face me. He gave a half-hearted smile. "You are loyal to your husband, I see," he said. "I suppose I cannot fault you for that, though you will rip out my heart." He stepped closer to me and kissed me on the lips;

I moved neither to encourage nor dissuade him. "Farewell, Simonetta," he said. He went to the door, but stopped, his hand on the latch, and looked back at me. "Will you not even consider it?"

Inwardly I laughed at his persistence, even as I shook my head. "My answer will not change, I am afraid."

"Would that it might, someday," he said. "Ah, God!" he burst out. "Would that I had found you before that fool Marco Vespucci!" With that, he left the room, shutting the door behind him.

I stayed where I was for a moment, standing alone in the now empty room. I let out a sound that was half sob, half laugh.

Yet the truth was, my refusal had less to do with my marriage vows and more to do with the fact that I did not wish to lie with any man but the one I loved. Even my husband, God forgive me. My illness had meant that Marco came far less often to my bed, and, sinful as it was, I could not help but be relieved. Even if it meant he found his pleasure with some French whore.

Collecting myself, I left the room and meant to return to the party, to find Marco and bid him take me home at once. Yet before I reached it, I encountered in the—blessedly empty—hallway the one man for whom I would betray my marriage vows. And the very sight of him threw me into a blinding rage.

"You!" I hissed, slamming my hands against Sandro's shoulders.

He grasped my wrists in his hands, gently. "Simonetta! Whatever is the matter?"

"How could you?" I all but shrieked.

"Simonetta, what has happened?"

I pulled away from him, beginning to laugh. "You know what has happened. You helped him in the whole sordid scheme."

His body tensed. "*Dio mio,*" he whispered. "Giuliano. What has he done?"

"What he has *done,*" I spat, "is ask me to become his mistress. To cast aside my marriage and my reputation and . . . and *fornicate* with him." I glared at him. "And you assisted him in his attempts to seduce me. You painted that banner he carried today with my likeness upon it. Why, my God . . ." I could feel the color drain from my face as a new thought occurred to me. "No doubt all of Florence thinks I am already his mistress, after that spectacle today."

"So you . . . you refused him?" Sandro asked hesitantly.

I wanted to slap him. "Of course I refused him!" I cried. "What do I look like to you? A common harlot who can be bought with poetry and pretty words and a painted banner? Am I thought to have no more virtue than—"

Sandro drew me into his arms, holding me against his chest as I shook in sorrow, in fear, in rage at this world that sought to use me as it saw fit. "Oh, Simonetta," he murmured. "I am so sorry. He asked—commanded—me to paint the banner for him. His family are my greatest patrons; I could not refuse, even though I wanted to. I had feared that he would want something like this. I know he has loved you long."

I drew back so that Sandro could see my face, now stained with tears. "I do not love him," I said quickly. I needed him to know that, more than anything. "I do not love him, Sandro. Not at all. Not in the least."

"I . . . I did not think you did," he said. I could hear the relief in his voice, and it was a balm to my worn and battered heart.

"I would not lie with a man I do not love," I said, lying my head against his shoulder again.

Sandro was silent, likely puzzling through my words. I, too, was puzzling through them. What, exactly, was I saying to him?

I drew away, suddenly cognizant of what this scene would look like if we were happened upon by anyone else—especially after I had just spurned the advances of a member of the ruling family of Florence.

If someone had happened upon us like that, they would have seen the truth. And that was the one thing that could not be known.

"I . . . I must go," I said. I was certain I looked a fright, but there was no help for it just then. "I must find Marco and have him take me home. I cannot bear to stay here any longer."

Sandro nodded, but then he caught my arm. "Wait, Simonetta. First I . . . I must know that you forgive me. For my role in this whole plot. Believe me when I say I am the last person who wanted any part in it."

"Of course," I said quickly, glad to be able to speak the words—for his sake and my own. "You, I think I could forgive anything."

And with that, I turned and left him, went back into the receiving room where a great number of guests still milled about.

I pushed my way through the crowd, craning my neck, trying to find Marco. When I did not see him, I left the room and made my way down the staircase to the courtyard, thinking that perhaps he was awaiting me there, but the courtyard was empty in the winter cold. I stepped past the statue of David and peered into the garden, only to find it empty as well, save for Judith with her sword forever raised, ready to strike down the evil in men. I might wish for such a sword, and for such courage, myself.

Feeling unspeakably weary by this time, I climbed the stairs again to the receiving room, still thronged with guests. Again, I did not see Marco. "Excuse me," I said, cornering a passing servant. "I am looking for my husband, Signor Marco Vespucci. Have you seen him?"

"Signor Vespucci left some time ago, Madonna," the man said, bowing.

"He . . . he left? You must be mistaken," I said. "I am his wife. He cannot have left without me."

The servant looked rather uncomfortable now. "I do not know why he may have done so, Madonna. All I know is that he ordered his horse to be brought 'round, and departed alone."

My heart began to pound in my ears. No more than a whisper of a thought coiled across my mind, and it was easy enough to shove aside. I was wrong. I had to be. "Very well. Thank you," I managed, and the man bowed and took his leave.

I did not know what to do. I would have to walk home, I supposed, now that Marco had taken the horse—or perhaps I might borrow one from Lorenzo? I looked about for him, or for Clarice or Lucrezia. But I spotted Sandro first. He must have come directly here after our encounter.

"Sandro!" I called out, heedless of who might overhear me using his Christian name.

He came toward me. "Did you find your husband?"

"He has left," I said, almost shaking with rage. "He has left without me."

Sandro swore. "Never mind that. I shall see you home."

"We shall walk?"

He smiled. "*Si*, Simonetta. Just like our strolls along the Arno. Your home is not far, is it?"

"No."

"Then let us go." He hesitated. "You go downstairs first, I suppose, so that we are not seen to leave together."

"Very well," I said, supposing I had to concede to this small nod to propriety, especially after the self-righteous storm I had broken over Giuliano's head just minutes ago. "Though should anyone inquire, I will be quick to tell them how my husband was so careless as to leave without his wife."

I went downstairs and to the front door, which a servant opened for me. "Do you need a conveyance brought 'round, Madonna?" he asked.

"No," I said, stepping outside. "I am just taking some air."

He bowed and closed the door.

Moments later, Sandro stepped outside and offered me his arm. We moved away from the *palazzo*, walking toward my house in silence. I knew that I should treasure these uninterrupted moments alone with him, and at any other time I would have. Yet that day and night had been too strange, too upsetting, and too confusing for me to be able to do so. The only thought on my mind was how to contend with my husband when I got home. How to contend with what he may or may not have agreed to.

Sandro and I barely spoke during the entire walk to my home. When we reached the door, I turned to him. "Thank you," I said. "Thank you for everything."

He bowed and kissed my hand, his fingers clasping mine tightly. "Anything for you, *carissima*," he said. "Anything." With that, he turned and went back up the street the way we had come, leaving me to bask in the glow of that one word. *Carissima.* Dearest one.

32

When I stepped inside, the house was dark. "Marco?" I called out tentatively.

No answer.

I felt my way down the hall, where I thought I saw some light coming from the dining room. As I drew closer, I saw a faint, flickering candlelight seeping underneath the closed door and into the dark hallway. I opened the door and stepped inside.

I did not know what I expected, if anything, but it was certainly not the sight of Marco, sitting alone at the head of the table, with only a single branch of candles lit, barely illuminating the room from their position in the center of the table. Lying on its side near Marco was an empty bottle of wine; another was in his hand.

"Marco?" I asked, stepping into the room. "What is going on? Why in the name of all the saints did you leave me alone at that banquet?"

He slammed his wine bottle down on the table, hard enough that I was surprised it did not crack. "Ah, Simonetta," he slurred. "What are you doing here?"

"I live here," I said sharply. "Now answer my questions, if you please."

He mumbled something that I could not make out.

"*Che?*" I asked, moving closer to him. "What did you say?"

"I said," he mumbled, somewhat louder this time, "why aren't you with Giuliano?"

The silence that fell over the room nearly deafened me. The roaring in my ears returned, until I realized that it was, in fact, my own heartbeat, pounding such that I thought it would explode from my chest in my anger.

"You knew," I said. The words came out dull and flat, yet they echoed in the silent room all the same.

"'Course I did," Marco said. "He asked me."

"He . . . what?"

"He asked me," Marco repeated. "Told me, more like, that he wanted my wife as his mistress."

I could hardly speak for my horror. "And you . . . what did you say?"

Marco shrugged. "What could I say? I told him he could have his way."

Red tinged the edges of my vision, nearly blinding me. Had I a knife or a dagger in my hand at that moment, I think I would have killed him, would have plunged it into his chest. "You told him he could have his way with me?" I screeched. I knew that I had probably just woken the servants, perhaps even Marco's parents, but I had never cared less about such a thing.

Let Marco's parents come to see what all the noise was about. Let them see the whoremonger their son had become.

"What could I say?" he asked again, louder this time.

"You could have said *no*!" I cried. "You could have told him to stay away from your wife, and you could have refused to agree to give me away as though I were chattel! As though I were a common prostitute!"

"What could I do, Simonetta?" he moaned, as though he hadn't heard me. "I didn't want to agree, but what choice did I have?"

"How *dare* you," I said. "How dare you give away the rights to my body, as though they are yours to give! How dare you make this devil's bargain, this whore's bargain, and not even consult me as to my wishes, my desires!"

"You are a fool, Simonetta," he said, rising from the table. "You understand nothing."

"Then *explain* it to me," I shrieked. "Explain to me how you dare—"

"I should not have to explain anything to you. It is politically expedient for me . . ." in his drunken state, he stumbled a bit over the words, "to have a wife who is the mistress of one of the Medici brothers. And, by extension, it is expedient for you as well." He laughed mirthlessly. "I thought you were smart, Simonetta, so intelligent. I thought you would have figured this out."

"No," I said. "No, I remained blissfully ignorant to the fact that my husband is no better than a common pimp, to whore out his wife for his own gain!"

Marco swiped the empty wine bottle off the table, causing it to fly against the wall and shatter. "How dare you speak to me so," he growled.

"How dare I?" I demanded. "You have no business complaining of my conduct ever again, after all this! Why, I do not know how I shall ever speak to you again, you unimaginable monster!"

He approached me and took me by the shoulders, shaking me. "Do you not see what this means for us? What this can do?" he asked. "Do you not see?"

I wrenched away from him. "I see none of that," I said. "All I see is my husband, who once professed to love me, and now only uses me for his own gain!"

For a moment he looked as though he would strike me, but then he stepped back. "And so why are you here?" he asked. He staggered back to the head of the table and took another swig of wine. "Was he done so quickly? Did he simply bend you over a table and take you? Up against a wall, perhaps, because he could not wait?" He laughed again, a cruel, empty sound. "Well, I suppose I could not blame him for not lasting that long, not his first time with you . . . even he has never been with a woman as beautiful as you before. . . ."

I stalked to him and slapped him across the face. "I said no!" I shouted. "I refused him! As you should have known I would do, since I am not some common harlot, to be bought and sold as you see fit!"

He swayed on the spot. "You . . . refused him?"

"Of course I did," I snapped.

He fell to his knees, his fingers grasping the hem of my gown. "Oh, Simonetta," he said. "You do love me. You must."

I snatched my hem away. "I did, once," I said. "But rest assured that any love I had for you is dead henceforth, after I have learned what you are capable of." I choked back my tears; I would not cry them here, not in front of him. "I cannot love you ever again, now that I learn how you truly see me." I turned to leave but stopped, looking at him, pathetically prostrate on the floor. "*You* are the fool, Marco Vespucci," I said. "For you have lost your 'political expedience' and the love and respect of your wife all in one ill-conceived wager." I left the room and went upstairs to the bedchamber where, only after locking myself in, did I allow myself to dissolve into tears.

Not long after, I heard the main door slam downstairs. Moving to the window, I saw Marco stagger out of the house and down the street.

No doubt off to visit his whore, I thought. For his wife, whom he treats as a whore, will certainly not have him. I turned away from the window, finding I did not care if he ever came back. I could only hope to be so lucky.

33

Even as winter began to somewhat lessen its grip on Florence and the surrounding Tuscan countryside, the interior of the Vespucci home may as well have been that of an ice castle. Marco was scarcely home—either to dine or to sleep—and when he was we spoke only when we absolutely had to. He had moved some of his things out of the bedchamber we had shared for our entire marriage and into one of the guest rooms. The servants—though they of course knew—did not remark upon it. No doubt some of them had overheard our row. And if Marco's parents knew the nature of our disagreement, they did not remark upon it either.

The thought that everyone knew the truth of matters in my marriage would, at one time, have embarrassed me, but no longer. I did not care if every servant in the house knew the sordid tale—I did not care if everyone in Florence knew. Let them know how my husband had sought to use me, how the darling, golden Giuliano de' Medici thought that I was his for the asking. The shame was all theirs, not mine.

What is it about beauty, I wondered one day, squinting at a bit of embroidery, which makes men think they have the right to desire you? That beauty means you automatically agree, somehow, to be coveted, to be desired? That your beauty belongs to everyone?

I had no answers for such questions.

I had run out of books in the house that I had not read, and I did not wish to venture to the Medici library for more, for fear of running into Giuliano. I knew Lorenzo would gladly send a messenger with any titles I might desire, but I did not know what titles those might be without browsing first.

So I returned to embroidery, which I had neither particularly liked nor disliked as a girl, and which I had not had much time for of late. When I could embroider no more silly patterns I begged Chiara to let me help her with the mending, so I might make myself useful. She protested at first, horrified at the thought of a lady doing her own mending, but I would not let the issue drop until she agreed to let me help her. So we stitched away and chatted mindlessly for many a chill winter day, while the throngs of men outside my window grew ever larger. Giuliano's tribute to me at the joust had, it seemed, only increased my fame.

"What do they say about me, Chiara?" I asked one afternoon, on a day when she had been to the market in the morning. "What do they say about me, out in the streets?"

Her hesitation before answering gave lie to her words when she eventually did speak. "They say nothing at all, Madonna," she said, not meeting my eyes.

"We both know that is not true, Chiara, so whatever it is, you had best tell me, before I hear it from someone else."

She paused again before answering. "They say you are the lover of Giuliano de' Medici," she said at last. "They say that the two of you are even as Venus and Adonis, blessed by the gods in your love and beauty."

I snorted. "Indeed. Have you ever noticed, Chiara, that whenever a man loves a beautiful woman, it is considered some great fairy tale of love? No one ever pays attention to how the woman feels. If she is worthy of being loved by a great or handsome man, why then, what could she do but return his love? How is anything else possible?"

"I had not thought of it that way before, Madonna," Chiara said.

I knew she was just humoring me, but I went on anyway. "Even Dante and Beatrice. Theirs is considered a great love story, a love for the ages, when, in fact, Beatrice never returns his love, not in any of the poems. What of that? Does how she felt not matter in the least? We remember only Dante's great love for her, as if that is all it takes to make a great love affair. And so she is remembered only as Dante's beloved lady. She did not have any choice in the matter."

"I suppose that is true, Madonna."

I sighed and bent back over my stitching. Where, indeed, was Sandro when I needed him? He would understand. "And what else do they say?"

"Not much of import, Madonna," she said. "They . . . some men have . . ."

"Yes, yes," I said impatiently, "out with it."

"There have been pamphlets circulating, Madonna. Some are written in support of you as the most beautiful woman in Florence, and some say that Lucrezia Donati—Signora Ardenghelli, as she is now—is more deserving of the title."

"She can have it." She can have my husband, too, if she wants him, I added silently, remembering the jealousy I had felt toward her on the night I first met her, when she and Marco had conversed so easily.

Chiara gave a small smile. She was well and truly settled in to gossip now. "I also heard that two men fought a duel a few days ago, right on the Ponte Santa Trinita. The cause of the duel is reported to be that one man insulted your beauty, and the other man could not let such an insult pass. And so they fought."

"*Dio mio,* but men are fools," I said. With that, we both went back to our mending and fell into comfortable silence.

It was some time before I was able to return to Sandro's workshop. He was finishing his commission for Santa Maria Novella and so had little time for our project, born of love and without the financial backing of a patron. I briefly considered approaching Lorenzo de' Medici myself and asking if he wished to finance the remainder of the painting, so that Sandro might be free to devote his time to it again, as I knew he dearly wanted to. But if Sandro had not already done so, he must have a good reason for it. Best to keep this particular painting private—just between Sandro and myself—for as long as possible.

Finally, one evening in early April, when his *Adoration of the Magi* was done and installed in the church, I was able to see him again. I half expected there to be some sort of awkwardness between us. When last he had seen me, I had been in quite a state; had gone from accusing him to seeking his comfort and help in a matter of minutes.

I should have known better, though. As soon as I stepped inside his workshop—the light dimming with the setting sun—he came to greet me and kissed my hand with a smile. "My dear Simonetta," he said. "How I have missed you."

My breath caught in my throat. It was just the sort of greeting one lover might give the other when they had not seen each other for some time.

"And I have missed you. More than I can say." Much as I wanted to, though, I could not go on from there; could not tell him, as much as I wished to, of all the things I had thought and pondered in weeks past and wanted to share with him. That I missed him because I did not see him every day. I missed him because he was not the one who was sharing my life, though he should have been. Instead, sighing, I turned to the business at hand.

A great canvas had been set up on a large system of supports, and I saw that he had begun to fill in some of the background color. The very center of the canvas beckoned to me, as though it had been waiting all this time for me to step into it.

I shivered, though the room was not cold, and moved to remove my clothes.

"Wait," he said, placing a gentle hand on my arm to prevent me. "There is something I must say to you, Simonetta, and I must do it before we begin our work."

"Now?" I asked stupidly, because that was all I could think to say.

"Yes. It cannot wait."

I turned to face him, my breath a bare whisper in my throat as I waited for him to proceed.

"I . . . they say in the streets that you are the mistress of Giuliano de' Medici," he said. "All of Florence accepts as fact that it is so."

Disappointment and even a bit of ire slipped into my heart at these words. "Yes, I know," I said shortly. "My maid has told me the gossip. You, of course, know that it is not true."

"Yes," he said. "And I . . . ah, Simonetta, I apologize. This is not how I wanted to start, not at all . . ." He spun away from me, his head in his hands.

Instantly my irritation vanished. I took a few steps toward him, placing a hand on his shoulder. "What is it, Sandro?" I whispered. "Whatever it is, you can tell me, *amico mio*."

He turned back to me, his eyes full of something heavy, as though he could not bear its full weight himself. "I . . . had I not been there, that day, and seen what a state you were in, perhaps I might have believed it," he said. "Not because you are a woman of easy virtue," he added hurriedly. "Not at all, never that. But because such a woman as you deserves a man of the station of Giuliano de' Medici. Even your own husband is a man in fine standing, from a well-respected family, with a fine name to offer you, and a good life to give you."

"I suppose that is true," I said, quite at a loss as to his purpose.

"But my life is not some tale of gods and goddesses, as the gossips would have it. Far from it."

"I know," he said. "I fancy that I, perhaps, know better than most. My point is . . ." He took a deep breath before continuing. "My point is that you are a woman who is entitled to the best of everything. You have all of Florence at your feet and so what I am about to say cannot possibly matter. It should not. But I must say it anyway." He looked up and met my eyes. "I am in love with you, Simonetta. I love you, I sometimes think, more than art, more than life itself. And even if every man in Florence has said such to you, I needed you to at least hear my voice saying it as well."

My whole body trembled where I stood. I wanted to dance with joy; I wanted to dissolve into a shower of tears; I wanted to kiss him, to touch him; I wanted to pray to God in thanks and to ask for forgiveness; I wanted to scream with frustration; I wanted to commence undressing and let him take me on the floor of his workshop, if he would.

I wanted to speak, but I did not know what to say.

Yet he was, it seemed, taking my silence in entirely the wrong way. "If you do not wish to stay . . . if you do not wish to continue the work anymore, or if you never wish to see me again . . . then I understand. I am sorry," he went on, fixing his gaze firmly on the floor. "But I had to say it. I could not go on without saying it any longer."

I knew that if I did not find my voice right then, all would be lost. "You must let me speak, as well," I said finally. "Know that of this chorus of voices you refer to, all of which claim to love me and desire me—know that yours is the only one I have heard, louder than the rest."

He looked up at me again, as though scarcely daring to believe it.

"Know, too," I went on, "that yours is the only voice I have cared to hear. Know that . . ." I trailed off, tears springing to my eyes, "know that I have loved you long, since before I was able to admit it to myself."

"Simonetta," he whispered. He stepped forward and cupped my face in his hands. "I have loved you since—"

"The moment you first saw my face?" I asked, then wished I had not.

He frowned for a moment, then chuckled. "No," he said. "I could see that you are beautiful. But I did not love you until that day when I first asked you to pose for me, when we spoke of philosophy and the Church and learning."

I felt as though my heart might burst from happiness.

We stayed there for a long moment, his hands gently cradling my face, our lips a mere whisper apart, breathing the very same air. He seemed to move closer to me, ever so slightly, and again I thought he was going to kiss me. I wanted him to, craving his lips to close the distance between us. I wanted to do it myself, but something held me back.

He was so near . . . we were so near . . . and there was no longer any doubt between us.

But we both knew that if we kissed at long last, we would never be able to stop there. And so we must stop before we ever started.

My tears had returned before he spoke. "It cannot be," he said, his voice ragged. "It cannot be, Simonetta. You know it as well as I do. Tell me you do."

I nodded, even as my heart screamed at me to deny it. "We cannot," I whispered. "I would not wish to endanger you. Marco, if he found out . . . I do not know what he would do. And you would lose the Medici patronage, surely, or . . ."

Sandro nodded. "Yes. And I fear for you, as well, if he were to learn you had been unfaithful. He does not seem a violent man, but . . . I cannot take such a chance with you, my beloved."

My tears were flowing freely as Sandro wrapped me in his arms, holding me tightly against his chest.

This is as close as we shall ever be to one another, I thought, weeping harder. This close, and no closer. There is no way. It is not meant to be.

But if just this once, just tonight, we might be together and have no one the wiser . . .

No. I cannot endanger Sandro and his talent in such a way. I love him enough for that.

Bitterly, I thought Marco had been willing enough to whore me out for his own gain; could he really complain, truly, if I gave myself to the man whom I loved? But he could. He could, and he would. It was not fair.

But I pushed my thoughts aside, not wanting to ruin this one, too brief moment with such vitriol.

Finally, we drew apart. "I . . . what I said before still stands," Sandro said. "If you wish to leave . . . I will understand."

Drying my tears on my sleeve, I shook my head. "I will do no such thing," I said. "You must finish this painting, Sandro. Even if no one ever sees it but the two of us. Someday we can tell the world that we loved each other, and your painting will be our message."

He nodded, and I saw that his own eyes were damp as well.

"Now, away with you," I said. "Gather your brushes and paints, maestro."

He laughed and went to do as I said.

I removed my clothes, as I had done so many times before, yet this time it was different. This time, as I stepped onto the pedestal where I took up my pose, the truth was as naked as I. This time, I marked the look of desire in his eyes as he beheld me, as he began to work, and knew I was not imagining it. This time, I let my own love and desire show on my face; I looked at him and thought of all those forbidden things I had dreamt of but knew could never be. And this time, I let him see them as well.

Perhaps, I thought, it is enough to love, and know that I am loved, truly loved, in return. Perhaps that is all I need. Perhaps it can be.

34

The next morning dawned warm and fair, as though Mother Gaia herself was in love. I met Chiara's eyes in the mirror as she dressed me and smiled. "Let us go out today, Chiara," I said. "We shall go for a stroll. It is such a lovely day."

She met my smile with one of her own. "Why, whatever you wish, Madonna. If you are certain that you are well enough."

Today, even her well-meaning concern would not irritate me. "I have never felt better," I said.

Her smile widened. "Indeed. I can see that is true. You seem exceedingly well, Madonna, and if I may . . ." She trailed off, and I nodded for her to go on. "Happier than you have been in some time."

I could feel the warmth of Sandro's words of love beneath my breastbone, where I carried them now and forever. "I am. Oh, I am."

Chiara did not, as I half expected she might, inquire as to the source of my newfound happiness. Perhaps she had made her own conclusions, and I cared not if she had. All she said was, "Then by all means, Madonna. You are right; it is a beautiful day, indeed."

Once we were both fittingly attired we left the *palazzo*, stepping out into the golden sunshine. "Perhaps a stroll along the Arno?" Chiara suggested. "Or did you have a destination in mind, Madonna?"

"I thought we might walk to Santa Maria Novella, to see Maestro Botticelli's new painting," I said. "It has been installed in one of the chapels there, I hear."

If Chiara had any private thoughts on my wish to see this painting, she kept them well to herself. "That sounds most illuminating," she said, and we set off through the narrow streets into the heart of Florence.

We were nearly sweating by the time we reached the Dominican basilica, presiding serenely over a large piazza. The exterior was adorned with geometric patterns in marble, and the interior—much like the Duomo or San Lorenzo with its plain, graceful arches—featured columns patterned in green-and-white-striped marble.

I had been in this church a few times before and had always liked it: it was simple but beautiful, and not so large that the light from its windows did not brighten and warm the interior. It was much less gloomy than the Vespucci family church of Ognissanti, where we usually attended Mass and which only let a minimum of light in.

As Chiara and I stepped inside Santa Maria Novella that day, I found that what I was looking for was not far to seek. We had just dipped our fingers in the holy water by the door when I saw the painting, adorning a chapel immediately to the left of the entrance.

I would have known Sandro's style anywhere. Eagerly I approached it, gazing up at it like a child might at a tray of sweets.

The canvas was a good size, large enough to dominate the small chapel but not, I noted, as large as the canvas for Venus. The scene of the Three Kings paying homage to the Christ Child was a riot of color, of movement, of action. Gold lined the robes of the kings, their large entourage, and the Virgin's blue mantle as well. The Kings knelt before the baby Jesus in the barn of crumbling stones and beams to which he had been consigned. The Blessed Mother, meanwhile, had eyes only for her beloved son, while Joseph watched over them both protectively.

As I stepped closer, however, I began to find some familiar figures. The king in the red robe, kneeling directly before the Christ Child with his hat cast to the ground, his face in profile—why, he looked much like the late Piero de' Medici. And in the far left corner was a handsome young man in a rich, gold-trimmed scarlet doublet, leaning on a sword with something of an arrogant expression on his face—Giuliano's face. Then, as my eyes swept back across the painting to the other side, I saw a young, dark-haired man in a black doublet regarding Christ with a thoughtful expression: Lorenzo. And, finally, in the far right-hand corner I was surprised to see a familiar blond man in a plain yellow robe, staring straight back at the viewer: Sandro.

I smiled widely, stepping so close to the painting that my gown brushed against the chapel's altar. I began to laugh, softly, almost gleefully, as I studied the figure of Sandro gazing out of the canvas, his painted eyes meeting my real ones. Slowly, I reached out and, ever so briefly, touched my fingers to his painted image.

For just a moment, I felt as though I might weep at the beauty of it all.

PART III

IMMORTAL

Florence, April 1476

35

"Good morning, Chiara," I said as she came in to open the shutters one morning.

"Good morning, Madonna," she said. "Why, it is so good to see you looking well. You are better every day!"

"I do not know if I should hope that it lasts, this time," I said. I bit my lip. "It has been so long . . ."

Chiara sighed and crossed herself. "Have faith, Madonna. God hears our prayers. Perhaps you shall finally be well again now."

"Perhaps," I said. I got up from the bed. "Send to the Medici *palazzo*, if you will, and see if Clarice would like me to visit her this afternoon."

"*Si*, Madonna." Chiara bustled away to send my message.

I heard a few cheers from the street below when the window opened, but nothing like it had been. My illness—a long one, this time, with only a few intermittent days of good health—had kept me out of the public eye for some months.

As though God were punishing me for my many sins, I was stricken again early the previous summer, soon after Sandro and I had declared ourselves to each other. Marco and I had not been able to go for a visit at the Medici villa, as we had been wont to do in years past. My world had shrunk to my bedroom; there were no more parties and dinners—or, rather, there were, but I was always too ill to attend. There had been a few frightful bouts, days of fever and coughing up blood that I scarcely remembered. Each time Marco—looking so haggard and worried, as though he still had some love for me left after all—told me both he and the doctor had thought it was the end. Yet always I rallied, always I came back from the brink. Then there would be some days—weeks, even, if I was lucky—where I felt perfectly well before the illness struck me down again.

What no one told me, but what I could divine for myself, was that I could not go on much longer like this. We had not known, when first the doctor had given his diagnosis, how much time I might have left; yet what seemed to be plain was that the consumption was determined to claim me before too much longer. It felt as though there were an hourglass lodged inside me, and the sand was beginning to trickle down at an alarming rate.

I had had much time to consider this on the days when I lay in bed, much time to rage and weep and beg and bargain with God. I had accepted my fate as fact, had accepted that my fears now seemed more likely than my hopes. Yet that did not mean that I was at peace with it.

If only I might live to see Sandro's painting. To see *The Birth of Venus*. If only I might live that long, at least.

Our work together had been very infrequent over the past year, since that one night that was seared on my memory. Perhaps only three more times after that had I gone to his workshop. We could correspond but little; only when I could send Chiara with a note—when I was well enough to write one—and when she could find him at home to deliver it in person.

Chiara returned to help me dress, and I went downstairs to break my fast. Meanwhile, I received a reply from Clarice that she would love for me to join her for the noon meal, if I desired. I sent back a reply in the affirmative, and went upstairs to gather the last few books I had borrowed from the Medici library—I would take them back and retrieve a few new ones while I was there.

Clarice, when I arrived, was well, if a bit harried from the demands put upon her by the ever-growing brood of Medici children. It had ceased to pain me quite so much that I had never conceived—no doubt due to my poor health, even if we did not know early on that this was the reason.

And perhaps it was just as well that I did not leave a child—or children—without a mother.

"You are looking quite well, Simonetta," she said, when she had passed off the children to their nursemaid. "I was so glad to receive your note. I have missed you."

"And I, you," I said. "I have been a poor friend of late, I feel."

"Do not say that," she said. "You have been ill." She reached out and took my hand. "I hope you know that I pray for you every day," she said softly. "I pray that God . . ." She broke off abruptly. "No, quite enough of that," she said briskly. "Quite enough gloom when you are looking so well."

"No, Clarice," I said. "Tell me what it is you wanted to say." I hesitated. "You may not have as much time as you think."

"Oh, Simonetta, no," she said. "Do not say that. I only meant—"

"Please, *amica,*" I said. "Do not play false with me. When I am not ill, Marco acts as though I am as well as I have ever been, and . . . somehow that is more grating than the consumption itself. Let us speak plainly to each other."

And so Clarice, with her quiet strength, took a deep breath and looked me straight in the eye. "Every day I beg God not to take my only friend," she said. "Because you are, you know, Simonetta. The only true friend I have had since I left Rome."

This time it was I who reached out and took her hand. "Then perhaps God will see fit to spare me after all, since it is you who beseeches Him," I said. "For I know of no better, kinder soul than you."

She smiled, blinking away tears. "If He hears any of my prayers, I hope it is this one." She shook her head slightly. "Now, though, it is enough of that. No doubt one day when we are old women together we shall look back on this day and laugh."

I smiled, releasing her. "Perhaps," I said.

I spoke the words, even though I did not believe them.

36

Later that night, I began to wonder if I should write to Sandro. I had last had word from him some weeks ago, when I was still ill, and thought he should know that I was recovered—for the time being, anyway. If there was a space of time when I might pose for him, we must take it while we could.

I went into my dressing room and opened the locked drawer in my dressing table. I pulled out Sandro's latest note and smoothed it out to read again. I knew I should burn such correspondence, but I could not bear to be rid of his letters right away. I had to save them for a short time, at least.

He had written that he hoped I would get well soon; that he prayed for my recovery. He wished that he could visit me, but knew Marco would not take kindly to such an overture. He ended by saying that he had continued work on the painting when he was able, and had begun to work on some of the other figures. Venus, he wrote, could wait for me.

Suddenly, Marco's voice came from the doorway. "Simonetta, Chiara says that—"

But I was never to know what Chiara said. I jumped when I heard him so near, and tried to hide the note back in the drawer, an instinct that only served to arouse his suspicion.

"What do you have there?" he asked, stepping closer to where I sat at the dressing table.

"Nothing," I said, trying to slam the drawer shut. "Just some old letters from home."

"Then why are you hiding them from me?" he asked.

"I am not hiding them—you startled me, that is all . . ."

"Then let me see," Marco said, catching the drawer before I could close it. He pulled out the note I had just been reading and quickly read through it. "This . . . this is from the painter?" he asked in disbelief. "He writes to you?"

"No—that is, not regularly, he just wanted to wish me well, since I've been ill, as you see yourself," I said. "We correspond about when I might come to pose for him, look there . . ."

"Then why lie to me, Simonetta, if it is as innocent as all that?" he asked. "'I have been on my knees day and night praying for your recovery' . . . that sounds a bit familiar, does it not?"

"He is a friend, that is all," I said. "I have known him for many years, as you well know—oh, Marco, no! Just leave it alone!"

But he had pulled out the rest of the contents of the drawer—another two notes from Sandro and, at the bottom, the sketch he had given me of his vision for *The Birth of Venus.*

Marco stared at it for a long time, and I could see by the way the paper shook that his hands were trembling. "This," he said at last. "He drew this."

It was not a question, and so I did not feel the need to answer him. I remained silent.

"Is this . . . is this the great, mysterious painting you are helping him with?" Marco demanded, his voice low. "This . . . this pornography? *This* is what you are posing for?"

Still I did not speak.

Marco slammed his hand down on the dressing table, and the

sharp noise made me jump again. "Is it?" he shouted. "You have been posing for him without your clothes on all this time?"

"I . . ." I began, not knowing what to say.

"Do not bother to deny it—I can see that this was drawn from life," he said, brandishing the paper in my face. "I know your body, after all, do I not? I am your husband. I am the only one who has any right to see it. But now I see that I am a cuckold after all, and that this painter has drawn what he has intimate knowledge of, though he has no right."

"How dare you," I said, rising from my chair. "He has no such knowledge. I have posed for him, yes; and in the nude, yes; but I have not lain with him."

But Marco seemed not to hear me. "You who were so high and mighty, who rejected Giuliano de' Medici out of hand, and called me a pimp—you are a whore after all!" he cried. "One of the richest men in Florence was too good for you, it seems, so you have sullied yourself with a common artist from the gutter."

"How *dare* you speak to me so!" I cried. "You are wrong, wrong about everything! Sandro is not my lover, we have never—"

"Oh, it is *Sandro,* is it?" he demanded. "You know him well enough to use his Christian name, at least."

"Yes, I do, because he is my friend, as I told you," I said. "I call Lorenzo de' Medici by his Christian name; do you accuse me of taking him as a lover, as well? Do you think I am betraying you and my friend Clarice all at once?"

Marco shook his head wildly. "That is not the point. *Dio mio,* that you should still deny . . . when I have the evidence right in my hand . . ." He glared down at the sketch once more, then crumpled it in his fist.

"No!" I gasped, lurching toward him.

He drew away, staring at me in astonishment as he stepped back out into the bedchamber. "Your actions belie your words," he said. "Can you truly not see that?" He opened his fist and looked at the now crushed drawing. "What woman lets a man other than her lover see her like this?"

"As incredible as it seems to you, it is true," I shot back. "I would swear on whatever holy relic you want that I am not Sandro's lover, Marco. Yet it does not seem that would help. You are determined to see me, your own wife, as a whore, even though I vow to you that it is otherwise!"

"Women are liars, all," he growled. "It has been thus ever since Eve tempted Adam in the garden."

I threw up my hands, nearly screaming in frustration. "Suddenly so pious, Marco! If you had had your way, I would have been a whore at your own hand long ago. And now you dare—"

"Enough!" he shouted, causing me to flinch. "I will not stand for you to speak to me so. This is how it shall be, Simonetta. Henceforth, you do not leave the house without an escort—either myself or my manservant. That maid of yours is not to be trusted; no doubt she has been assisting you in your harlotry all along."

"Indeed!" I cried. "I will not be condescended and dictated to as though I were a senseless child! I am—"

"And most importantly," he continued, "you are never to see that painter again, am I understood?"

"I will not—"

"You will do as I say!" Marco cut me off before I could go any further. "You have proven that you cannot be trusted, and so you will abide by my will as though it is law. I am your husband and I say that my word *is* the law."

"Get out!" I shrieked, beyond all patience, beyond trying to reason with him and make him see his error. "Get out of my chambers this instant! I cannot bear the sight of you, you false friend!"

Surprisingly, he did in fact move to leave. "No doubt it is best that I am gone before I do something I will regret," he snarled. "But you will heed me, Simonetta, or, so help me God, you will be sorry."

With that, he stalked out, slamming the door of the bedchamber so hard behind him that the very walls rattled.

I remained where I was, trembling with rage and anguish. Moments later, I heard the main door slam downstairs. I hurried to the window just in time to see Marco stalk off down the street, practically running in his haste to be away from the house. From me.

It had come to this. Our marriage, our life together, all our hope and love and pain and struggles, had come to this. Who knew if we would ever put it right? Though I had stopped loving Marco long ago—if indeed I had ever loved him in the true sense of the word—it filled a part of me with sadness all the same.

We might not have the time to put it right. *I* might not have the time to put it right.

But the rest of me could not care. The majority of my heart did not want to set eyes on Marco ever again did not want to have to put up with this farce of a marriage for another instant.

Did not want to remain in this house—his house—for another moment, even though he was not here. Even though he had forbidden me from leaving. What did I care for that now? Did he mean for me to spend the rest of my life—whatever was left of it—trapped in here like a prisoner?

I refused.

Scarcely thinking about what I was doing, I strode back into the dressing room and pulled out a cloak. I exited the bedchamber, flinging open the door Marco had slammed in my face. I half fell, half flew down the stairs in my haste to be away.

I had not taken for myself the one thing, the only thing in all my life that I had truly wanted, truly yearned for, despite multiple temptations. I had resisted, and yet I was to be blamed and scorned and punished and shamed just the same as if I had not.

Might I not have him, then? Might I not make myself happy, while I still had the chance?

Just as I reached the front door, I heard a man clear his throat behind me. "Ah . . . Madonna Vespucci . . ."

I spun around to see Giovanni, Marco's manservant, step into the entryway. "Yes?" I asked impatiently. "What is it?"

"*Allora*, you see, your husband, he . . . he has given me instructions that I am not to let you leave the house," he said. "Or that, if you tell me where you are going, I am to accompany you."

I laughed at him outright before turning back to the door. "This is absurd, Giovanni. I shall leave this house if I choose to."

"I . . . I am afraid I cannot let you, Madonna. Your husband, he—"

I whirled around to face him. "Oh, you cannot, can you?" I demanded. "Tell me, Giovanni, what are you going to do to stop me? Will you lay hands on me, and bodily restrain your master's wife from leaving her own house? Is Marco's temper so fearsome that you would mistreat me so, so as not to disobey him?"

His moment of hesitation told me all I needed to know.

"No," I spat. "I thought not."

With that, I yanked open the door and stepped out into the chill evening air.

37

I had never been out alone in the streets of Florence after dark before. I should have been nervous and on edge, jumping at every sound and shadow, yet my mind had no space for such things. I nearly ran the entire way to Sandro's workshop, so intent was I on getting there.

A part of me wondered what I would do if he was not home, or if his apprentices and assistants were there with him.

Yet it was almost as though he knew I was coming, as though he had been waiting for me. When I arrived he was all alone, working on a painting with candles lit all around him—some commission or other.

I stepped inside without knocking, and he turned at the sound of the door opening. I must have looked quite a sight, for he dropped his paintbrush on the floor with a clatter at the sight of me. "Simonetta," he said, concerned. "What—Are you well? Is everything all right? What are you doing here?"

"Yes, I am well," I said. "And no, everything is not all right. Nothing is." I drew a deep, shuddering breath. "But it can be."

We stared at each other for a long moment, then I moved forward toward him, even as he came to meet me. I flung myself into his arms, and his lips descended on mine as he crushed me to him. My mouth opened underneath his, and I moaned deep in my throat as his tongue slid hungrily into my mouth.

It had been so long that we had resisted, so long that we had gone without so much as touching each other in any intimate way. So long that we had gone without even a kiss. Now, finally, that long-awaited kiss had come, and I felt that the world around me was suddenly rendered in even more brilliant colors, as though we had stepped into one of his paintings and away from our own imperfect world.

Yet even such a kiss was not enough. Mouths still working, I shrugged off my cloak and let it fall to the floor. He lifted me easily in his arms, and I wrapped my legs around his waist as he took me to a small pallet against the wall—no doubt a place where one of his assistants slept when they worked late into the night.

But as he laid me down on the pallet, sudden doubt overtook me, an almost paralyzing fear—not for myself, but for him. "Wait," I cried out. "I . . ." I struggled to catch my breath, to form the words I knew I needed to say. "If we do this, we are both adulterers," I said. "And even if no one ever knows of it, your soul will be—"

He leaned over me and placed a finger across my lips. "Don't," he said roughly. "I do not care, not if you do not. It is worth my immortal soul to spend one night with you."

We spoke no more.

It had been too long that we had waited, and we could wait no longer. I hastily unlaced his breeches, and he pushed them down even as one hand pushed my skirts up around my waist. His mouth met mine again as he lowered himself atop me. I clutched him to me hungrily and arched against him as he thrust into me. I cried aloud with joy and pleasure and relief simply at the feel of him inside me.

He moaned as he entered me, as he began to move within me. "Simonetta," he said, his voice ragged. "Simonetta, my Simonetta."

I wrapped my legs tightly around his waist, drawing him deeper and deeper inside me, feeling the warmth building within me, ready to shatter me. "Yes," I sighed. "Yes, Sandro. Please."

In the next instant, pleasure wracked my body, a pleasure so acute and consuming it was almost painful. My voice felt ripped from my throat in an animalistic cry, and I did not care who may have heard, nor could I have stopped it had I tried.

As I surfaced, I felt him shudder against me as he reached his own pleasure, heard my name as he groaned it in my ear. Then he was still; we were both still for a long moment as I held him to me as tightly as I had as we made love, holding him inside me. Then he lifted himself off of me and rolled onto his back, wrapping his arms around me and drawing me tightly against him, as though he could not bear to let me go. I laid my head on his chest, and I could hear the rapid pounding of his heartbeat, not yet slowing down.

I do not know how much time passed before he spoke. "Oh, Simonetta," he said. "My Venus, my goddess. What have we done?"

I drew away slightly so that I could see his face. "Do not tell me you regret this."

"Never," he said immediately. "And though I might burn in hell for it, it was worth it. I shall laugh in Lucifer's face when he greets me."

I smiled at the image, blasphemous though it was.

"No," he went on. "That is not what I meant at all. I mean that I . . . I have been with women before. But never was it like this."

My eyes, inexplicably, filled with tears. "Nor for me."

He kissed my neck. "It is because neither of us has ever loved anyone the way we love each other," he said. "They call it the act of love, but it has never truly been so for me until this moment."

"Nor will it ever be for me again," I said, "unless I am with you."

We lay there for some time, our arms and legs loosely entwined, hands lazily roaming over each other's bodies. Finally, I drew myself into a sitting position. "You know, Sandro, it is not quite fair," I said.

He propped himself up on one arm. "What is not?"

I reached out and pushed a lock of hair out of his eyes. "Why, you have seen me wearing nothing at all," I said. "Many times. And yet I have not had the same privilege. I have not seen you."

An irresistibly alluring smile curled around his lips, the one that always transformed his already handsome face. The smile that I loved so much. He leaned forward and kissed me, then rose from the pallet. "Come, then," he said. "And I shall show you all you wish to see." He pulled me to my feet, kissing me again. "And it is only right that I make love to you in a proper bed," he said, drawing me through the workshop and toward the staircase in the back, snatching a branch of candles off one of the tables in the workshop as we went.

I giggled. "That improper bed seemed to serve us well enough."

He led me into his bedroom at the top of the stairs. It was a simple, small room, the size of my dressing room. A large, roughly hewn bed took up most of the space, but even here sketches and bits of parchment were scattered all about.

I did not care. Dante had never visited such a paradise as that room was to me.

He shut the door behind us, though there was no one to discover us. Somehow, just that simple act made everything seem much more intimate: we were alone together in his bedroom, a room that I had never before entered but had imagined many times. Just us.

He set the candles down on a small table beside the bed. "As you wished," he said, smiling. He pulled his shirt off over his head and dropped it on the floor. The flickering candles created shadows in all the lines and planes of his lean chest. I stepped closer to him and ran my hands over his bare skin, feeling the hard muscles beneath.

He drew in his breath sharply as my hands touched him. "Careful now," he murmured. "Or I shall never be able to remove the rest."

He pushed down his breeches, and I saw that his manhood was

already swollen and erect again. I could not resist; I stepped closer again and took him in my hand.

He groaned. "Simonetta, please."

I smiled and stepped back, slowly withdrawing my hand. "Very well," I said. "Though this time, I confess that I shall need your help."

He chuckled, and I turned my back to him so that he could unlace my dress. I let it slide to the floor and faced him again. I drew my shift off over my head, as I had done so many times before in his presence.

Yet this time was different, still. This time his eyes took me in as carefully, as hungrily as ever, but I knew that soon his hands would trace the path his eyes had taken. I closed my eyes, feeling heat bloom between my legs.

When I opened them, he was kneeling at my feet. "My goddess, my Venus," he whispered again. "I worship you just as surely as if you were a goddess in truth, and not mortal at all."

"No," I whispered. "I am as mortal as you, Sandro. And perhaps we are luckier than the gods, for we are but a simple man and woman who love each other."

He rose to his feet and stepped close to me, and this time his hands traveled slowly all over my body, cupping my breasts, moving down my waist to my back, my buttocks. His hands traced fire in my skin as they moved. He toyed with my hair, letting it slip through his fingers like silk.

It was everything I had imagined and dreamt of so many times, and better. And I could not bear much more of it. I stepped away from him, moving toward the bed. "Do not make me wait much longer, please," I whispered. I was as hungry for him as I had been when I had first walked in his door. More so.

I lay back on the bed and drew him down to me, but he was determined to torture me a bit more. He kissed my neck, my breasts; his mouth closed around one nipple, teasing it with his tongue as I gasped and writhed beneath him, then he switched to the other one even as he moved one hand between my legs, and he slid two fingers inside me. Sweat broke out on my skin, and I thought I could bear it no longer when he suddenly withdrew his hand. "No," I moaned. "Oh, please."

He eased himself atop me, and this time he slowly slid into me, keeping his eyes locked on mine as he did so. Our gazes never broke even as he moved within me, gently at first, then faster as his breath and mine began to come in short gasps.

Not once did we look away as our bodies moved together toward ecstasy, so that it seemed that he was not simply making love to me, nor I to him. We were making love to each other's souls, could see each other deeply and clearly as we joined completely.

We reached our pleasure at the same time, and it ripped through me with even more force than before. I saw my pleasure reflected in his eyes, watched his own move through him. We cried out together, our voices mingling in one perfect moment that seemed to go on and on, and even so it was over all too quickly.

Oh, far too quickly.

Afterward, he held me as I wept silently. I did not need to explain. He understood.

We slept for a time. When I awoke, rain was pounding on the walls and roof of the building. I wanted to huddle back within the blankets; curl up against Sandro's side and stay there. I wanted to never leave, and damn the consequences.

Yet I knew all too clearly what the consequences would be, now that my haze of love and desire no longer blinded me. If I did not return home, Marco would look for me here first. And nothing good could come of that. Not for me, not for Sandro.

When I returned home, Marco—if indeed he was there and not out whoring—would no doubt know where I had been, but he would have no proof. And I would never say a single word. I would never speak of this night to anyone: not Marco, nor my confessor, nor to God himself. It belonged to me and Sandro and no one else.

Quietly, I slipped from the bed and groped about in the dark for my clothes. The candles had burned out long since, so it was something of a struggle to get into my shift once I found it, before my eyes adjusted somewhat to the dark.

"Simonetta," Sandro said in a whisper behind me. "What are you doing?"

"Dressing," I said simply. "Help me, please." I stepped into my dress and turned my back to him so that he might do up the laces.

Reluctantly, he rose from the bed and did as I asked. "You are not leaving?" he said.

"I have to."

"It is pouring rain outside, Simonetta," he said. "You will be soaked, and then you will take ill again. Stay. Stay until it passes."

I could barely look at him. "No. I cannot."

"Please, Simonetta. Do not make me beg you."

I sighed and turned to face him. "I must get home, or else it will not go well for either of us," I said. "Marco . . . he would know where to find me."

Even in the dark I could see the questions in Sandro's eyes, but thankfully he did not ask them. "Then at least let me accompany you. It is not safe for a woman alone out on the streets at this time of night."

I shook my head. "No. If we reach my house and Marco were to see you . . ." I shuddered. "I have never known him to be a violent man, Sandro, but even so I do not want to think what he would do."

"I do not care about my safety," he said. "I care only about yours. He will never see me, and I will make sure you are home safe."

"No!" I cried. I could not tell him the other reason I was refusing so vehemently. If I did not leave now, leave him behind, I was afraid I would never be able to do so. "No. Please, do not ask it of me."

"Simonetta . . ."

"No," I said again. I took his face between my hands. "This has been the most sublime, perfect night of my life. We cannot ruin it with an argument."

I kissed him, and he kissed me back, deeply. Then I pulled away and made for the door, going back downstairs.

In the dim light of the dying fire in the workshop, I found my cloak on the floor and settled it about my shoulders. Sandro followed me right to the door.

"When will we see each other again?" he asked, cupping my face in his palms.

My eyes filled with tears. "I do not know. I do not know, my love."

He kissed me one last time, desperately, and then I broke away and stepped outside and into the driving rain, knowing that if I did not do it then, I would never be able to.

38

The rain soaked me to the skin within minutes, and at first I welcomed it, letting it wash the scent of sex and sweat from my skin so Marco would not know where I had been and what I had done. But I began to shiver when I was just out of sight of Sandro's workshop. It was a chill April night, that time of year when spring is in every ray of sun during the day, but winter still seeks to claw its way back after dark. I began to cough, as though the rain had settled into my lungs and I needed to expel it.

The walk between my own house and Sandro's workshop had never before seemed so long. When finally I dragged myself onto the right street, I could have wept with relief, yet I did not even have the energy for that. It took me a few tries to pull open the door, as my hands were slick with water and trembling violently with cold.

I managed to get upstairs to my room which, of course, was empty. "Chiara," I croaked. Just the effort of using my voice caused me to begin coughing again. "Chiara!" I called again, only slightly louder this time.

She came bustling into the room, wiping sleep from her eyes. "Madonna?" she asked, sounding confused. "What has happened?

Oh, my . . ." she said, as she took in my wet cloak, my soaked hair and clothes, my glistening skin. "*Dio mio,* Madonna, you are nearly blue with cold. Where have you been? Oh, no matter. Come here, we must get those wet things off. Quickly, take that cloak off, and I will get you something dry." She went into my dressing room and came out with a thick woolen shift. I dropped my sodden cloak to the floor, but that was as much as I could do.

"Oh, Madonna," Chiara said. With deft fingers, she removed my wet clothes and dried my naked body with a length of cloth, as though I were a child after a bath. Then she pulled the shift over my head and led me to the bed. "I shall get the extra coverlet," she said. "You shall be warm in no time."

I only remembered shivering.

I had thought before that each bout of illness was God punishing me for one of my many sins—for loving a man other than my husband, for desiring that man, for not cleaving to my husband, for vanity. Whether I was right or wrong, it seemed fitting that the worst illness yet would come upon me after my gravest transgression.

Still I did not regret it. In those moments when I was lucid enough to consider it, I knew that I would do it all over again.

It is worth my immortal soul to spend one night with you, Sandro had said. I had not told him then, but I felt the same way. It began to seem as though it had been a mistake not to tell him.

I spent several days—I cannot say how long—in a haze of fever, sometimes waking myself with the force of my own coughing. I saw flashes of blood, black against the sheets. Chiara's face, then Marco's, then Sandro's, always Sandro's, came to me. Sometimes when I awoke, I was freezing and thought myself still out in the rain; at other times I burned so hot that I thought I was already in Lucifer's hellfire.

I know Marco was there sometimes; I know the doctor was as well. Chiara hovered over me always, bathing my brow with cool cloths and bringing me water and diluted wine. If I awoke long enough to speak to anyone, it was her.

Yet one night when I awoke, it was no mystery what had roused me: two men's voices, arguing loudly and strenuously.

"I forbid it, do you hear me? You scum who has laid hands on my wife, who has defiled her with your filthy drawings."

"You may kill me yourself if you like, Vespucci; I care not. Just let me see her first!"

Sandro. Even in the throes of a fever I could not mistake his voice.

"You would need to kill me first," Marco shot back. "Only when you step over my dead body shall you enter her chamber."

Slowly, as my wits returned to me, I realized they must be just outside my bedchamber. Sandro must have forced his way in and gotten this far before Marco intercepted him.

"Do not tempt me, signore. You cannot keep me from her."

"Marco," I called past my ravaged throat, through dry lips.

Both voices fell silent.

"Marco," I called again.

He opened the door and stepped inside. "Simonetta? You are awake?"

Even after everything, it nearly broke my heart to see the pain and sorrow on his face. He looked as though he had aged ten years since that night when he had found Sandro's sketch of me, when we had argued. It was the last time we had really spoken, I realized. "Marco, please," I said. Over his shoulder, I could glimpse Sandro through the open door. "Let him in. I wish to see him."

Marco's eyes hardened. "Simonetta, please. This is hardly—"

"Please," I said. "This is the last thing I shall ask of you."

At that, his expression crumpled, and he dropped his head into his hands. "Very well," he said. Abruptly he turned and stalked out of the room. "You may go in," I heard him say shortly to Sandro. "She wishes to see you."

Sandro stepped into the room, closing the door behind him. He rushed to my side, sitting on the bed next to me and taking my hand in his. "Simonetta, my Simonetta," he said. I could hear the tears in his voice.

I closed my eyes, recalling when he had sighed my name as he moved within me. It seemed like it was decades ago, and yet it was one of the last things that I remembered clearly. If I could have no other memories left to me, I thought, then that one would be enough. "Sandro," I said, my fingers curling around his. "You are here. You knew."

"I did, my love," he said. "I knew. Nothing could have kept me from your side."

"I have wanted to see you," I said. "You must promise me something."

His strong hand tightened on mine. "Anything."

I opened my eyes, taking in his beloved, handsome face: his wide eyes, his beautiful features, his tousled blond hair. "You must promise me that you shall finish the painting," I said. "*The Birth of Venus.*"

"Oh, Simonetta," he said, his emotions nearly choking him. "I . . . I do not know if I can. Not without you."

"You must," I said, raising my voice. "You must, for me. It will be a testament of our love. So that all the world might know. Remember? So that no one will ever forget. Promise me."

Tears slid freely down his cheeks. He nodded. "I promise, Simonetta. I swear on my life that I shall do it, for you. So that you may live forever, as I told you once that you would."

I closed my eyes again. "Thank you. Thank you, my love."

We both fell silent for a moment, then I opened my eyes when he spoke again. "When I die," he said softly, so softly that if he had been any farther away, I would not have heard him, "I shall be buried at your feet. It will be my last wish."

I smiled and let my eyes drift closed. "I shall await you in Elysium, my love. I shall save a place for you. I will wait for you there."

When I awoke again, he was gone. And I wept.

I do not know how many days have passed since Sandro came. I wish that I might have slipped away with him there beside me, holding my hand, yet I was denied that comfort. If that is to be the punishment for everything I have done, so be it.

I drift in and out of dreams, though I cannot always tell that they are so. I dream of *The Birth of Venus,* dream that I stand before the finished canvas with Sandro at my side, and that I weep at its beauty. I dream myself into another life, one where I am not ill, one where I am not the daughter of a noble family from Genoa, one where I am not Marco Vespucci's wife. In this life, I am a simple Tuscan peasant, and free to marry Sandro for love. I keep his house and tidy his workshop, and we make love every day and he holds me all through the night.

I see our children, beautiful and golden-haired, the children that we would have had together, the children I was never meant to have with Marco. I see them grow up to be artists and poets and statesmen, and there are tears in my eyes, tears of pride and of sorrow for these magnificent children that never came to be.

I pose for Sandro, and he creates the greatest works of art that the world has ever seen. This last I know, at least, is true.

And now I have woken from these dreams, from these other lives I've lived even as I am dying, and I am alone, save for one figure. For Death is beckoning to me at last, and I see now that he is blind: blind to my beauty, blind to my youth, blind to what my destiny should have been; blind to all but my soul and, no doubt, the sins that mar it. But I am not afraid.

Sandro promised me that I would live forever.

AUTHOR'S NOTE

Simonetta Cattaneo Vespucci died on the night of April 26, 1476, at the age of 22 or 23 (her exact date of birth is not known) of consumption, which we today call pulmonary tuberculosis. She was indeed regarded as the most beautiful woman in Florence and, according to some, in all of Italy. Thousands followed her funeral procession through the streets of Florence, where her open coffin was carried so that the populace could view her famed beauty one last time—a fact that strikes me as incredibly morbid. She is buried in the Vespucci's parish church of the Ognissanti, which still sits on the bank of the river Arno and is open to the public.

Marco Vespucci remarried shortly after Simonetta's death. He was a cousin of Amerigo Vespucci, the famed explorer who gave his name to the New World.

Clarice Orsini de' Medici also died of consumption, in July 1487. While her relationship with Lorenzo is nowhere described as being a particularly loving one, they did have ten children together, six of whom survived to adulthood. Their son Giovanni de' Medici would go on to become Pope Leo X, the first of two Medici popes.

Nowhere in my research did I come across any explicit evidence that Clarice and Simonetta were close friends, but they would certainly have known each other, and so I took the liberty of making them so in my story.

Lorenzo de' Medici was, as I have described him here, a true patron of the arts and of learning, cultivating the careers of many artists and writers—Leonardo da Vinci and Michelangelo Buonarroti being the most notable among them. His political genius was perhaps unmatched in his age, and all these factors combined to give him the nickname of "Magnifico"—or Lorenzo the Magnificent. He reigned as the de facto ruler of republican Florence until his death in 1492, at the age of just 43. Like his father Piero, he was plagued by ill health in his later years, notably by gout, which ran in the Medici family.

Lorenzo's eldest son, Piero, attempted to take the reins of power after his father's death, but he lacked his father's sharp intelligence and political savvy. Piero and the rest of the Medici family were soon driven from the city of Florence altogether for a time by the Dominican friar Savonarola, who had for years been preaching against the Medici family in particular, as well as against the sinful excesses, artwork, pagan learning, and decadence of Florence—in essence, against everything that made the Renaissance what it was. In the absence of the Medici family, he briefly ruled Florence as a theocracy, and famously hosted Bonfires of the Vanities, in which citizens were encouraged to throw their worldly goods on the flames: clothing, works of art, books, jewelry, and furniture were among the things Florentines burned at Savonarola's behest. Sandro Botticelli himself burned at least one of his own paintings on such a bonfire. In true Florentine style, however, the people soon grew tired of living without their books and fine clothes and artwork, and Fra Savonarola was eventually ousted—with a little help from Pope Alexander VI, who had the friar burned at the stake for openly defying and preaching against the Vatican on more than one occasion.

Oddly enough, Giuliano de' Medici died exactly two years to the day after Simonetta's death—April 26, 1478. He was stabbed to death during Mass in the Duomo, as part of a plot that became known as the Pazzi conspiracy. The Pazzi were a rival Florentine banking family, and after a series of political and business-related slights at the hands of the Medici, they decided to eliminate their rivals once and for all—with the tacit blessing of Pope Sixtus IV, who had long been feuding with Lorenzo. The assassins succeeded in dispatching Giuliano, but were not able to kill his brother, who was their true target. Lorenzo escaped with only a few wounds thanks to his friends and supporters who managed to fend off the attackers, and in the days following ruthlessly punished those who were found to have any part in the plot.

The exact nature of Giuliano de' Medici's relationship with Simonetta Vespucci is unknown. Some sources say that she was his mistress; others that he was her lover only in the more chaste, courtly sense; and others simply concede that we will never know for certain. For my story, I made the choice that I thought made the most sense based on how I had written Simonetta as a character.

And writing about Simonetta was both a joy and challenge. Very little information is available about her; she is quite literally a footnote, or mentioned in only a sentence or two, in many books on the period or on the Medici family. At times this was very frustrating, as I could not confirm certain simple facts one hundred percent—where her wedding to Marco took place being one such example. However, this was also very liberating in many ways, as I could build her story around those few facts and events that I did know for certain—the joust where Giuliano carried a banner of her painted by Botticelli did actually take place, for instance—and fill in the blanks with my imagination. In those instances where I was presented with conflicting information I simply chose the version I liked best or that best suited the story. This book is, after all, a work of historical fiction, and with fiction comes many freedoms.

Sandro Botticelli, of course, went on to paint many of the great masterpieces of Western artwork, including, of course, *The Birth of Venus* and *Primavera,* which are no doubt his two best known works. He was also one of the artists commissioned for the paintings on the walls of the Sistine Chapel. The women in many of his paintings look alike, and so it is speculated that he went on painting Simonetta his whole life. That she is the woman pictured in *The Birth of Venus* is accepted as fact by many, though some art historians disagree and claim that this is nothing more than romantic nonsense. Obviously, I thought it made for a pretty good story.

All of the artwork described in this novel is real, except for the scandalous portrait of Lucrezia Donati that Botticelli was said to have painted for Lorenzo de' Medici—that is a juicy rumor of my own invention (though Lucrezia Donati was in fact Lorenzo's mistress). In the novel most of the artwork is in its original place as well—the Donatello statues of David and Judith did grace the Medici family's courtyard and garden, respectively. Botticelli's *Adoration of the Magi* was indeed commissioned for the church of Santa Maria Novella and was placed in a chapel near the entry there. Where I have taken liberties, though, is with the timeline of when some of Botticelli's works were painted. The first painting for which Simonetta poses is Botticelli's *Portrait of a Lady* (which is also widely believed to be of Simonetta Vespucci) and which was not, in reality, painted until sometime between 1478 and 1490—after Simonetta's death. As well, *The Birth of Venus* was not completed until 1484, as I describe in the novel's prologue. Whether Botticelli ever asked Simonetta to pose for the start of such a work during her lifetime is unknown, but I like to think that he did, and that she accepted.

Sandro Botticelli did in fact request to be buried at Simonetta's feet, and on his death in 1510 his wish was granted. Many visit his burial place in the Church of the Ognissanti today and leave flowers, messages, and notes, without knowing that his great muse is buried just feet away.

When I originally had the idea to write about Simonetta Vespucci, it was going to be a story about her as Botticelli's muse and Giuliano de' Medici's mistress. Yet some preliminary Googling led me to the above fact—that Botticelli had requested to be buried at her feet, and actually was—and immediately I knew that this was the story I had to tell: that of her relationship with Botticelli, whatever the truth of it may have been. That he is buried with her certainly suggests more than a simple artist-muse attachment, but we will never know the truth for sure. And that, of course, is where historical fiction comes in.

Many of the paintings described in this novel—*The Birth of Venus, The Adoration of the Magi,* and Botticelli's two panels telling the story of Judith—are located today in the Uffizi Gallery in Florence, along with many other Botticelli paintings and the works of other Renaissance masters. I absolutely recommend visiting the Uffizi if you are able, as its collection is absolutely unparalleled and contains some of the most beautiful works of art in the world. For my American readers, if a trip to Florence is out of the question, I highly recommend paying a visit to the National Gallery in Washington, D.C. They have an incredible collection of Italian Renaissance art, including many paintings by Botticelli, the only Leonardo da Vinci painting in North America, and busts of Lorenzo and Giuliano de' Medici. And, as the gallery is part of the Smithsonian, admission is free. I happened to visit with a friend while working on this novel and didn't know much about their collection; I was in Italian art history nerd heaven when I walked into that wing and saw the embarrassment of riches on the walls.

For further reading on the Medici family, Botticelli and his work, or the Italian Renaissance in general, I recommend the following books, which are just a few of those I consulted in writing this novel.

Basta, Chiara. *Botticelli* (Art Classics Series). New York: Rizzoli, 2005.

Frieda, Leonie. *The Deadly Sisterhood: A Story of Women, Power, and Intrigue in the Italian Renaissance*. New York: HarperCollins, 2013.

Lee, Alexander. *The Ugly Renaissance: Sex, Greed, Violence and Depravity in an Age of Beauty*. New York: Doubleday, 2013.

Lucas-Dubreton, J. *Daily Life in Florence in the Time of the Medici*. Trans. A. Lytton Sells. New York: Macmillan, 1960.

Tinagli, Paola. *Women in Italian Renaissance Art: Gender, Representation, Identity*. Manchester, UK: Manchester University Press, 1997.

Unger, Miles J. *Magnifico: The Brilliant Life and Violent Times of Lorenzo de' Medici*. New York: Simon & Schuster, 2008.

ACKNOWLEDGMENTS

This book was not an easy one to write for many reasons, and as a result there are many people to whom I owe my thanks now that it has all finally come together.

First, of course, my infinite thanks to Lindsay Fowler, friend, critique partner, and writing therapist. Your input has made this book orders of magnitude better than it was, and your friendship has made my life better than it was, too. And thanks for all of the *Hamilton*, *Game of Thrones*, and *Pirates of the Caribbean* reference-laden banter.

All my thanks and appreciation to my fabulous, one-in-a-million agent, Brianne Johnson, for loving Simonetta as much as I do and for believing in this book even in those moments when I didn't. Your support, insights, and pep talks keep me going when the going gets tough. I can't thank you enough for all that you do.

I am so, so fortunate in my editor, Vicki Lame. She is the actual, literal best. Thanks for completely getting my work and giving me the best notes so that it can shine brighter than I ever thought it could. Let's do this again sometime!

Thank you to the whole team at St. Martin's for being so supportive of me and of my work, and for bringing my books to different countries around the world. Thanks especially to Staci Burt and Jessalyn Foggy for doing such a great job spreading the word about *The Violinist of Venice*. And my undying gratitude to Danielle

Fiorella for the absolutely gorgeous cover—I think I am the luckiest author ever when it comes to covers!

Thanks, as always, to the Canisius Alumni Writers, aka CAW: Joe Bieron, Cara Cotter, Brittany Gray, David Klimchuk, Caitie McAneney Klimchuk, and Ryan Nagelhout, for all the support, pep talks, and hilarious off-topic conversations over wine/beer/pizza/brunch/all of the above.

Thank you to the Wednesday night writers for keeping me on track and making me show up and get the work done and for all the encouragement and publishing talk: Adrienne Carrick, Jenn Kompos, Kate Karyus Quinn, Dee Romito, Claudia Seldeen, and Sandi Van.

Infinite gratitude, love, and appreciation to my friends, family, and friends who may as well be family for your unending love and support: Amanda Beck, Andrea Heuer Bieniek, Bob and Marcia Britton, Alex Dockstader, Jen Hark Hameister, Sandy Hark, Lisa Palombo Moore, Jen Pecoraro, and Tom and Mary Zimmerman. You all keep me sane, make me laugh, and are always there when I need you. I am so, so fortunate to have so many people in my life who wish me well and are always up for sharing a bottle (or two) of wine.

My heartfelt thanks and appreciation to the Canisius College English and creative writing departments for their continued support, especially to Mick Cochrane and Janet McNally. I owe so much of who I am as a writer to your wisdom!

Of course, I would be remiss if I didn't give a shout-out to all the amazing bands whose music inspired me while writing this book: Nightwish, Delain, Kamelot, Flyleaf, Xandria, In This Moment, Epica, Evanescence, Stream of Passion, and Serenity.

Thank you to the guys and gals at Public Espresso in downtown Buffalo, for letting me work in your beautiful space and for keeping me deliciously caffeinated with cappuccinos just like the ones in Italy.

Thank you to my brother, Matt Palombo, for always being happy for and supportive of me. Sorry this book still doesn't have any duels, car chases, or explosions—but there is a joust, so we're moving in the right direction.

Thank you to Fenway, the very ferocious silky terrier, for sometimes keeping me company while I write and sometimes making me get up from my chair, because someone has to.

Thank you to my grandparents, Mike and Kathy Zimmerman, for telling everyone about my books and for being so proud of me. I love you guys!

There are no words for the love and gratitude I have for my parents, Tony and Debbie Palombo. Infinite thanks to my mom for being my biggest fan and for being an excellent publicist—I'm going to have to start paying you soon! Boundless thanks to my dad, who went to Florence with me while I researched this book and took excellent pictures of everything we saw. Thank you both so, so much for everything you have done and continue to do for me. I couldn't do any of this without you.

And last but certainly not least, thank you to everyone who has bought, read, reviewed, or recommended *The Violinist of Venice*. Your love and support for that book have meant so much to me, and it's so amazing to see my work resonating with so many. I hope you've enjoyed *The Most Beautiful Woman in Florence* just as much.

1. What do you feel was Simonetta's strongest motivation for marrying Marco? Do you think she truly loved him, or did she only convince herself that she did? Could she realistically have refused to marry him?

2. Simonetta is sometimes frustrated by the effect that her beauty has on those around her, and at other times she uses it to her advantage. Did both of these reactions feel reasonable and realistic to you? How might you have felt in her situation?

3. Simonetta is widely proclaimed the most beautiful woman in Florence, and men wait outside her house, leave her gifts, and recognize her in the street. Do you see any similarities between the Florentines' reaction to Simonetta and our own celebrity culture today?

4. What do you think Marco hoped for in marrying Simonetta and bringing her to Florence? Do you think he got what he wanted?

5. Simonetta is a friend of both Lorenzo de' Medici and his wife, Clarice. How is her friendship with each of them different? How is it similar? What does she value about each friendship?

6. Simonetta feels as though, by posing for Botticelli, she becomes a partner in his creative work. Do you think he sees her that way as well? Why or why not? How do you see her participation in their artistic relationship?

7. At one point in the novel, Simonetta asks herself the following questions, only to realize she does not have the answers: "What is it about beauty which makes men think they have the right to desire you? That beauty means you automatically agree, somehow,

St. Martin's Griffin

to be coveted, to be desired? That your beauty belongs to everyone?" Do you think these questions are still relevant to the way in which our culture perceives beauty, especially female beauty? How are women who are considered beautiful still treated similarly to Simonetta? Where is the line between objectification and empowerment?

8. Simonetta refuses Giuliano de' Medici's advances and claims that she cannot violate her marriage vows. Yet she later does just that with Sandro. How did you feel about her decision? Did you feel she was justified?

9. In the last line of the book, as she is dying, Simonetta says, "Sandro promised me that I would live forever." Do you think she has, in fact, been immortalized? How do you think she would feel about the fact that *The Birth of Venus* is one of the world's most famous and beloved works of Western art?

10. Were you familiar with any of the works of art described in this novel before reading it? How did your familiarity (or lack thereof) influence your reading of the novel? Did you look up any of the artwork as you read? Which were your favorites, and why?

Discover a world of unforgettable passion, music, and secrets in Alyssa Palombo's *The Violinist of Venice*.

Read on for more.

Available now from St. Martin's Griffin

1

THE MAESTRO

The gondola sliced silently through the dark water of the canal. My hired gondolier pressed the craft close against the wall of one of the buildings that lined the waterway, allowing another boat to pass us.

"Ciao, Luca!" he called to the other gondolier, his voice echoing loudly off the stones of the narrow canal, causing me to start.

I drew the hood of my cloak closer about my face, hiding it as we passed the other gondola.

We drew up to a bridge, and I spied a set of stone steps leading up to the street—*the* street. "Stop," I said, my voice low from within the hood. "Let me out here, *per favore*."

The gondolier obliged, bringing the boat close to the steps and stopping so that I could gather my skirts and step out, giving me his hand to assist me. I pressed some coins into his palm, and he nodded to me. "*Grazie, signorina. Buona notte.*"

I started down the street, peering at the houses, looking for the one where the man I sought was said to reside. I crossed a bridge over another small canal, the water beneath looking deep enough to swallow both my secrets and me and leave no trace of either.

Just beyond the bridge I found it. I took a deep breath, banishing the last of my nervousness, pushed open the door and, without knocking, boldly stepped inside.

The room I entered was not large, and appeared even smaller by its clutter. Sheets of parchment covered the table a few paces in front of me, some written upon, some blank, and many with bars of music scrawled on them. A harpsichord sat against one wall, scarcely recognizable beneath the papers heaped on it. I counted three instrument cases throughout the room that each looked to be the right size to hold a violin, or perhaps a viola d'amore. A lit lamp sat on the table amongst the papers, and another on the desk against the wall to my right. These, plus the slowly dying fire in the grate to my left, were the only sources of light in the dim room.

At the desk, bent over a piece of parchment, quill in hand, sat a man in worn-looking clerical robes. He looked up, startled, and I was able to get my first good look at him. He had hair as red as the embers in the hearth and wide dark eyes that, when they caught sight of me, narrowed on my face in anger, then bewilderment. From what I had heard, he was only in his early thirties, yet the strain of childhood illness and—or so I guessed—the trials that life had seen fit to deliver him had given him the weary demeanor of a still older man. And yet beneath his somewhat haggard appearance there was a spark of liveliness, of fire, that made him appealing all the same.

"Who are you? What do you want?" he demanded, scowling as he rose from his chair.

I took another step forward into the room, pushing my hood back from my face. "I seek Maestro Antonio Vivaldi," I said. "The man they call *il Prete Rosso*." The Red Priest.

"Hmph." He snorted derisively. "You have found him, although I do not know that I rightly deserve the title maestro anymore. After all, I have been sacked."

"I know," I said. All of Venice knew that about a year ago, Maestro Vivaldi had been removed, for reasons largely unknown, from his position as violin master and composer at the Conservatorio dell'Ospedale della Pietà, the foundling home renowned for its superb, solely female orchestra and choir. He had spent the past year since his dismissal traveling throughout Europe—or so the gossip said. Having heard of his return, I took the first opportunity I could to seek him out. "I was thinking that as you are currently out of a job, you might be willing to take on a private student."

His gaze narrowed on me again. "I might be," he said.

Clearly he was expecting me to bargain. The corners of my mouth curled up slightly into a smile as I reached beneath my cloak and extracted a cloth purse that was heavy with coins. I closed the remaining distance between us and handed it to the maestro. His eyes widened as he felt its weight, and grew round with disbelief as he opened it and saw how much gold was within.

"I trust that will be sufficient for my first month of lessons," I said, "as well as your discretion."

He looked back up at me. "Who are you?" he asked again. When I failed to answer immediately, he went on. "If you can afford to pay me so much, then surely you can afford to have some perfumed, mincing fop or other come to you in the comfort of your own palazzo and teach you. Why come here—in the middle of the night, no less—to seek me out?"

"That is quite a lengthy tale, padre," I answered. "Suffice it to say that I have heard that there is no better violinist in all of Venice than yourself, and that is why I have gone to such lengths to find you."

He frowned, not satisfied with so vague an explanation, but he let the matter rest. "You wish to learn the violin, then?" he asked.

I nodded. "I used to play, years ago . . ." I shook my head. "It has been a very long time." Five years, to be exact; five years since my mother had died and taken all the music in our house with her.

Vivaldi nodded absently, then turned to remove a violin and bow—which I took to be his own—from a case that sat open on the floor next to the desk. He handed them to me. "Show me what you know," he said.

Oh, it had been so long since I'd held a violin in my hands, had felt the smoothness of the wood beneath my fingers, had smelled the faint, spicy scent of the varnish. I had not practiced before coming to see the maestro, thinking it best not to tempt fate before I could secure his help. I closed my eyes, savoring the feeling of being reunited with an old friend I had believed I might never see again. Then I began.

I started with the simplest scales: C major and A minor. My fingers were stiff and clumsy on the strings, but after playing each scale twice, the old patterns and habits began to return. When I felt more comfortable, I began to play a simple but pretty melody I remembered playing when I was younger. My memory was imperfect; there were several points where I forgot what note came next and simply skipped ahead to the next one that I could recall. It was rather unimpressive, but it was all I could think of to play. When I came to the end, I began again, this time improvising to repair the sections I'd forgotten. So intoxicated was I with simply playing a violin again that I forgot Vivaldi's presence altogether, until he lightly placed a hand on my shoulder to stop me.

"Good," he said, more to himself than to me. "Good; not bad at all. I can tell that you have a natural talent. And you certainly play with passion." He smiled, and the expression transformed his face. "I shall teach you. I assume you have an instrument of your own?"

I nodded, thinking of the untouched violin I had stolen from my brother Claudio's room. It had been given to him as a gift and was of the finest craftsmanship, though he had never played or shown any interest in learning. "Yes, I do," I answered. "Though it will be . . . difficult for me to bring it here with me."

The maestro waved this aside. "I have one that you may use. You wish to come here for your lessons, then?"

"Yes," I replied quickly. "Yes, if that suits."

"Very well," he said, his eyes bright with curiosity. "Shall we say two days hence, around midday? If that is agreeable to you?"

I thought for a moment. I could perhaps get away unnoticed for a time then. "Yes, that is agreeable."

"Though I do not suppose you will tell me the reasons behind such need for discretion?" he asked.

I smiled. "As I said, that is quite the long story, padre, and one that would be better saved for another time." *Or never.*

"I see," he said.

"Two days hence, then," I said, moving toward the door.

"Wait," he said, and I stopped. "May I at least learn your name, signorina?"

I glanced at him over my shoulder. "Adriana," I said. I could not risk him recognizing my surname; so, before he could press me further, I pulled my hood over my face again and stepped outside into the late April rain, leaving him to think what he would.